TKO . . .

Zank listened at Jill's door. Inside he heard her say, "I haven't said anything to anybody." Then he heard what sounded like a slap.

Zank had a stupid impulse to smash the door in, but held himself in check. All he had to do was follow these clowns and they'd take him right to Vernon Cole, and Vernon Cole would lead him to the missing kid. So they beat Jill to a pulp, so what? Life in the big city.

The conversation started up again: "Move it, Jill."

"I'm not going anywhere with you."

Another slap, this one louder. A muffled cry.

Suddenly the door in front of Zank flew open at about the same time he realized it was his foot that had blasted it.

Three men were trying to get Jill up off the floor. Zank grabbed the nearest man by the back of his collar, spun him around and slammed him into the wall, face first; he bounced back, stumbled, and crashed on the floor.

The next closest took a swing at Zank that glanced off his cheek. Zank counterpunched with a shot to the man's soft, voluminous belly that dropped him to the floor with an "ooph."

Number three was not going to be so easy. He'd drawn a knife.

THE LONG WAY TO DIE

JAMES N. FREY

BANTAM BOOKS
TORONTO · NEW YORK · LONDON · SYDNEY · AUCKLAND

THE LONG WAY TO DIE

A Bantam Book / September 1987

All rights reserved.
Copyright © 1987 by James N. Frey.
Cover art copyright © 1987 by Bantam Books, Inc.
This book may not be reproduced in whole or in part, by
mimeograph or any other means, without permission.
For information address: Bantam Books, Inc.

ISBN 0-553-26564-4

Published simultaneously in the United States and Canada

Bantam Books are published by Bantam Books, Inc. Its trademark, consisting of the words "Bantam Books" and the portrayal of a rooster, is Registered in U.S. Patent and Trademark Office and in other countries. Marca Registrada. Bantam Books, Inc., 666 Fifth Avenue, New York, New York 10103.

PRINTED IN THE UNITED STATES OF AMERICA

O   0 9 8 7 6 5 4 3 2 1

FOR SUSAN ZECKENDORF

James N. Frey worked his way through a number of occupations before he discovered he was a writer. He ran a newspaper, was a dishwasher, warehouseman, lifeguard, and the world's worst life insurance salesman. He now teaches novel writing and suspense fiction at the University of California, Berkeley Extension and is at work on his next Joe Zanca novel. In addition to his Joe Zanca series, James N. Frey is the author of three suspense novels and a non-fiction book called HOW TO WRITE A DAMN GOOD NOVEL. He lives near San Francisco with his wife Elizabeth and three children.

One sin doth provoke another . . .

—Shakespeare

1

Zank smelled trouble when he saw the young black come into Murray's Gym that afternoon. There was something in the cocky way he held his head high, the way he rolled his shoulders, the way he looked around the gym with half-closed eyes that said: I'm royalty and you're all gonna have to bend a knee or there's gonna be trouble.

Not trouble for Zank, just trouble for somebody. Trouble for somebody who would maybe want to debate the issue. Somebody like Jaime Gonzo, who was skipping rope in front of a mirror, with a Walkman plugged in his ears. Yeah, Gonzo had already spotted him and was curling his lip. Gonzo, Zank figured, didn't go in much for paying homage to visiting royalty. Neither would Tiger Torres, a hot-tempered Cuban who was a little slow-witted but had a right hook that could stop a bulldozer. Now where the hell is he? Zank turned around and spotted Tiger doing sit-ups in the corner. He was already giving the young black an icy stare. Gonna be trouble, Zank thought, sure as wine comes from grapes.

What the hell, trouble comes, I just go on pounding the heavy bag and keep minding my own business. Got nothing to prove to nobody. Somebody wants to play at being royalty, that's copasetic.

Zank came to Murray's Gym every day he could, put on his baggy red sweatsuit, and got in a good workout. Murray's was Zank's kind of place. Nice Nautilus machine. But that was about it as far as modern equipment went. The mats scattered about the unpainted floor were stiff and yellow with age, frayed around the edges. The cracking plaster on the walls, the paint peeling off the ceiling, the smell of sweat, canvas, and old resin gave the place an air of history. Murray's Gym was not a *fitness center:* no aerobics classes, no ten-day shape-up programs taught by blondes in leotards, no pamphlets given out on how to measure your optimum pulse rate.

Zank usually started his workout on the speed bag, going through his rhythms for ten, fifteen minutes, then he'd jump rope or pedal the old Schwinn Exercycle for maybe a half hour until he was good and warm and sweat ran down his face.

Then he'd pound on the heavy bag for half an hour, which is what he was about to get started on. He shadow-boxed his way over to the heavy bag, keeping his head turned toward the windows and away from the visiting royalty. It was overcast outside. Gloomy.

He'd start easy, doing combinations. A left, a left, a left, then bamo! a right, step back, dance little stutter steps. Zank never was naturally good at footwork, but he knew that's what made the great ones great, and he always tried hard to get it right. He'd even studied ballet, but he never became good at it. Zank had the body of a large, armor-plated vehicle. "Zank the Tank" they called him. He was six feet even, with a twenty-inch neck and broad, powerful shoulders. His reach was seventy-two inches, a distinct disadvantage for a heavyweight when up-and-coming guys like Angel Moran and Jesus DeVera had almost ninety.

A left, a left, bamo! a right, now circling backward, fending off imaginary punches, bobbing his head from side to side.

Zank was a Rocky Marciano–type slugger in the age of finesse. He had the face of a slugger too, and at thirty-six was puffed and scarred from thousands of jabs and hooks he should have blocked. He had a large chin, and his nose was flattened and pushed slightly to the right. He'd had severe acne as a kid, and his face was pockmarked even before he started letting guys use it for target practice with their fists. The Italian kids in the West Oakland neighborhood where he grew up called him Grattalora—cheese grater—which didn't bother him, he said. What the hell, what's in a name?

His hair was short, curly, and dark, and his coal-black eyes had Sicilian stoicism and oxlike, bovine directness in them. Sometimes he'd squint, trying to look ruthless, the way he felt a Sicilian ought to be. Like Luca Brasi in *The Godfather*, the guy who used a garrote rather than a gun. The guy with all the *force*. The Godfather's one-man army. But Zank couldn't hold the squint for long, and in the end he was never able to intimidate anyone with his Luca Brasi impersonation.

Even though his boxing career was over, Zank went on slamming the bag as hard as he ever did, as hard as he did when he trained to fight Salvatore Pedrone, the Argentinian champion. Zank figured some day he was going to be an ace trainer, and an ace trainer ought to keep up his skills to the day he died. Besides, in his new line of work it paid to stay in shape. His new line of work didn't really have a name. He thought of it as just helping people who were desperate. And sometimes to help people you had to get *real* physical.

So two, three, sometimes four times a week, he came here to Murray's Gym in the Marina District with a pal of his, Harry Chow, who never boxed but liked to work out on Murray's twenty-five-thousand-dollar Nautilus. Zank did some leg work on the Nautilus once in a while, but most days he spent his workout time warming up, then punching the heavy bag until he was arm weary. Bamo! Bamo! Bamo!

"You Joe Zanca?"

Zank turned around. "Could be," he said. The question had come from a pencil-thin little creep in a brown suit with gold wire-rimmed glasses stuck on his beak of a nose. "Then again, maybe I'm his grandmother." Zank kept his legs moving because he didn't want to cool off.

"You know me, Joe?" the man asked, lighting a cigarette with a bright gold lighter. The smoke smelled sweet.

"Yeah, sure, I know you. You're Skimpy Shenazy." Shenazy was a sometime fight promoter and sometime loan shark. Zank backed away a few steps, like the guy had a bad odor, and kept dancing.

"You know my boy over there?" Shenazy's thumb jerked in the direction of the ring. A grinning face stared back at

Zank from the other side of the ropes. The face belonged to the young black Zank had seen come in a few minutes before. It was a sharp-featured face. Eager.

Zank said, "Don't know him."

"Name's Davy Swan," Shenazy said. " 'Kid Swan,' he likes to be called."

"He looks good," Zank said.

"He *is* good. Tops. Real tops. He's gonna be up there in the not-too-distant future." Shenazy's chest swelled.

"I wish him luck," Zank said, stepping back up to the bag and smashing it with a couple of looping rights. Bam! Bam!

Shenazy didn't move. He took a drag on his cigarette. "The kid would like to have a light workout today," he said slowly. "We was planning for him to go a few rounds with a rummy, but the rummy didn't show. Supposedly got sick or something. We was wondering if you might oblige."

"Sorry."

"A little sparring is all," Shenazy said, twirling two fingers to imitate a sort of waltz. "We'd pay ya a slam, maybe a slam and a half if you go, say, three."

"Nobody pays that kind of bread for a light one."

Shenazy shrugged. "We was thinking, with Zank the Tank the kid might have to work up a sweat. I mean you was up there and all. And it wasn't all that long ago."

"Two years, seven months, fourteen days."

"That ain't so long." Shenazy wiped his glasses with a silk handkerchief and hung them back on his nose. Then he crushed his cigarette out on the floor with the tip of his pointed black shoe.

"I ain't in condition, Shenazy."

"You look better than the night I seen Morgan Ralston lay you down on the canvas." His smile was almost a sneer.

Zank said, "You can keep on talking all you want, but I ain't listening." He turned back to the heavy bag and smashed it with a hard right.

"You lost your guts, Tank?"

"Fuck off!"

Zank unleashed a flurry of blows on the bag, bamo! bamo! bamo! bamo! Shenazy backed away. Zank breathed easier, but he had a tingling feeling deep in his gut that Davy Swan wasn't going to take no for an answer. All of a sudden he was back in grammar school and the new tough on the block was calling him Grattalora, goading Zank to prove he was tougher than Joey Zanca. Shit. If I got a brain in my melon, I head for the showers and get on home, he thought. But I walk, then what? Word gets around I got the balls of a hummingbird, and then every dork in the world wants to try me. But maybe they won't press it. Maybe they'll go a few rounds with Gonzo, who could use the bread. Zank glanced back toward the ring; Shenazy was telling the kid something, who was nodding and grinning, but wasn't looking at Zank. Looked like they'd lost interest. Hey, okay, everything's copasetic.

Zank started dancing again, and stepped up to the bag, jabbing with his left, throwing hard rights. He was quickly back into the rhythm. Left, left, left, bamo! a right to the old rib cage. He liked those body shots. Loosen up the organs. A trainer named Mole Allen had told him that maybe a million times. Mole Allen was the best trainer in the world, Zank thought. Mole knew everything there was to know except how to stop popping bennies into his mouth. Mole told Zank life was good but with bennies it was the fast lane all the time. Mole didn't make it much past forty-one. Goddamn idiot.

Zank had to concentrate hard because his mind was on the kid, and he was no longer enjoying himself. Harry Chow drifted over to his side, ringing wet with sweat. Harry was a few inches shorter than Zank and forty pounds lighter. He had a spindly body, and despite working out every day of his life, never got a bicep bigger than a pea. But he was strong and agile and at thirty-five could still play basketball all day long with the high school kids at the Chinatown Boys Club.

Zank stopped punching and dancing and wiped the sweat off his face with his sleeves. "You want to know something?" he said. "Sweat is uric acid, salt, and water. It's the body's air-conditioning system. It's produced by tiny glands in the skin—"

"I give a shit not, but let me guess—*The World Book, S*."

"You ought to get yourself one Harry, teach you a lot."

"What'd Shenazy want?"

"A proposition. I turned him down." Zank returned to his punching, just lightly jabbing the bag high with his left.

"He want you to do loan shark collections for him?"

"Nope. Wanted me to spar with junior over there."

"That's Davy Swan! He knocked out Woolly Thompson in Sacramento in the first goddamn round."

"Then the kid must be good. Woolly Thompson is one tough son of a bitch." He threw a couple of hard rights at the bag, chest high.

"How much Shenazy offer you?"

Zank took a couple of deep breaths. "A hundred and fifty bucks."

Harry's eyes shifted over to the ring, then back to Zank. "You could take him."

Zank stopped punching and glanced at the kid who was shadow boxing in the ring, getting warm. "Looks like God intended him to box."

"Sure would be something to see you take him, Zank."

"No, no, no, no, no, no, no," Zank said, a punch accompanying each no.

"Okay, Zank. But I'd sure love to see you knock that chip off his shoulder." Harry drifted off toward the Nautilus machine.

"Somebody'll do it, Harry, it don't have to be me."

A sudden break in the clouds brought bright afternoon sunlight flooding into the gym. Outside, Zank could see the tall masts of sailboats docked at the San Francisco Yacht Club, their pennants and flags waving in the breeze. He figured maybe he'd let Harry take his motorcycle and he'd jog home. It had been raining and foggy for a week, and now that the weather had broken, he felt like being outside. Bamo, bamo, bamo! The blows were solid and crisp, the heavy bag jumping to the one-two-three-four count of his punches.

A couple of women in warm-up suits walked past him. He'd seen them together at Murray's many times before. One was round and fleshy with a ponytail to her waist; the other small and pretty. Zank figured they were lesbians. They went over to a mat by the barbell rack and started some stretching. Zank never could get used to women in the gym. He used to come to Murray's because it was the last place that kept them out. But then Murray got sued and it was either let the women in or close the door for good. Murray told everybody not to be rude to them. He said it was best just to ignore them and maybe they'd get the message. It had been six months, and here they were, Zank had told Murray, still infesting the place like cockroaches. Murray said these cockroaches had constitutional rights and you couldn't buck the damn Constitution.

The pager in the pocket of Zank's sweatsuit sounded. He usually only got paged when he had a job to do.

He went into the small office near the showers where Murray was going over his bills. Murray always rubbed his bald head when he went over the bills, and his bifocals usually fogged up.

"Gotta use your phone, Murray."

"The black kid, Davy Swan, didn't cause any trouble?"

"Not a bit." '

"Shenazy's a shit," Murray said, looking at Zank over the top of his glasses. "Anybody he'd bring in here's got to be a shit too. Don't mess with him."

"You know me better than that."

"I know you, that's why I'm saying it." He went back to his pile of bills.

Zank dialed his answering service.

A woman answered: "Phone guard, Mary."

"Joe Zanca."

"Hi, Joe. Charlotte called, she says she's got a job."

"Hey, at last! Thank you, Mary. Talk to you later." He hung up and dialed again.

Charlotte answered on the first ring: "Yes?"

"You called? It's me, number seventeen."

"Got a rush job, can you handle it immediately?"

"Be there in fifteen minutes. What's the job?"

"Client wants us to arrange a homecoming."

"Piece of cake."

"Depends on how you handle it, I suppose, Mr. Z." The line went dead.

Zank hung up and said, "Thanks, Murray."

"Don't mess with Davy Swan."

"You already told me."

"So I'm telling ya again."

Zank came out of the office, turned the corner to head for the showers, and found himself face to face with Davy Swan.

"You the one called Chickenfuck Tank?" the kid said.

"Zanca. Joe Zanca."

"Used to be maybe. Now you noooo-body. Now you a chickenfuck." He brought his face an inch from Zank's. The kid's ebony skin was smooth over his angular features. His breath smelled of mint. His eyes were big and cool. He rolled back his upper lip, showing his wolfish teeth as he squeezed out: "Chickenfuuuuuuuuuuuuuck."

Zank felt a jolt of anger go through him, but he didn't let it show. "I ain't fighting today," he said evenly. He stared straight into the kid's dark eyes. A prickling sensation shot up and down his back.

The kid said, "Come on. Jez spar around a little."

"You came here looking for me, didn't you, kid?" Zank said. "I mean, you came to Murray's because Shenazy knows I work out here. Shenazy wants to up your reputation quick."

The kid licked his lips and ignored the question. He said, "Zank the Tank. Hmm." His big eyes rolled up and down. "Looks to me like the tank turned into a pile of chickenshee-it."

"I just called in to my boss, I got a job to do."

"All chickenfucks got jobs to do." He grinned.

"Some other time, kid." Zank started to maneuver around the kid, but the kid wouldn't let him.

"Chickenfuck, chickenfuck, chickenfuck, chickenfuck . . ." the kid kept chanting, dancing in front of Zank now, throwing mock punches. Everyone in the gym had stopped what they were doing and watched.

"You can only push a Sicilian so far and then you get all the trouble you've been asking for," Zank said. "You're gonna keep it up until I have to get into the ring and give you a boxing lesson, ain't you?"

"Got a fight coming up. Got to get in fightin' trim. Step right up, I won't hurt ya much, gramps."

"Just get your damn gloves on and let's get it over with."

*　　*　　*

In the locker room Zank put on his protection, changed into his trunks, laced his high-tops tight. He took his cloth scapula—a small, square picture of Christ showing his sacred heart—and pinned it to the inside of his trunks. His sister Maria was a nun and she said the scapula would protect him. To him it was superstitious nonsense, but she said it was blessed by an archbishop, and she made him promise he would always wear it. What the hell, what could it hurt?

When he came out of the locker room, he noticed everyone in the gym had stopped their workouts and were setting up folding chairs around the ring. Besides Harry Chow, Tiger Torres, Jaime Gonzo, and the two women, there were a couple of body builders, Jerry and Wesley, who usually came together and kept to themselves at Murray's. Gay, probably, but who gives a squat? At least, he thought, they ain't women. Zank climbed into the ring. The little crowd was growing. Even a couple of the businessmen who came to Murray's to grimly fight the middle-age spread like it was their religion stopped doing deep knee bends by the window and came over.

Murray came out of his office, grumbling that he'd warned Zank, then took a seat to watch, arms folded across his small paunch. But he had an eager look on his face, as if he couldn't wait for it to get started. The spectators talked among themselves in hushed tones, creating the tense, excited atmosphere that traditionally surrounds public hangings, stonings, prizefights, and other authorized bloodlettings.

The blinds were closed and the lights turned on over the ring, leaving the small audience in the shadows.

Zank and the kid put on Everlast headgear and pulled the chin straps tight. Zank gave his pager to Harry Chow and told Shenazy to give Harry the hundred fifty dollars. Shenazy took a roll of bills the size of a cantaloupe out of his pocket and peeled off three fifties. Harry stuffed the bills in his pocket, then taped Zank's hands and helped him on with the gloves. They were lightweight seven-ounce gloves and had seen a lot of combat. For sparring, fighters usually used gloves as big as pillows. Shenazy, Zank thought, wanted to test his boy. "Hey, Shenazy," Zank said. "I damage junior here, I don't want no lawsuits."

"The kid's like a ghost, Zank, you can't hit him."

While Harry laced Zank's gloves, the kid pulled on the ropes to stretch his muscles. When the kid bothered to look at Zank at all, it was with a slight smile on his lips and a glint in his eyes.

Zank felt an old fire being stoked back to life someplace deep in his soul. Harry Chow shoved a mouthpiece into his mouth. Zank bit down hard. The rounds were three minutes. The old man who did the cleaning up around the gym was assigned the job of timekeeper. He looked at Zank through horn-rimmed glasses to see whether he was ready. Zank nodded. The old man looked at the kid. The kid nodded and grinned.

The old man rang the bell.

The kid came out dancing, dodging, moving in and out and left to right, circling. And as he moved in, he jabbed. The jabs were light, but fast—it was as if he were shadow boxing and Zank wasn't even in the ring. The kid was as fast as Zank had ever seen. He could shoot moving either right or left, varying his attack, keeping his chin tight to his chest and his eyes on the target.

The kid was schooled and he had the instincts, an unbeatable combination. Zank tried to stay in the center of the ring, throwing feather-light counterpunches, and for a while he relaxed and enjoyed watching the kid glide around. As the kid's punches got crisper, Zank threw his counterpunches with a little more authority, just to let the kid know he had a little something.

Then wap! Zank's head snapped back from a phantom blow. He shook off its effects and tried to figure out where it came from. Goddamn kid is good.

The kid jabbed twice; Zank countered, then got wapped on the forehead. This time he saw it. The kid could throw a punch backpedaling, which made counterpunching hazardous. The kid jabbed, Zank countered, the kid struck hard again, backing away, looping the blow high, over Zank's extended arm. Zank slipped the punch with a quick turn of his head. The kid danced around him.

Zank admired the kid's style and quickness. And his ring presence. Like it was his territory and he was in charge. His black skin glistened, and under his skin the muscles were taut and lean. He had speed, grace, and obvious smarts. The fucker's gonna be up there, Zank thought with a jealous pang, no doubt about it. All the way, maybe. Champion of the world. That's if he had the killer instinct. A desire to win more than anything on earth, more than a woman, more than money, more than goddamn *anything*. Not just to win, but to beat his opponent into *total* submission.

The kid was flicking stinging little jabs at Zank now, but Zank blocked most of them and landed a few slapping rights the kid didn't bother to block.

With a minute to go in round one, the first hard right landed on Zank's forehead, a surprisingly stiff jolt, a message: Look, Kid Swan has a hammer. The kid grinned at Zank. One of the women called out: "Let him have it good, Kid!"

Fun and games were over.

Zank felt the adrenaline flow, the surge of strength. Exhilarating. He stepped up and took a mean swipe at the kid that missed, but it brought a gasp from the spectators. The kid moved even faster now, dancing, unleashing flurries of lefts and rights in a blur. Zank covered up and moved to the corner, hoping to conserve his strength while the kid wasted his. But the kid kept up the pounding, landing heavy blows against Zank's arms. Then he backed away, dancing around the middle of the ring, daring Zank to come out, taunting him with his eyes. Zank caught a glimpse of Shenazy smiling from the kid's corner. Wants the kid to win with a goddamn knockout, Zank figured. Word would get around. Kid Swan creams former contender Joe Zanca.

The kid kept punching, and Zank kept himself covered up until he heard the bell sound. Zank watched his opponent bounce into his corner, continually moving to stay loose while Shenazy wiped him down. Zank headed for his corner.

Harry Chow, holding the water bottle to Zank's mouth, said: "I think you made a mistake getting in the ring with this guy."

Zank rinsed his mouth and spit into the bucket. "You were fucking all for it!"

"Worry not, I seen Rocky One, Two, Three, and Four, and the good guy always wins."

Zank took some deep breaths and said, "The only thing Rocky has in common with the fight game is the ring has ropes." He took another swig of water and looked around. Most of the spectators were standing in the kid's corner, admiring him. Only the two gay body builders and Tiger Torres were watching Zank.

Tiger Torres said, "Zis kid, he tough."

Harry Chow said, "Zank's just fucking around."

"Za kid fucking around with Zank's head, I think." He chuckled.

Zank got up from the stool. His arms were tired and sore. His skin, out of punching condition, was peppered with tiny welts. Zank's legs were already tired, and he'd only had a light workout and sparred for one round. He thought of Archie Moore, who was light heavyweight champ at fifty. Goddamn made of iron. Zank took another mouthful of water, rinsed, and spit into the bucket.

"The kid is having target practice," Harry whispered to Zank. "Why not just lay down for him, take a nap."

"A Sicilian don't take naps in public—tell them this is the last round."

Harry nodded and went over and talked to Shenazy. Zank slapped his biceps with his gloves to loosen them up.

Harry came back looking grim. "They say they paid for three rounds. They either get three rounds or they want their money back."

"Fuckers."

"Let them have it."

"And have 'em telling everybody I'm a fucking candy ass? Had to buy my way out?"

"Better to be a live candy ass than tomato paste."

"Up yours!"

The bell rang. Harry shouted, "Wait a friggin minute!" Then to Zank, he whispered: "You better do something, Zank."

"Yeah, like what?"

Zank glanced at the kid, who was waving to his newly won fans.

"You know what you have to do, Zank." Harry said, closing his eyes halfway.

"What evil is cooking in your pot, Harry?"

"When Ninja fights, he uses both claw and teeth—old saying."

"You made that up."

"Nevertheless true. When I played football at Lincoln High, the coach said: be a good sportsman unless you are losing, and then fuck that sportsman shit."

Zank glanced over at his opponent's corner again. The kid was dancing, throwing mock punches, looking goddamn confident. "I did promise the kid a boxing lesson."

"Well, then, give it to him. There ain't no ref to say you can't."

Harry slipped Zank's mouthpiece into place. Harry yelled, "Okay!" and the old man rang the bell again. The kid came after Zank, chasing him into a corner. Zank was slower now, holding his gloves an inch or two lower. The kid unleashed his blows in stinging combinations, contacting solidly on Zank's forehead. Zank pushed forward, trying to get to the center of the ring and cut it off, but the kid kept dancing around him, peppering him with jabs. Then: Whumph! The kid landed a hard right in the center of Zank's face. Goddamn. The room spun like a top. Zank thought: time to fuck the sportsman shit. Time to give the kid some real boxing lessons.

Zank retreated, inviting the kid to come in, and when he did, Zank stepped on his foot. Lesson #1.

The kid stumbled. Zank darted forward, wrapping up the kid's left and holding his right against his body while pounding his kidneys with stiff body blows that couldn't be blocked. As he pounded away, Zank kept throwing his left shoulder into the kid's jaw to annoy him. Lesson #2.

"Hey, keep it clean! Break! Break!" Shenazy shouted.

Zank loosened his grip and let the kid pull back. As he did, Zank suddenly lunged forward and head-butted him squarely in the face. Lesson #3.

The crowd booed. Shenazy cried, "Foul! Foul!"

The kid whirled, blood gushing from both nostrils. Zank's head felt like it'd been split open, but he just smiled, watching the kid trying to keep his feet. "When they wobble, wap 'em," Mole Allen had always said. Zank charged after the kid, who seemed confused. He blocked punches, but couldn't seem to throw one back with any force.

"Hey!" Shenazy shouted. "That's it!" He threw a towel into the ring. Zank backed off.

The kid stood in the center of the ring and didn't move for a moment, then suddenly a look of determination swept across his face and he kicked the towel out. He shook his head, trying to clear out the cobwebs, but he was steady on his feet. Zank glanced at Shenazy who didn't seem to know what to do for a moment, then Shenazy signaled the kid to keep fighting. The kid put his fists up in front of him and stood in the far corner, blood still gushing from both nostrils.

Zank went after him, jabbing, jabbing, jabbing—trying to set him up for the big right, and when the kid tried to move on the attack, Zank wrapped up his arms and started kidney punching him again. Zank outmuscled him easily, but the kid wasn't beaten by a long shot.

Someone booed, followed by a chorus of boos. Zank ignored them. His head felt like it had been split in two from the head butt, but he managed to keep coming at the kid, throwing stiff lefts and rights in controlled patterns. When he hit the kid, blood rained over the ring.

The kid started moving and deflecting Zank's blows now, roaming the ring, not letting Zank cut him off and fence him in. Zank was tired and dizzy. He paused to catch his breath. The kid stopped too, his eyes glowing. His face dripped blood and sweat, which ran down his hairless chest. Blood bubbled from his nose. He snarled, then he came at Zank in a flurry, directly, not dancing, not bobbing or weaving, but straight on, throwing punches like a maniac. The boxer had become a brawler. This was Zank's fight now. This was the way he liked it; slugging it out, toe to toe.

Zank tied the kid up again with his arms, this time slashing at his left eye with the laces of his glove. Lesson #4. The kid backed off and kept throwing punches, but even a kid gets tired. The punches were badly aimed and ill timed. Zank could move inside now, unleashing smashing body blows to the kid's midsection that took the wind out of him.

The kid's body was awash in the blood streaming from his nose. The smell of the kid's blood gave Zank a surge of strength. Zank was like a bull now, charging repeatedly after the bullfighter. The kid stumbled over his own feet.

Then the bell rang to end the second round. The kid hit Zank a glancing blow off the chin after the bell. Okay, the kid was learning.

The woman with the ponytail came over to Zank: "You're a bully!"

"Mind your own business!" Zank spat at her. "Find yourself a goddamn husband. Mend socks. Do dishes!"

"You should be reported!" she screamed, red-faced.

She went back to the kid's corner. Zank dropped onto his stool, rinsed his mouth, and kept his eyes on the kid, who had his back to Zank and was huddling with Shenazy. Three minutes of boxing to go. Shenazy was probably telling him not to lose his head. Zank grinned at him. Lose your head, you bought yourself a ticket to the goddamn canvas. The kid had lost his head, Zank figured. Ain't no way in hell to get it back once it's lost.

Tiger Torres gave Zank the okay sign. He was beaming.

Harry Chow rubbed Zank down. "Jesus, Zank, this is better than the Forty Niners winning a Super Bowl."

"This round, I take him out. Remember Pedrone, the Argentinian?"

"Yeah, sure."

"The kid's a hothead, just like Pedrone. I'll take him out the same way." He got up off his stool and started dancing, light on his feet. He felt nineteen again.

"Be sure to save a little something for defense. Old Ninja saying."

"Man, I'm so pumped up I could take King Kong."

The bell for the third round sounded. The two fighters came out into the middle of the ring and touched gloves. Zank thought the kid looked surprisingly alert and fresh. No bleeding. Eyes clear. Goddamn.

Zank wasted no time. He jumped in close, wrapped up the kid's arm, hooked his leg inside the kid's, and muscled him over backward. The kid stumbled and started to fall. Zank hit him on the chin with a good left uppercut.

The kid bounced onto the canvas and scrambled to his feet. Boos filled the room. "You fucking tripped him!" Shenazy shrieked.

Zank had expected to see the kid wild with rage. Figured he'd lose his head completely, start throwing goddamn hay-makers. Instead, he quickly regained his balance and shook himself. He took three deep breaths through flared nostrils. Then he came at Zank hard and fast, but well controlled, pummeling Zank with good, fast combinations to the head and body, coming in and circling and not letting Zank move in on him.

Zank tried to tie the kid up, but when he lunged the kid floated away, banging out punches as he moved. Suddenly Zank could feel his arms drooping, and he was breathing hard. Goddamn Archie Moore musta been taking steroids. Zank backed into a corner and tried to cover up, hoping to get his strength back. The kid moved in and hit him with thundering blows to the top of his head, his biceps, his rib cage. Zank felt like he was caught in a windmill.

Frantic, Zank pushed the kid back, but it left him open and the kid landed a big right square in Zank's face. Then another. Goddamn, goddamn, goddamn. The room shuddered. Lights flickered in Zank's head. His knees buckled under him.

The kid was just a shadow now. All Zank could see were fists in his face. A blow to the side of his head rocked him. A loud buzzer sounded someplace in the middle of his brain. He tasted blood in his mouth. The canvas floated beneath his feet. Wap, wap, wap, the blows rained on his head. He bent at the waist and covered his face. The kid bent low too, and kept pounding away. The crowd cheered him on.

Goddamn, Zank thought, I'm going down. But then he remembered how Jackson Hill had knocked him out in his first pro fight, and maybe the kid was just as cocky as he had been. Cocky can get you killed. Here, kid, watch this.

Zank stood straight up, suddenly dropping his guard, and took a blow to the chin. A gasp went up from the spectators. Zank turned to the side and stumbled, bending his knees, pretending he was going down. The kid dropped his guard, ready to raise his arms in victory. That's it Davy Swan, Zank thought, here's the greatest lesson in your life, coming right up.

Zank's right was cocked behind him and he swung with all he had.

And missed by a foot and a half.

Zank felt a blow to his chin. And then another. The kid was all over him. Wap, bam, bam, pow. Goddamn. Surrender, surrender, gotta surrender. Everything was whirling around now. Put your hands up, this is a stickup. Surrender or die. The Spartans at Thermopolae, 450 B.C. Lee at Appomattox Courthouse, April 9, 1865. Here's my sword, General Grant. Keep the damn thing, General Lee. Lee, Robert Edward. Born 1807. Son of Henry Lee, superintendent of West Point . . . Wap, wap, bam, bam . . . Ceiling lights flashed blue and green. Goddamn pretty . . .

He heard a bell sound. Somewhere. It kept ringing.

A voice: "That's it, kid, you don't want to hurt the guy."

That you, Murray? Cockroaches have constitutional rights. Ratified June 21, 1788.

"You okay, Zank?" It was Harry, throwing water at him. What happened to the black guy? Harry took Zank's arm and put it around his shoulder. "Easy there, big guy."

Zank looked around. The room came into focus. His gaze settled on the two women, who were applauding the winner. So was most everyone else. "Never did go down, did I?" Zank asked.

"Hell, no, you had him on the run."

Zank spit his mouthpiece into the water bucket, then rinsed his mouth. Harry sponged his face and gave him a towel.

"Hold up some fingers," Zank said.

Harry held up three.

"Sixteen."

"You're okay."

The kid came over to Zank, still dancing. "Zank the tank, eh?" he said. "More like Zank the toilet tank."

"Watch the smart mouth!" Harry snapped.

"Or what? Your boy here gonna spank me? We already proved who's the man and who's the asshole."

Zank said, "I had the flu all week." Goddamn lame

excuse, and he knew it. But he was too shot to think of something better.

"Yeah, man," the kid said, "that flu can be *real* bad." He danced off toward the shower, chuckling.

Zank's ears were ringing. The skin on his face smoldered. Tiger Torres came by and patted him on the shoulder. "Zank, my friend, is no so bad. My wife give me a black eye when we having a nice fight and she never let me forget it." He shook his head in sympathy and went over to use the Nautilus machine.

Zank opened a window, then sat down on a bench and let the breeze cool his face while he breathed air into his lungs. Harry told him his pager had sounded about halfway through the round.

Zank struggled to his feet. "That'll be Charlotte. She's probably one pissed-off lady by now."

"Charlotte's no lady, Zank. She's Adolf Hitler with tits."

"Don't make no difference to me. I just work for her, I ain't gonna father her children."

2

Zank parked his black Kawasaki 750 in front of a red-brick mansion with white shutters near Pacific Heights. He had showered and changed into his street clothes: black slacks, white sport shirt, dark blue windbreaker. He took off his helmet and secured it with a bicycle lock to the rear frame of the bike. Then he put the windbreaker into the side compartment, locked it, and started up Cimmarron on foot. He'd used half a styptic pencil on his face to clot the small cuts. His skin burned. His legs and arms were still weary and his ears rang, but the fresh air was reviving him. He felt good to be getting an assignment. It had been six weeks since his last job. A young woman, Annette Turner, had an old boyfriend who wouldn't leave her alone. His name was Waldo and he loved three things: hot cars, cocaine, and hurting women. A real prize, that one, Zank thought. Waldo hounded Annette at work and at home, even got her unlisted telephone numbers. She got a court order telling him to leave her alone. He ignored it. Kept telling her he was going to cut her breasts off if she saw another man. And the cops weren't no goddamn help. Told the woman she had a domestic dispute, and unless Waldo hurt her, there was nothing they could do. One cop said she should have been more careful about the men she slept with. Cops, what a bunch of assholes. So Zank had tracked Waldo down in two days and convinced him that if he wanted to continue walking upright, he should move to Chicago. Zank begged him to give him an argument, but Waldo just looked Zank up and down and said he thought he'd love it in the Windy City. Zank had felt great after that one.

Looking north and west now, Zank could see the Golden Gate Bridge, rust red in the afternoon sun, half smothered by a glacier of fog pushing into the bay. In front of the fog the bay was a deep blue, flecked with whitecaps. An oil tanker with the Chevron logo was making its way past Alcatraz Island, heading for the refinery at Richmond.

Zank walked past the mansion and through a gate at the end of a wrought-iron fence. The gate led to a path which ran between two tall hedges. The path sloped downward behind the mansion, leading to a refurbished carriage house secluded by trees. A small brass sign read: RENALDO GOODFELLOW, ARCHITECT, *by appointment only*. Only there was no Renaldo Goodfellow, and you didn't come to this place if you needed an architect.

The two-story carriage house was covered with freshly painted charcoal-gray shingles and a gray roof; the trim was a glossy white. A patch of manicured lawn surrounded it. It projected an image of tradition and good taste, the kind of place an architect would have for a studio. That meant, Zank figured, it was good cover for The Agency.

Zank went up the steps and through the front door without knocking. No one was waiting in the waiting room. No one was ever waiting. The waiting room was furnished with a couch embroidered with a seascape pattern, a walnut coffee table, two chairs to match the couch, two end tables, two lamps. A *Time* magazine with two ICBM's on the cover lay on the coffee table. The same magazine had been there for four months. A picture of a sailing ship in a storm took up half of one wall. Next to it was a thermostat. Zank opened the face of the thermostat and pushed the buzzer hidden inside. Then he went up a circular stairway to the second floor and knocked on a heavy metal door.

"Enter," Charlotte said through an intercom. The door clicked open. The room was large and sparse, containing two chairs, a desk, a couple of lamps, no windows. On the desk was a sculptured jade cat with a smooth, long neck and fire-red eyes, rubies the size of peanuts, a jeweled cigarette box, a jade ashtray, and a gold lighter the size of a tennis ball. Charlotte sat behind the desk smoking a long, dark cigarette. She was thin and chronically pale. She wore a plain black dress, no jewelry, no watch, no makeup. Her black hair was cut short and combed straight down the sides. She had plain features and a perpetual neutral expression. Zank guessed she was in her mid-forties, maybe older. It was hard to tell.

"Sorry I'm late, Charlotte. I ran into a little problem."

"Your face looks like orange rind." Her features remained neutral.

"I had a boxing lesson. A guy was trying to teach me how to duck."

"So far, looks like you haven't caught on. Sit down." She let some smoke escape slowly out of her nostrils.

He sat down in the chair placed directly in front of her desk. His shadow on the wall looked elephantine.

"How ya been, Charlotte?"

She ignored the question. "Are you ready to go to work, Mr. Zanca?"

"Sure. What's this homecoming deal?"

"Client wants us to bring back her missing daughter."

"The daughter a minor?"

"Sixteen."

"Sounds like a job for the cops."

Charlotte's tight mouth drew tighter. "We're in business, Mr. Zanca, we do not refer clients to public agencies."

"Who's she taken up with?"

"At the moment, it appears no one knows. It will be your job to find out."

"Look like she might be in a cult?"

"Her mother suspects so." Charlotte leaned her head back and blew some smoke toward the ceiling. "You did a cult snatch last year, I recall."

"I had *two* cult jobs last year," Zank said, "both a piece of cake. One here, one down in L.A. One was the Moonies. The other, Buddhist or some damn thing. They ate brown rice, burned candles, shaved their heads, wore bedsheets."

She took an envelope out of her desk drawer and slid it across the desk to him. "Here you are, Mr. Zanca."

Inside there were twenty-five one-thousand dollar bills. "The price go up?" he asked.

"We consider this job as possibly high risk."

"What is it you ain't telling me, Charlotte?"

"Why nothing, Mr. Zanca." She smiled with her lips, but her eyes were cool.

Zank put the envelope in his pocket.

"What do you do with your money, Mr. Zanca? You don't drive a Porsche, you haven't moved into a penthouse. Why is it you still live like you pump gas or bus tables?"

"That ain't none of your business, is it?"

"Everything about you is our business, Mr. Zanca. You and The Agency are married. Married people should be completely open, don't you think?"

"I don't even know your last name, Charlotte."

"You don't even know my *first* name." Her smile was as icy as January in Minnesota. She took a drag on her cigarette and slid a note across the desk to him. "The client," she said.

He picked it up and read: "Fisk, Gertrude, Marsden Road, Gehenna, California. *Gehenna,* that's what they call hell in the bible."

"It never ceases to amaze me, Mr. Zanca, how much trivia you know."

He didn't know if she was complimenting or knocking him. That's the way it was with Charlotte, you never could tell. He started to smile as if it were a compliment, then said, "Who's this Mrs. Fisk?" He handed the paper back to her. He'd remember the address.

"She's a fifty-two-year-old lonely widow. Her husband was a small-town minister. You'll find her a pathetic little creature."

"How can she afford us?"

"By mortgaging her house."

"She must want her daughter back real bad."

"Guess she must." Charlotte took another cigarette out from the jeweled case. She tapped the end of the cigarette on her thumbnail. "Gertrude Fisk has inoperable cancer. She says she doesn't want to go to the next life without settling things up with her daughter. We've agreed to find the daughter and bring her home. She will fill you in on the girl's description, last known address, that kind of thing. We told her an operative would contact her today."

"How's she going to keep her home when we bring her back?"

"That isn't our concern, is it, Mr. Zanca?"

"Suppose not. Where the hell's Gehenna?"

"It's past Stockton on Highway 4. Take you about three hours—unless you ignore the speed limit."

"I always ignore the speed limit."

Zank got on the Embarcadero Freeway at Broadway heading south, then turned east and crossed the Bay Bridge. He was wearing his leather jacket now, buttoned tight up to the collar. Rush-hour traffic was heavy but moving on the MacArthur Freeway. When he turned off toward Walnut Creek, it was lighter and going at the limit, which was fifty-five by law and seventy by custom. The Kawasaki hummed and smoothed out at seventy-five as he streaked through the tunnel on 580 and down into the valley, past Walnut Creek, Dublin and San Ramon. As the miles stretched out behind him, his mind cleared, and after a while his stiff and sore muscles relaxed and the world fell away. The bike, the road, the hum of the engine, the whoosh of the wind in his ears were all that was left.

He refueled at a 76 Station in Stockton and went into a McDonald's for two Big Macs, a hot cherry pie, and a large coffee. While he was eating he watched a young couple holding hands and making eyes at each other across a shake with two straws sticking out of it. The boy was maybe twenty, with acne and thick glasses. The girl was a little plump and her face was plain, but glowing so with love that Zank thought it was beautiful. Enjoy it, kids, 'cause it ain't gonna last.

It hadn't with him, anyway. Her name was Arlene. She was a black-eyed fireball he'd married when he was on top and it looked as if he was going to get a shot at Larry Holmes. The money was pouring in like a fountain. On their wedding night they took twelve people to dinner at the Four Seasons in New York. Afterward he took her back to the Pierre and filled her bathtub with Dom Pérignon.

But then the following year he got cut over his right eye in a fight in Jersey and it never healed right. The next fight he lost on a TKO—the blood wouldn't stop when the old cut opened and couldn't be closed. The skin specialists said the scar tissue was thin and there was nothing that could be done. After that the purses were smaller, the losses regular. He sunk from contender to has-been in six months. And Arlene didn't want to be married to a has-been. Her last words to him when she was leaving were: "Hey, Joe, nothing is forever."

The girl was kissing the boy's fingertips. They giggled at each other. Bombs could go off in the driveway and they ain't gonna notice, Zank thought. He smiled, even though his jaw was tender and it hurt to smile.

The McDonald's manager was taking a survey and came over to Zank's table and asked him what he thought of the service.

"You want to know what exactly?" Zank asked.

"What you thought of your meal, you know, how is it?" The manager was bald and wore a white shirt emblazoned with: YOU DESERVE A BREAK TODAY.

Zank said, "Truthfully, I thought it lacked something."

"Oh?" the manager asked, pen ready. "What?"

"Surprise."

"Surprise?" He knitted his brows.

"Yeah, *surprise*. You've taken all the surprise out of eating."

"Don't think I get you," he said, slowly shaking his head.

"Every time I been to McDonald's what do I get? It ain't never burnt. It ain't never raw. It ain't never nothing except what it was the last time."

"We pride ourselves on our quality control," the manager said, smiling now.

"That's just it!" Zank hit the table with his palm. "Too damn much quality control. You eat one quarter pounder with cheese, you've eaten a million of 'em."

"You're having fun with me, aren't you?"

"No, sir, I mean what I'm telling you. McDonald's makes an okay burger, but it's boring. You guys ought to be bad sometime, just to show you're only human."

The manager gave him a blank look. "I'll suggest it to our district manager. Have you been in some kind of accident?"

"You ever heard of face bowling? I'm the world champion."

The chair Gertrude Fisk offered Zank, she said, had been her husband's favorite. It was an old leather-covered easy chair, stuffed with horsehair, well worn and sagging. It was situated next to the window, looking down from the second floor on the untended apricot orchard that surrounded the ancient wood-frame farmhouse. Mrs. Fisk had an apartment upstairs and rented rooms on the first floor to tenants. Zank lowered himself into the chair cautiously. It groaned under his weight, but seemed sturdy enough, and comfortable. She looked over at him from a high-backed rocker.

"You people sure do work fast," she said with a raspy voice. "I only just got the money over to you today."

"We're the Federal Express of the business," Zank said. He spoke slowly, trying to remember as best he could the vague and confusing rules of English grammar.

She smiled, showing uneven teeth.

Gertrude Fisk looked perhaps fifty; but she had a pallid, sickly complexion and stringy white hair. She wore a faded blue print dress, and a large gold cross on a chain dangled around her neck. She coughed harshly, and her body seemed to slump. After a moment she said, "You're not a detective, are you?" as if she already knew the answer.

"No, ma'am, The Agency just helps people solve their problems for a fee."

"I don't think I got your name."

"Conrad," Zank said. "Richard Conrad."

She was studying him now with a steady gaze, fingering the cross and rocking gently in her chair. He thought for a moment she was going to ask him what happened to his face, but she didn't. Instead, she said: "I'm very happy indeed to make your acquaintance, Mr. Conrad." She took a couple of deep breaths, holding her hand flat against her chest. Her skin was almost transparent. "Can I get you anything, Mr. Conrad? Tea, milk? I don't partake of alcoholic refreshment, I'm afraid, so I don't keep liquor in the house."

"Nothing, thanks. I hope you don't mind answering a few questions," Zank said.

"It's expected."

"Could you tell me a little something about your daughter? What kind of person is she? Her interests, hobbies, things like that . . ."

"Where to begin," she said with a sigh, as if there might be a million good places. "I guess you should know Cleomona is rather stubborn. More than just a little." She bit her lower lip, as if she wanted the admission to be painful. "She was always a difficult child. Moody, ill-tempered. Nothing ever seemed to please her. Lord knows I tried to make her happy. I gave her everything we could afford—certainly as much as any other child in Gehenna. She had *four* Barbie dolls at one time. Imagine. Used to play with them dolls morning, noon, and night. She was a lonely child, but in her way she was a loving child too." Gertrude Fisk paused and breathed deeply.

Zank waited; he didn't want to interrupt her thoughts. He looked out the window at a rusting old Buick on flat tires in the dirt driveway along the side of the house. He could see the peaks of the High Sierras in the distance, glittering like gold in the setting sun. He looked back at Gertrude Fisk. She scratched her neck and continued.

"Cleomona was never a good student at school," she said slowly. "Just never cared much for it. She left high school when she was fourteen—a few months after her father died. They were very close. I think her father's death had a very terrible effect on her." She paused for a moment to scratch her neck some more. It was red and raw. Then she said, "I don't know exactly how to explain it. She was just so . . . different. I don't know what else to say. She seemed sort of lost inside her head." Gertrude Fisk's eyes were glassy now, staring straight ahead.

"How about the rest of the family? You say her father died. Any brothers or sisters?"

"Cleomona is an only child."

"Close friends?"

"Just one. A boy named Charlie Plummer. Him and his family moved back east, oh, about four years ago, and she never heard from him again." She coughed harshly, then spit into her handkerchief. Then she waited, as if she expected another burst of coughing, but it didn't come. She settled back into her chair.

Zank said, "No other friends?"

"We're pretty isolated here, Mr. Conrad. About all Cleomona had here was her loving family." She pointed to a portrait on the wall. "That was my mother," she said, as if it were important that he know. The woman in the portrait had a severe expression; she was wearing a black dress with a tight white lace collar and a small cameo brooch. "To understand our family, you've got to go back some. We have a lot of tradition behind us, most of which Cleomona has chosen for the moment to ignore." Her voice had a hard edge to it.

Looking over his shoulder at the portrait, Zank said, "Lots of character in that face," but he was thinking it looked like a face that could stop a freight train.

"My mama was the famous evangelist, Phoebe Tanner," Gertrude Fisk said. "She denounced sin from one end of America to the other. Drew fifteen thousand people in Chicago in nineteen and thirty-eight."

"Must have been something."

She smiled with obvious pride. "I'm telling you so you'll know what kind of a family Cleomona comes from. Her father was a minister too. Pastor of the Community Church here in Gehenna. That's why it's so hard to believe she would run off."

"Could you tell me something about her running off?" Zank rubbed his sore chin and wondered if it might not have been the smartest thing Cleomona Fisk ever did. Living in a house with freight-train-stopping grandma on the wall could drive a young girl bats.

"Part of her leaving was my fault," Mrs. Fisk said, sighing deeply. "I'm not denying that. I didn't encourage her to go out with people her own age. She was so upset with her father dying that, well, I don't know, I just sort of let her mope around. After a while it just seemed like the natural state of things." Her mouth began to quiver. "We had words, Mr. Conrad. Hard words. I'm a Christian woman and I don't want to go to my grave with things unsettled in regards to my daughter, can you understand that? She's out there alone in the world, and I got to know that things are set back to normal with her. In a few days I'll be going into a nursing home. I only got maybe two months left on this earth." She wiped her eyes with the twisted handkerchief. "Please, Mr. Conrad. Find her. Bring her home to me."

"Tell me how she left. When and why exactly."

She thought it over for a long moment, her face wet with tears. "I don't know if I ought to tell you this—I don't want you to dislike Cleomona." Her face tightened, her body pulsating with hiccuplike sobs. "It was so terrible, Mr. Conrad. I'm so ashamed." She stiffened suddenly. "No! You should know. I want you to know what happened." She took a couple of deep breaths, then looked away from him as she said it: "I found an, ah, *unpleasant* book in her drawer."

"You mean, like naughty?" He stopped rubbing his jaw. It was only making it worse anyway.

She nodded slowly. "I don't know where she got it. It was disgusting. Men and women were doing unspeakable things."

"And you fought about it?"

Gertrude Fisk nodded. "She said it was educational. Filth! I told her I didn't want it in the house. I may have said more than that—I was beside myself with anger at the time."

"Then she left?"

Her eyes shone, stared out fixedly. "I went into her room one morning and she was gone. Packed up everything she owned and just disappeared. She never came back. She sent one postcard that said, 'So long.' That was it. I called the police, of course. They put her down as missing, but what can they do? They told me there's two, maybe three hundred runaways a week coming into San Francisco. I hired a private detective named Stroud to look for her. Now she must have got word that she was being hunted because she called me one night and told me she was happy and didn't want to come home."

"Stroud find where she was living?"

She took a piece of paper from her pocket and read: "Two ten, number A, Cedarwood, in San Francisco . . . She was staying with a woman named Jill Stanyan. This Stanyan woman claimed she didn't know where Cleomona went, but that's probably a lie. Stroud said there was no way he could force her to talk. He gave me The Agency's phone number—aren't you going to write any of this down?''

"We never put anything in writing, Mrs. Fisk. Two ten, number A, Cedarwood, right?"

"That's right." She seemed pleased he remembered.

He said, "Have you got some recent pictures of Cleomona?"

"I'll get them for you."

Zank stood up and stretched. The stiffness was gone, but he was feeling sore and numb, and his skin burned. He took a look around. Mrs. Fisk's living room had high windows and antique furniture cluttered with newspapers. There was an old TV set with bent rabbit ears in the corner. Next to it sat a large potted plant with colorless leaves. A pale yellow cat slept on top of the bookshelf. It had an old wound on its scalp and its left ear had been hacked off. Mangy goddamn cat. There were a lot of photographs on the wall, many featuring the preaching grandmother and the preacher father and Mrs. Fisk. Nobody smiling. Tightasses all, Zank thought. Then he realized there was no young girl in any of the pictures. No Cleomona. Banned from the goddamn family gallery.

Gertrude Fisk returned with a large envelope and a small brown bag. She handed him the envelope. Inside were half a dozen photos of a blond girl with long straight hair, sulky eyes and a hard mouth. Bad tempered, Zank thought. Bad tempered and sassy, and tough as Smokin' Joe Frazier.

"You can tell just by looking how difficult she is," Mrs. Fisk said.

"Yeah, just what I was thinking. If I don't find her through this Jill Stanyan, where would she go next? Any idea?"

"No, I really haven't." She looked puzzled. "Stroud thinks she may have joined a cult or something. He said in San Francisco the cults hang around the bus depots and just wait for young people with no place to go. It'd be just like her to do something like that."

"That time she called, did she give you any clue as to where she was or who she was with?"

"None at all. I begged her to come home, but she's as stubborn as a pine board."

"Was it collect?"

"No."

"Was it from a pay phone or a house?"

"A pay phone. The operator interrupted for more money and that's when Cleomona hung up."

"You tell her you were sick?"

"She didn't believe me." Her eyebrows went up.

"Think she can come home if she wants?"

"I have no way of knowing."

Zank nodded. He could see she was getting tired so he started gathering up his stuff to leave. On his way toward the door he said, "Before we start, I think I should warn you that when we bring your daughter back and she don't want to stay, that'll be between the two of you."

"You bring her back, I'll see to it she stays," she said with surprising firmness. "I'll guarantee it."

"If she's been in a cult, she's maybe been brainwashed."

"Stroud told me."

"You got a deprogrammer lined up?"

"Don't you worry none." Anger rising in her voice now. "I understand what has to be done, Mr. Conrad. Just what are the chances of your bringing her back?"

"If this Jill Stanyan knows where Cleomona is, I'm sure she'll tell me. After that, it'll be a piece of cake."

"She wouldn't tell Stroud, why would she tell you?"

"We have our ways."

The woman smiled for the first time. "I feel better already—oh, wait!" She handed him the brown bag she'd brought from the other room.

"What's this?"

"For the trip back—oatmeal cookies." She smiled.

He promised he would keep in touch and report his progress. Then he headed down the stairs.

From the top landing Mrs. Fisk said, "It's the Lord's will that you bring her back to me, I know it."

Outside it was now nearly dark. Zank got onto his motorcycle, buttoned his leather jacket, and put on his helmet. He kicked over the engine, then throttled it down, letting it warm up. He drove to the end of the drive and looked back at the house; it was a high-peaked Victorian, long ago fallen into a state of neglect. A light came on in an upstairs window. Mrs. Fisk was standing there with the light behind her, looking almost transparent, like a ghost. Zank waved to her, but she must not have seen him because she didn't wave back.

There was no traffic on the two-lane country road back to Gehenna and the interstate. He was still sore, but relaxed. A little tired. Things, he thought, are okay. As long as the girl's trail ain't too cold, it's gonna be easy. As easy as getting Waldo to take the bus to Chicago.

Suddenly there were headlights following him. He didn't remember passing any side roads or driveways. Where the hell did they come from?

He slowed to forty. So did the car. He sped up to seventy. So did the car.

As he entered the town of Gehenna he spotted a shopping center off to the right. Only Pay and Save Discount Drug was open. Only a few cars in the parking lot. He swung into the parking lot, spun around, and headed back in the direction he'd just traveled. No headlights coming at him. He drove a mile or so back up the road. No cars, no trucks, no nothing. He figured the car might have pulled into the driveway of one of the small cottages at the edge of town, or it might have driven into one of the apricot or peach groves that lined both sides of the road. Either way, there were too many possibilities to check out.

Besides, he thought, it was possible he might not have been followed at all. Might have been just some kids screwing around. Might have been a drunk. Might have been anybody. Might have been Davy Swan gave him too many thumps on the melon, and Zank was getting punchy.

He went back to the Pay and Save to make a phone call.

"Hello, Stroud?"

"Who's asking? " There was a TV on in the background. A cop show. Lots of shooting.

"This is Joe Zanca, Stroud. How's things?"

"What are you doing, calling me at home? I've got an office, you know."

"Wanted to wish you a merry Christmas."

"This is May, minibrain."

Zank chuckled. "I wanna be the first. While I got you on the line I thought you might shovel me a little something about Cleomona Fisk."

The TV in the background went off. Stroud said, "You drew that one, eh? Cleomona the minister's daughter who's run away from the farm. Yeah, how could I forget that one. I traced her to San Francisco, she stayed briefly with a sometimes registered nurse name of Jill Stanyan, then vanished. Jill Stanyan is the lush of the century."

"I never knew you to chuck a case before, Stroud."

"Sometimes you just hit a dead end. It isn't ethical to take a client's money if you can't make reasonable progress."

"When you start sweating the ethics, Stroud, the Giants will be winning the World Series. What happened, somebody tell you to buzz off?"

There was a pause, then: "Yeah. Okay, I don't mind telling you, there was a warning."

"From who, or whom?"

"Person or persons unknown dropped a note in my wife's grocery cart at the supermarket. It said, 'Cleomona is free and happy and wants to stay that way.' "

"Doesn't sound all that scary that you should drop the case."

"This case didn't have the profit potential, let us say, that I felt warranted the risk. I got a family."

"I'm getting half of twenty-five large ones, what the hell you talking about?"

"Discretion is still the better part of valor."

"Falstaff," Zank said.

"Pardon?"

"Falstaff said discretion was the better part of valor. He was the fatso coward in a play by Shakespeare. I had this cellmate who was a nut about Shakespeare, taught me a lot. Falstaff also said, 'To the latter end of a fray and the beginning of a feast, fits a dull fighter and a keen guest.' "

"I'm going to bed. Good night."

"Wait a minute, Stroud, give me all you got on this. You

ain't going to walk away from twenty-five large ones just because of a note.''

"I told you I hit a dead end!''

"What do you know about the mother?''

"Isn't your assignment to get the daughter back?''

"Yeah, but it might help if I knew something about the mother. You must have dug around a little. I know how you guys work.''

There was another pause, then a sigh. "Okay, the old lady is dingdong. That's another reason I didn't want to go on with it. She's had two trips to the monkey house.''

"She's claiming she's got cancer.''

"We verified that—lymphatic cancer, spread to the pancreas. She'll be a statistic by the end of June.''

"What's Cleomona like?''

"A real space cadet, okay? You now know what I know. Good luck, Mr. Zanca, and good night.''

Zank came out of the Pay and Save and found his motorcycle lying on its side. He looked around but couldn't see anyone who might have been near it. He walked over and lifted it up.

Both tires had been slashed. The saddlebag was open and his tool kit gone. Gertrude Fisk's oatmeal cookies were scattered on the ground. Goddamn motherhumpers.

He laid the bike down and looked around. An old couple were getting into a car; a woman with a baby was going into the store. "You seen anybody touch my bike?'' They hadn't. There was nobody else around, as far as he could see.

"They think this kind of whoopee would scare off a Sicilian,'' Zank said under his breath, "they gotta be retards.''

3

His alarm sounded at six-fifteen the next morning. He swatted it with a pillow, sending it to the floor. It stopped ringing. He felt his arms and legs. Stiff as overstarched shirts, but they worked. He rolled out of bed, did fifteen painful minutes of stretching, then took a long hot shower. Afterward he lathered and shaved. In the mirror his eyes looked red and puffy like he'd been on a six-day bender. His skin was tender. Goddamn Davy Swan.

He splashed himself with Aqua Velva, combed his hair and got dressed quickly. He put on a pair of brown corduroy slacks, brown dress shoes, a sport jacket, a dress shirt, and a tie. The tie was striped and too fat to be in style. He couldn't see why men wore the goddamn rags anyways, but today he had to have one.

Then he fixed breakfast—two fresh oranges cut in wedges, six slices of sourdough bread with crunchy peanut butter, and strong French roast coffee.

While he ate he read his *World Book*—the section on William Clarke Quantrill, the Confederate guerrilla leader during the War Between the States. The part about the bloody raid on the sleepy little town of Lawrenceville, Kansas, made him shudder.

Zank lived in a one-bedroom apartment near Broadway and Polk. He lived alone and had no pets. Comfortable. Nothing fancy. The furnishings were mostly bought at Sears when there was a sale; he had a small-screen color TV, a

VCR, a stereo. And a complete set of the *World Book Encyclopedia*.

There were hundreds of pictures on the wall chronicling his fight career from his first amateur bout, when he was fourteen and creamed a kid from Oakland, to the night he knocked out the champion of the Argentine. He liked to look at the pictures. Remember every win. How good it felt.

When he was through with breakfast, he went across the hall to his neighbor's apartment and let himself in.

"Morning Zank."

"Morning, Nolan. I never seen you up this early, or I'd of knocked."

"Haven't been to bed yet. What happened to your face?"

"Allergy to after-shave."

Nolan smiled. "Two-fisted after-shave, no doubt."

Nolan Wollenski was in his seventies, and, Zank thought, looked it. He had a full white beard and long white hair. One of the few guys in the world who knew what the fuck he was talking about—and he looked like he knew what the fuck he was talking about. His face was a plowed field of deep wrinkles. A pair of gold wire-rimmed glasses surrounded his small, serious eyes. He was wearing a blue smock with big pockets.

The sparsely furnished room was lined with shelves full of Nolan's sculptures, mostly heads and hands grotesquely twisted in anguish and full of despair. They always gave Zank a strange, prickly feeling on the back of his neck. Nolan was working on a small piece of clay that had been transformed into a fist mashing a globe of the world.

"What do you think of my new child, Joseph?"

"I never know what to think, Nolan. I got no idea what you're doing with all this stuff."

"Art is a statement about life, Joseph, a statement that's made in a language other than speech."

"So what's the statement?"

Nolan shook his head. Then an eyebrow went up. "That's just the point. If it could be said with the mouth, I wouldn't have to do all this damn work." He took a Gauloise cigarette out of a pack in his smock pocket and lit it with a kitchen match.

"I got no idea what you're talking about, Nolan."

"As your world widens, you will come to know."

"Right now I got a case to worry about. I'll widen my world afterwards."

Nolan's small eyes narrowed. "What kind of case?"

"Finding a missing girl. I got my tires slashed last night, Nolan. They're going to have a kid drive the bike down from Stockton today sometime. I told them to leave you the key. I hopped a ride home with a trucker."

"What a business, what a business," Nolan said, slapping some clay onto his sculpture.

"I got to get some stuff out of the safe."

Zank went into Nolan's kitchen, stashed most of the twenty-five thousand he'd gotten from Charlotte in a secret place behind the sink and took out what looked like a small black wallet. Inside was a plastic ID card with his picture and a gold San Francisco P.D. detective's badge #7117 in the name of Sgt. Sergio Veracruz. He had a .38 snub-nosed revolver hidden there as well, but he didn't take it. Zank had been twice convicted of felony assault and didn't want to be caught in the City with a gun if he could help it. Next time they'd throw away the goddamn key.

He used Nolan's phone to call Harry Chow at his home. Harry's sleepy voice answered: "This better be good news."

"It's me, Harry. Zank."

"What the fuck you want at this hour?"

"Remember that little black box you showed me a month or so ago?"

"Yeah."

"I want to rent it."

"It's not for rent, it's for sale."

"How much?"

He could hear Harry's wife telling him to hang up and go back to sleep. Harry shushed her and said, "Two hundred, Zank. Special price."

"Two hundred fortune cookies?"

"Dollars."

"That's a lot of soap."

"I make them up special." Harry yawned. "You can't get them anyplace else on the West Coast."

"Ain't I the best friend you got in the world, Harry?"

"Otherwise it'd be four hundred."

"Let me borrow it, how's that? Try it out."

"Okay. Try it out. Buy, rent, or lease, the price is still a double slam."

"With a busload of friends like you, Harry, I'd have a nice ride to the poor house."

"If I was making your kind of bread, I'd want to share it. What did Charlotte have for you yesterday?"

"Missing kid, right here in town looks like."

"When you want the box?"

"Right away."

"You'll find it in the usual place."

Zank hung up and turned to Nolan, who was studying his creation while he fingered his beard and sucked on a cigarette jammed between his lips. Zank said, "Okay, Nolan, I got to shove off. Thanks for everything." He put a hundred dollar bill on the table.

"For the services I perform for you, Joseph, I am paid exorbitantly."

"Even artists got to eat."

"You fight for every penny with Harry, and then you throw it away on me."

"Harry's greedy, you ain't."

Nolan smiled. "Good luck finding the girl."

"Piece of cake."

"Unless whoever slashed your tires shows up."

"You got to think positive, Nolan, otherwise you get bitter. My old man told me that and he was the bitterest son of a bitch you ever met."

Zank took a bus downtown and rented a blue Ford sedan from American West rent-a-car. He drove out to Twenty-fourth Street in the Mission, to a Chinese laundry by the name of City Shirt Company. At the counter was an ancient Chinese with hair to his shoulders and a face cast in plaster.

"Harry call?" Zank asked.

The counter man produced a package the size of half a carton of cigarettes. Zank handed him two hundred dollars. "Nice doing business with you." The man smiled mutely.

Zank put the package in his pocket, got back in his rented Ford, and headed for the Excelsior district.

Two ten Cedarwood was a plain, boxy, stucco apartment building that looked, Zank thought, something like San Quentin Prison. Phony-baloney Spanish type. Red tiles on the roof, wrought-iron trim around the door. Goddamn California crackerbox. There were a couple of palm trees planted in the lawn out in front, their lower leaves brown and wilted. Zank parked in an empty space on the street and went up to the front door and rang the bell for the manager. The name on the brass plate over the bell said the manager's name was Albert Nostrum. Zank pushed the buzzer; a voice answered: "It's your nickel."

"Sergeant Veracruz, San Francisco P.D."

"Who is it really? Jerry? That you, Jerry?"

"Let me in, pal, I ain't in the mood to be playing twenty questions."

A buzzer sounded; Zank opened the door and went in. A head popped out of a doorway down the hall.

"You Nostrum?" Zank asked, marching toward him.

"Yessir, yessir." Nostrum waited at the entrance to his apartment. He was bald, fiftyish, and nervous. Probably, Zank thought, in awe of cops. Good. Very good. You could always count on the awestruck.

"I'm sorry, Officer," Nostrum said timidly, "I thought you were a friend of mine, Jerry Paltz, a real crazy guy. Always pulling stunts."

"Yeah, okay," Zank said, pushing the man into his kitchen. Nostrum had been eating breakfast. A big red box of Cap'n Crunch sat in the middle of the table. A woman, no doubt Mrs. Nostrum, sat on the far side of the table reading the *Chronicle*. She was a squat, moon-faced woman, wearing a red robe. She looked at Zank, smiled a sort of good-morning-to-you Officer Veracruz smile, and went back to her toast and marmalade. She wasn't in awe of anything, least of all cops. But she was the kind who wouldn't make a fuss, Zank figured, unless you wanted her to move out of her chair. Zank held out his Sgt. Veracruz ID for Nostrum, who looked at it with squinting eyes.

"Got some questions," Zank said, slipping the ID back into his coat pocket.

"Yessir," Nostrum said.

"Jill Stanyan lives here, does she?"

"Apartment A, yessir—right down the hall, first one on the left as you come in the front."

"How long's she lived here?"

"Two years."

"Two and a half," Mrs. Nostrum said without looking up from her newspaper.

Zank said, "Where's she work?"

"She's a nurse," Nostrum said. He put his hands in his pockets, jiggling some keys.

"Special care, but it's too much for her," Mrs. Nostrum said. "She's a little too high strung, if you ask me—for that kind of work."

"She home now?"

"Don't know," Mr. Nostrum said.

Mrs. Nostrum looked up. "She should be, she's working evening shift over at Walker Memorial. Works the trauma center."

"She has a friend, Cleomona Fisk. You know her?"

"No," Nostrum said, shaking his head. His wife shook her head too.

"Jill isn't the type to have many friends," Mrs. Nostrum said, turning a page of her paper.

"She's sort of a loner," Nostrum agreed. "Has a little problem too," he said, glancing at his wife as if to ask permission to go on.

"Wet lips," his wife said.

Nostrum gestured as if he were taking a drink.

"Bad?" Zank asked. Stroud had already told him, but he thought he should ask, because cops always asked a lot of questions.

They both nodded.

Zank produced a picture of Cleomona, one Mrs. Fisk had given him. "That's the girl we're looking for, Cleomona Fisk."

Nostrum shook his head. He showed it to his wife. She

chewed toast while she eyed it, then shook her head. "Sorry," Nostrum said.

Zank said, "You know where the phone company puts their junction boxes?"

"Yeah, sure."

"Show me."

Nostrum looked at his wife. "Do what the officer says," she said.

"Don't he need a warrant or something?" Nostrum asked. Maybe he wasn't awed after all, Zank thought. Fear ain't awe. Maybe he was growing forbidden mushrooms in the basement.

"You make a cop go get a warrant," she said, "it only makes them mad. Just do as the man says, Albert."

"This way," Nostrum said gloomily.

Zank followed him down a hallway and then down the stairs into the basement. Along the way Nostrum said, "She's really a sweet gal. Kind of shy. Wasn't for the bottle, she'd be a star. Yes sir, a star."

The telephone junction box was in a small utility room. Zank took out a penknife and pried the cover off. Inside he found two dozen connections, labeled by apartment. From his pocket he removed the small box he'd picked up at the City Shirt Company and connected it to the terminals for apartment A. He set the gadget inside the junction box and said, "That ought to do her."

"What's that?" Nostrum asked.

"Police business."

"Oh."

"Go back to your apartment, and tell no one that I've been here. Just go about your business, that understood?"

"Yessir."

Zank went back upstairs and watched Nostrum go into his apartment, then he headed for Jill Stanyan's place. Zank took out his Sgt. Veracruz ID and knocked.

It took a moment before there was an answer. "Yes?" Her voice was quiet, sweet-sounding.

"San Francisco Police Department—Sergeant Veracruz."

"Just a minute."

He shuffled his feet. He put his hands in his pants pockets and then took them out. He knocked on the door again.

"I'm coming." He heard movement inside. The clanging of china or glasses. Finally the door opened. The woman standing in front of him was maybe thirty-five, of average height, a little thin, with messy short blond hair and pale blue eyes floating in a sea of pink. Morning-after eyes, Zank thought. A lush, all right. Goddamn shame. She was wearing a white robe with a red rose pattern along the sleeves and hem. She looked closely at his ID. "Sergeant Veracruz?" she said. He nodded. She stepped aside for him to come in.

The apartment was a one-room efficiency with a kitchenette. Zank glanced around. A white nurse's uniform was thrown over a chair. The sofa bed in the living room was open, unmade. Next to it was a portable bar with half a dozen vodka bottles. A breeze fluttered the drapes. Pretty neat, Zank thought, for a lush. Maybe she ain't totally gone. No dirty dishes in the sink. No clutter.

She said, "I was sleeping—I must look a mess."

"Sorry to disturb you."

"Would you like coffee or something?"

"No thanks. I'm here about Cleomona Fisk."

"Has something happened to her?"

"No, why do you think something may have happened to her?"

She shrugged. "It's a dangerous place, this old world." She closed the top of the portable bar.

He said, "You have a little taste from time to time?" He said it to let her know he wasn't judging her.

"Guess I do have a fondness," she said. She lit a menthol cigarette. She smiled at him. It was a curious, friendly smile. Nice. A cheerful, nurse smile. He thought she ought to smile all the time.

He said, "Cleomona Fisk was here, was she not?" He said it as coplike as he could. Stiff, cold, like he was accusing her of something. He added, "We know she lived here."

"She just stayed here for a while. Only for a week." She answered quickly, like she couldn't wait to get it out.

"How'd you happen to know her?"

"We met quite by accident on a Muni bus. She looked

sad and lonely. She was obviously a runaway. I invited her to stay with me and she did. She was sort of mixed up, you know, like most kids are these days. I got some good food into her, we saw some movies, then one day she just said she had to go. She told me she was going back to her mother in Gehenna. What's this about? What has Cleomona done?''

"What makes you think she's done something?"

She folded her arms and shifted her weight to one leg. "Why would you be looking for her if she hadn't done anything?"

"She's been exposed to a very serious disease and if she doesn't get a shot from a doctor real soon, she might get real sick. It's very important that we find her.'' He knew it sounded like bull. He wanted her to be suspicious, maybe shake her up. Maybe she'd call Cleomona to warn her.

She said, "What disease?"

"Something like AIDS. We have to have her checked out.''

"I see . . .'' She took a drag on her cigarette. She wasn't buying it, it was obvious.

"This is serious,'' Zank said.

She was nodding—not, Zank figured, like she believed him, but like she'd figured something out. "Why don't you leave me your card,'' she said. "I'll call you if I hear from her—which I don't think I will.''

Zank gave her a business card with the name of Sgt. Veracruz. The number on the card was for his answering service in North Beach. "My private line. It's an extremely delicate matter, very hush-hush. There's a five hundred dollar reward for information leading to her, ah, whereabouts.''

She looked at the card, then looked at him and said, "Tell me the truth, why do you want Cleomona?''

"I told you all I can.''

"Okay, Sergeant, I'll hold on to this card and let you know if I hear anything.''

She opened the door for him and he stepped into the hall. He started toward the front door, but when he heard her apartment door close behind him he hurried back down into the basement to the utility room and took the cover off the phone terminal junction box. Inside, the little device was flashing. He took off his tie and shoved it into his pocket. He stood there tapping his feet for a few minutes and waited for the device to stop flashing, then pressed the button on top that rewound the cassette tape cartridge inside. He pushed the play button.

"Hello," a man's voice said.

Jill Stanyan's voice: "Let me talk to Cleomona."

"She's busy."

"It's an emergency!"

"Who is this?"

"Jill. The police were here looking for Cleomona."

"Hold on, Jill, wait a minute."

Goddamn, Zank thought, it's working!

Another man's voice: "Jill? Vernon. What's this about the police?"

"A guy claiming to be a police officer was here and said Cleomona had some disease and he had to find her."

"What disease?"

"AIDS, something like that—it was a put-on job if ever I saw one."

"Are you certain he was with the police?"

"I've got his card. Veracruz, he said his name was. Detective Sergeant Sergio Veracruz."

"Did he show you any ID?"

"Yeah. It *looked* real."

"He have a partner with him?"

"No."

"You see his car?"

"No."

"What did he look like?"

"Big, tough looking. Beat-up face—I don't know how else to explain it. Crooked nose."

"Sounds like the gentleman who was in Gehenna yesterday. Definitely not an officer of the law. We'll check it out. Give me the phone number on the card."

"It's 526-7010."

"Thanks, Jill."

"Wait a minute, Vernon, she might not act like it, but Cleomona is a minor. Maybe you ought to send her home before you get into trouble."

"Go have a drink, Jill. Steady yourself down."

"Good-bye, Vernon."

Zank disconnected the box and rewound the tape, then pushed another button and took a look at the digital readout panel where a series of numbers flashed in red: 707 566 9472.

On his way downtown he stopped at a phone booth and dialed a number. When a woman answered he said, "Area code 707, prefix 566, number 9472."

"Authorization code?"

"The Agency, number seventeen."

After a moment she came back on the line and said, "Endless Horizons, Eagleston, Mendocino County, California."

Zank turned down an alley off Third Street in the Hunter's Point district, near the old wharfs, and cruised by an apparently abandoned concrete block building. A weatherbeaten sign on the building read: OWNER WILL BUILD TO SUIT. Most of the windows facing the alley had been smashed out, target practice for the local vandals.

Zank left the rented Ford in a vacant lot half a block away, walked down the alley past a dumpster, and found the steps that led down into the basement of the old factory. Broken glass crunched under his feet. Old newspapers and beer cans littered the steps. The door showed rot underneath the peeling green paint. The sign over the door said, GORKY SHIPWRIGHTS, EST. 1942. The sign looked old, and Zank wondered how they made it look like that when it had just been put up in the last week or so. Zank knocked twice, paused for a moment, then knocked again, twice. The door creaked open.

"Hello, Charlie."

" 'Lo Zank."

Charlie Kirk was tall and lean and wore thick, leather suspenders. He was in his early sixties, had a ruddy complexion, white hair, and he limped when he walked. Zank followed him down a long, dank hallway and into a musty storeroom.

"I got a memo you had an assignment," Charlie said, clicking on a naked light. "What you be needing?"

"The usual field gear. Glasses, a Ruger .44, and you still got those .32 automatics you can put on your ankle?"

"Lot of firepower for a lousy snatch."

"I ain't taking no chances, they already slashed my tires. Outfit by the name of Bright Horizons. Ever hear of 'em?"

"Nope."

Charlie opened a drawer in a large metal cabinet and took out a gun-metal-blue Ruger, field glasses, a .32, two holsters, and two boxes of shells. He said, "The ankle gun jammed the last time out. Wasn't cleaned proper by the operative. We got her fixed up, new barrel and all, but it ain't worth much over about ten feet."

"I know."

"I just want to make sure you do. You want some Armorwear?"

"Makes me sweat, and I might have a lot of walking to do."

"Suit yourself." He shrugged.

"I'll need a field knife and a knockout kit," Zank said. "And some foul-weather gear in case I got to spend the night."

Charlie pulled a couple of boxes out of a drawer and handed them to Zank. "Okay, here you go. That be all?"

"As far as equipment goes."

"Sign here."

Zank signed by spelling out the number seventeen.

"I'll need transportation too, Charlie."

"What kind of transportation?"

"A fast car with a big trunk."

"We got the '69 Ford LTD with interceptor engine, how'd that be? She's old, but she's got low mileage and a lot of speed. Good for a snatch. Giant trunk, well ventilated."

"Guess she'll do."

Charlie handed Zank a set of keys and made out another form for him to sign. As he signed it, Zank said, "Need some ID. The usual."

Charlie Kirk reached below the counter and searched through a small file, pulling out a billfold with a driver's license, credit cards, and a concealed weapons permit. "Richard Restin Conrad. Here you go."

"How long you worked for The Agency, Charlie?"

"Longer than I care to remember."

"You ever do assignments yourself?"

"Nope."

"You ever meet anybody, I mean any bosses, other than Charlotte?"

"Didn't they ever tell you not to talk to nobody about The Agency, Mr. Zanca?"

"Sure, and I don't."

"Well then, *don't*."

Zank headed out of the city and over the Golden Gate Bridge to Marin County. The day was spectacular: blue, cloudless skies over the emerald-green San Francisco Bay, a gentle breeze churning up tiny whitecaps. The traffic was light heading up the Waldo Grade and through the tunnel and down into San Rafael on U.S. 101. The LTD purred, its interceptor engine loping along at sixty. He played some old Hank Williams eight-track tapes he found in the glove compartment and chewed Juicy Fruit gum. Copacetic. He wasn't thinking of the assignment now, but it was ahead of him, and assignments always made him a little jumpy. He stopped for gas in Santa Rosa and had a rawhide-tough steak sandwich in a place called Bernardo's, then got back on 101 and continued north. The sun was high by the time he got to the turnoff for Eagleston. He drove through rolling hills of tall grass and grazing cattle and occasional vineyards, then turned east and followed the valley of Amador Creek, gushing with snowmelt from the Sierras.

He came over a small hill where the trees grew thick and close to the road, and then the road dipped and he came to the town. First he passed a few small wood-frame houses, most of them needing paint, the grass overgrown on their lawns, a few old cars on flat tires sitting in the driveways. Next were a few gas stations, an AM/PM Arco, a Mohawk self-service, and an old Texaco with a sign that said MECHANIC ON DUTY, but the place looked closed. Next came an IGA and a 7-Eleven, two bars, and a volunteer fire department. That was it. Nothing that said Bright Horizons. He passed a sign that read, COME AGAIN, EAGLESTON APPRECIATES YOUR VISIT, and turned around and found a place to park. He got out of the car and stretched. He'd stiffened up again. Goddamn creeping old age. He crossed the street and went into the bar called Nellie's because there was a sign in the window that said, *Friendliest place west of the Rockies between here and anywhere.*

Inside, there were some cowboy types at the bar playing with dice cups. Seated by the window a couple of women were having an animated discussion. The woman behind the bar pointed a spindly finger. "What'll it be?" Zank guessed she was maybe sixty, sixty-five, with bags under her eyes and dentures as white as a refrigerator. Nice small-town howdy smile on her lips, he thought. Suspicious eyes.

"A draft," Zank said.

"Coors or Oly?"

"Oly."

"Big or small?"

"Big."

She poured the beer from a tall spigot and put it down on a cocktail napkin in front of him. A hand-painted sign on the wall said, FIESTA FOLLIES, EAGLESTON, JULY 17-21.

"What's the tariff?" Zank asked.

"Buck even."

He counted out four quarters and slid them across the bar to her. She rang it up on an antique crank cash register. Somebody threw five aces with the dice and a couple of the cowboys gave a whoop. The lady bartender made a face, but didn't tell them to quiet down. She came back down the bar to Zank.

"Don't think I ever seen you in here before," she said.

"Never been near the place."

"Just a-visiting?"

"Yeah. I need some information."

She rolled her tongue around in her cheek. "You a cop? I figured you for a cop when you came in the door."

"I ain't a cop."

"Then you must be insurance or credit, something like that."

"Something like that. You know an outfit called Bright Horizons?"

"Sure, everybody around here knows Bright Horizons. They do charity work with welfare kids."

"How about a guy name of Vernon?"

"Vernon Cole, must be. He's the founder, one of the leading educators in the world. Head straight up the country road, then turn on Creek Road. You'll see a sign, can't miss it."

"This Bright Horizons, what are they, a club? Something like that?" He said it casually. Just making conversation.

"I guess, sort of. They do seminars and stuff. Just a hell of a nice bunch of people. Vernon Cole used to teach at Stanford. And they are kind to kids. They love kids. They take in kids that are troubled, not doing good in school. A lot of Bright Horizon people will be coming to the fiesta." She pointed at the sign on the wall. "They do puppet shows. Two years ago they bought the town a fire truck."

"Anybody around don't like 'em?" he said offhandedly. He took a couple swallows of beer. It was cold.

The lady bartender's eyes darkened. "Anybody don't like Bright Horizons? No . . . not that I know of."

Zank wiped his mouth on the back of his hand. "You wouldn't happen to know a sixteen-year-old girl staying with him by the name of Cleomona Fisk?"

She fished a toothpick out of her shirt pocket and put it in her mouth. "If I was you, mister," she said in a subdued tone, "I'd just forget about making trouble for Vernon Cole."

"Hey, if I've said something wrong, I'm truly sorry. I didn't come here to get nobody mad, that's for sure. Cleomona's my little sister. Her mama and me would like to see her come home."

"You saying she's being held against her will?" She eased away from him. Her suspicious eyes were thin lines now.

"No, nothing like that." He gestured with his hands that he meant it.

"Sister, huh?" She was still backing away from him.

"Yeah. My little sister."

"You prove that?"

"Don't see any reason I should."

She stared at him blankly for a long moment. Then she

said, "You know what? You ought to talk to Al and Russ."
She turned and called out to two cowboys at the other end of
the bar. "Fella here asking questions about Bright Horizons.
Says Cleomona is his sister." The cowboys came lumbering
down the bar like, Zank thought, two trained attack dogs.

Goddamn, Zank thought, now I got trouble in the friendliest place between the Rockies and anywhere. What the hell is
it about trouble that found him even in the most unlikely
places? He felt a shot of adrenaline go through him. His
muscles tensed. He took a couple of deep breaths and stepped
back a little so he wouldn't be hemmed in by the bar stools.
He smiled and kept his hands at his sides like a man who
wanted to be friendly and wasn't ready for trouble.

One of the cowboys hiked up his pants. The other put his
hands in his pockets. The one with his hands in his pockets
was beefy and short, with a thick neck and hairy arms. Zank
guessed he was in his early thirties. He'd be strong, a bar fighter.
He'd be a little trouble, maybe. The other was six-two or
-three, lean and muscular, and maybe twenty-five. He was
smiling a forced, caustic-as-Drano smile. Zank judged him to
be the more dangerous of the two. He'd be quicker. And he
had the air of a man who liked inflicting pain. He could be
goddamn big trouble if he knew how to handle himself.

The other half-dozen cowboys who had been playing dice
filed in behind. The two women who had been sitting by the
window joined them also. Blood-sport time in Eagleston.

"Sister, you said." This from the short one.

"Well, maybe I was kidding about that," Zank said.

The short one smiled and said over his shoulder, "Somebody call up to Doc Cole and tell him we got a big nose here
asking questions."

One of the women went to the phone.

Zank took a drink of his beer without taking his eyes off
the two men in front of him.

The tall one said, "Everybody in this town's a friend of
Dr. Cole." He sucked some air through his nose.

"We like him," the short one said. His grin was growing
wider, his eyes narrower.

Zank said, "Nice."

"What's nice?" the tall one said. He stepped closer to Zank.

"That Bright Horizons is so well liked by everyone. Like I said, I was just curious to know what they were up to, you know."

The short one said, "That's so much turkey squat."

"Who are you, mister?" the tall one asked.

"Name's Richard Restin Conrad. I'm in the athletic equipment business down in San Francisco. Used to box. I'm very tough. I ain't the toughest guy in the world, but I'm up there."

"A real blowhard," the short one said, turning to the small collection of friends behind him. "He used to box, he says." He took his hands out of his pockets and shifted his weight to the balls of his feet like he was getting ready for a little game of hardball. He flexed his muscles. They bulged like kiddie balloons. A pumper of iron, Zank thought. He'd be strong and slow, with no snap in his punches. He gets his first. A pulse of excitement went through him.

Zank said, "I'm required by law to warn you that my fists are registered with the state as lethal weapons."

"You're scaring us to death," the tall one said, chortling.

Zank said, "You two step aside and I'll be on my way."

"Empty your pockets on the bar," the short one said.

The woman who had made the phone call said, "Dr. Cole says he sounds like some guy who was in Gehenna causing trouble last night."

The short one said, "Looks like we might have found ourselves a private dick. And he plans on grabbing Cleomona."

Someone said, "Let's tar and feather the son of a bitch."

Nervous, anxious laughter.

Zank felt his heart beating fast now in his chest. He could take two of them, maybe even three or four, but he couldn't take them all. He said, "I ain't no private dick. I'm telling you two guys, I don't want to hurt you, but I ain't about to empty my pockets for nobody."

"Oooooooooo, he do sound tough," the short one said, taking a step closer to Zank. The tall one said, "I'm pissing in my boots right now."

Zank drained the last of his beer and stepped back from

the bar with the empty glass in his hand. He looked at the tall one, smiled, then flipped the glass to the short pumper of iron, who reflexively lurched forward to grab it. Goddamn dummy. Zank stepped up and hit him on the tip of his jaw with a short, chopping left, snapping his head back. The blow stunned him. He shook his head and blew air out his mouth. To keep Zank away he clumsily fanned the air with his fists. That's it, dummy, go crazy. Zank stepped in quickly between the blows and hit him again with a stiff left hook. He staggered around for a few steps in a tight circle, then dropped to his knees and rolled onto his side, twitching. He wasn't getting up.

Zank shook the sting out of his fist, stepped back and stood ready for an assault, but no one moved. No one spoke.

"Now if you'll just step back and put your hands in your pockets," Zank said to the tall one, "I'll be on my way."

The man looked to his friends for help. Everyone was staring at Zank, but no one was volunteering. "Well?" Zank said to the tall one, who suddenly had the look of a very lonely man.

"You sucker punched him!" he said.

"I'm full of tricks. You gonna get out of the way or ain't you?"

Zank watched the man's eyes. He was calculating the odds. Should he be a hero or a coward? Finally he puffed out his chest and sucked in as much oxygen as he could. He'd made up his mind, Zank figured. His stare became fixed. He said, "You aren't leaving quite yet, motherfucker."

He moved away from the bar, cautiously circling. Zank kept his guard down and loose in front of him and waited. He circled too. He feinted, but didn't throw a punch. He kept murmuring, "Come on, come on." Zank was a better counterpuncher, and the man had a couple of inches of reach on him so Zank wanted him to throw some punches. But his opponent didn't seem all that willing. Zank waited him out. He dropped his guard even lower, inviting attack.

Finally the tall man made a clumsy forward move and swung at Zank, a fast, looping right. Zank ducked, then ducked a left, then two quick rights. The man had swung four times without landing a blow. Zank smiled. Goddamn amateurs. Enough horsing around. Zank faked with a right, then slapped him twice in the face with his left to humiliate him.

"Motherfuck," the man growled, and swung wildly at Zank. He missed. He missed again. Then he put his head down and charged. Zank landed a perfectly timed right on the side of his jaw that took him down hard. A Budweiser sign fell off the wall from the jolt. The small crowd stepped back as one.

The man lay still for a moment or two, then got up on his knees, breathing deeply and spitting blood and pieces of tooth. His friend was just beginning to stir. They looked at each other without seeming to know what planet they were on, Zank thought, their eyes like tropical fish darting around in cloudy little bowls.

Zank looked over the rest of them. Mostly they looked stunned. Zank's hand stung maddeningly, but he didn't let it show.

No one spoke. No one moved. Some shook their heads in disbelief.

"Please stand clear of the door," Zank said. As he walked out he heard the lady bartender saying: "Dr. Cole will pop his balloon, don't worry none."

4

Zank thought of the LTD he was driving as a sled, but it had a modified suspension, air shocks, and the fuel-injected interceptor engine. It would top out at about 135, Zank guessed. Be no good on mountain curves against a good road car like a Porsche or a Ferrari, but it could take any standard production sedan on earth on the straightaway. The battered old Chevy pickup that followed him out of town would be no problem at all.

He kept his speed at forty-five and waited for the two guys in the pickup to make a move. They seemed content to hang back and just follow. The waiting game continued for a couple of miles, then Zank sped up just to see what would happen. They matched his speed, staying back maybe half a mile. He slowed to twenty miles an hour. So did the pickup, keeping its distance. Finally, with a grin, Zank hit the accelerator and felt the surge of the engine's enormous power: the LTD knelt low in the rear and shot forward, the speed climbing quickly—seventy, eighty, ninety, ninety-five. The pickup shrank to a dot in the rearview mirror. Zank slowed, took a couple of curves, then headed into a long flat stretch alongside a reservoir and slowed down to twenty-five. He checked the rearview mirror again. No pickup. Piece of cake.

Zank kept going for a few miles, then turned westward again on Creek Road. He found the entrance to Bright Horizons a couple of miles farther on. It was in a wooded area of rolling hills. Past the entrance was a dirt road heading into the woods. He couldn't see any buildings or people. A sign said, ADMITTANCE BY INVITATION ONLY. No one around, far as he could tell. He continued on the road for a mile and a half and parked in a cluster of scrub pine on a flat spot thirty yards off the road. His right hand still throbbed. He wondered what the man's jaw felt like. He hoped it was broken in six places.

He took the ankle gun from beneath the seat and pumped a shell into the chamber. It was a lightweight Bersa Model 644. He flipped on the safety, put it in the holster, and fixed the tie-down strap. Then he reached up under the dash and took out the big gun, the Ruger Super Blackhawk single-action .44 revolver. It weighed maybe two-and-a-half pounds, but he knew that carting it around, it would feel as heavy as carrying a bowling ball in your pocket. He didn't like guns. He'd never shot anyone and couldn't imagine himself doing it. But a .44 magnum makes a hell of a bang. Scare a lot of pigeons. Scare a college professor outta his shorts.

He swung the barrel open and checked the cylinder. It was loaded. He took off his jacket and slipped on a shoulder holster. Next, he put two speed loaders and a box of shells in his jacket pocket. He put his jacket back on, picked up his light-collecting, infrared binoculars and a knockout kit (containing two syringes, alcohol, cotton, and two ampules of barbiturate), and got out of the car. He opened the trunk and found boxes of survival gear, food, heavy clothing, sleeping bags. He stuffed a bottle of high-energy tablets into his sport coat pocket and left the rest. He wasn't figuring to camp out.

There was a quiet breeze blowing from the southeast and somewhere off in the distance Zank could hear a single-engine plane. That was the only sound, except for the chirp of the birds in the trees. He stepped back a few paces and took a look at the car. It was nearly completely hidden by the pine trees, but that wasn't good enough. He tore off a few pine branches and covered the trunk. His hands were sticky now with strong-smelling tree sap.

He crossed the road, went up a small hill, and looked back toward his car. No part of it showed. Satisfied, he moved off over the hill and down the other side, making his way in a northerly direction. He stopped every few minutes to listen and scan the area with his binoculars. Ahead of him, off in the distance, a couple of deer grazed on the side of a hill, but he didn't see any people. Surely someone from town would have called and they'd be on guard. He wondered where they were. He kept walking.

He'd gone about a mile and a half when he came upon a well-worn trail circling downhill and to his right. He followed it down the hill to a road that led eastward, into the hills. Figuring if they were waiting for him, they'd be waiting along that road, he stayed a few hundred feet off, keeping to the high grass and pine groves. It was rough going. Burrs stuck to his socks. He was sweating. His hand hurt. His sinuses were clogging up and his eyes watering. The bugs were lunching on his neck. Zank was not an outdoorsman. He never even liked picnics. His ex-wife Arlene had liked picnics, he remembered. That should have tipped him off as to the kind of person she was. He cursed at the burrs stuck in his socks, then cursed Arlene.

For a long time he'd had a vague dream of starting his own training camp for young boxers away from the city where there'd be no distractions. As he trampled through the trees, he made up his mind that when he made his training camp he was going to cement it over, put a wall around it, and stay inside. Nothing would get in but the clean air and sunshine. No nettles, no wood ticks, no rabid squirrels.

There was a curve in the road ahead. He went around a small hill and looked down. He saw a gate with four men hanging around. Waiting for him? Another one stood lookout halfway up the hill, behind a tree. All five were athletically trim, had short hair, and wore white: white shirts, pants, jackets, and shoes. They looked a little jittery. Amateurs. Good.

Zank considered his alternatives. He could talk to them, maybe see if they'd just let him have Cleomona. He could plunge in and knock a few around, try to force them to take him to Cleomona. Or he could avoid them. He decided to avoid them. He retreated up the hill and continued east, keeping parallel to the hill. A little farther on he found a parking area with two cars. One was a Lincoln Continental Mark VII, the other a Datsun. They were both new and shiny and had California plates. He memorized the license numbers, just in case.

He circled around through a stand of tall pines, and came to a sandstone cliff. He made his way along the edge of the cliff for a few hundred yards to where the cliff became a hill. Below the hill was a small cluster of buildings: a large clapboard house and half a dozen cottages. He took a look through his binoculars.

A small gray dog was barking in the yard. No one paid any attention to it, so Zank figured the dog just liked to bark. He watched for half an hour. Nothing happened. Then two men came out of the house, walked around behind it to a cottage, and knocked on the door. The door opened. A girl wearing a white sweatsuit stood in the doorway and spoke to the two men. Cleomona? Zank looked at the picture he had in his pocket. The girl's hair was shorter and she was older, but it could be her. Sure, gotta be. Gonna go home to mama, Cleomona, just sit tight.

One of the men went inside the cottage. He had gray hair and wore gray slacks and a gray sport coat and tie. Not dressed for camping out, Zank thought. The other had a beard and wore his blond hair shoulder length. He was wearing slacks and a white shirt, white shoes. He carried himself straight and stiff, like the head guards at Quentin carried themselves, and looked around with his head tilted back. Like he owned the place. Zank figured he was Vernon Cole. The man went back into the main house after a few minutes.

Zank waited another half hour. Nothing much happened. A woman in a lavender jumpsuit came out of the main house through a side door, put something in a garbage can, did a little stretching, then went back inside. Zank moved down the hill and took up a position behind a tree fifty yards from the big house. It was dusk now. In the cottage behind the house the lights came on for a few minutes, then went off. Zank chewed some high-energy tablets.

The deep shadows of twilight turned to darkness, the moon rose and then disappeared behind clouds. Zank was grateful for the darkness. It would cover his moves, but he'd still be able to see through his light-collecting binoculars.

Lights came on inside the main house. No one came or went. He heard a kid crying. Somebody sang a song.

Zank could hear voices inside the house now. Laughter. Running water and the clacking of plates—someone was doing the dishes. The dog was barking again. He circled around the clearing where the buildings stood and came up alongside the main house. A telephone line rose out of an underground pipe and went up the side of the house. He took out his knife and cut a two-foot section out of the wire so that if he managed to get Cleomona, no one would be calling ahead for roadblocks. Unless, Zank thought, they got a two-way radio. He figured they probably didn't.

Then he circled behind the cottage where the girl he thought might be Cleomona had gone inside with the gray-haired man. There were no lights on. He listened for a long while, then heard the man say, "You asleep?"

"No," the girl said.

"I should be heading back," the man said.

"What about the intruder?"

"If he was coming, he'd have come by now."

Zank heard the creaking of bedsprings. The light came on. He made his way around the side of the building and found cover in the brush along the walkway. He didn't get a good look at the man's face when he came out a few minutes later, but he could see the girl clearly in the light. It was Cleomona Fisk, and there was no mistake. Zank's heartbeat quickened. Gonna be a piece of cake.

He waited until the man had gone down the path and into the big house before he went up to the cottage and tried the door. Not locked. He stepped inside and closed the door behind him.

"Who the fuck are you?" She stood in front of him, still as a statue of Venus, still and naked—except for a pair of pink silk underpants. She was slender and shapely, with small breasts and fire-red nipples. He sensed not an iota of fear in her. Nor shame.

"Be quiet," Zank whispered. "Get something on." He handed her a sweatshirt and a pair of white tennis shorts lying on the table next to the bed. She didn't move.

"Put 'em on or I make you put 'em on—your choice."

She was smiling faintly at him. "Anything you say." She slipped the sweatshirt on over her head.

Zank took a look around. The cottage was small and tidy; the furniture, the kind they sell cheap at Goodwill, was sparse. The lace curtain on the window gave the place the feel of a doll house. On the wall was a picture of Jesus Christ pointing to His Sacred Heart.

She said, "You gonna tell me what the hell you're doing here?"

"Come to get you out of here. Your mama sent me."

"Why? She tell you why?" She didn't seem surprised, Zank thought, and didn't seem not surprised.

He said, "She wants to see you real bad. She's sick."

"Oh, yeah? How sick?" She didn't seem to believe it.

Zank hesitated, then said, "The doctors don't give much hope."

Her eyes softened. She nodded and said, "I feel bad about that, but I can't go. Believe me, you try to take me out of here, there's going to be blood spilt."

"That's up to them."

"You got a gun?"

"Think I might need one?"

"Cole knows you're here, you're going to need an army."

"Then let's get going before he finds out."

"Promise if I go along there'll be no shooting."

"You got my word."

She took a pillowcase from the bed and started stuffing her clothes into it. This all seemed strange to Zank. In the two snatches he'd made before, both subjects kicked and screamed and made a hell of a fuss.

"What's your name?" she asked, still stuffing things into her pillowcase.

"Richard Conrad."

"Nice to meet you, Rick." She smiled at him. Not a girl smile, a woman smile. A woman-who's-interested smile. Zank didn't like it. If she was going to try to seduce him, she better get grown up first.

Zank said, "Who was that guy who just left here?"

"Don't know his name. Don't care, either." She tied the pillowcase into a knot. "Okay, I'm ready."

"You bed guys you don't know who they are?"

"When Vernon tells me. That's just the way things are around here."

"I get it. Maybe you ought to learn to say no."

She looked at him as if he were an idiot child. "Everybody earns their keep around here."

"You got a jacket?"

"I'll be okay. I'm warm blooded."

He clicked off the light and waited a moment for his eyes to adjust. Then he took a look through his infrared binoculars. No one out in front. He checked the back window, keeping hold of Cleomona. Two figures were in the trees on the hill above them. Maybe men, maybe deer.

"They're waiting, aren't they?" Cleomona said.

"Can't tell." He checked again out the front. "Looks okay this way."

"You hope."

"Ready?"

"Sure."

Zank took her by the wrist. "Hope you don't mind I hold onto you."

"You got to do your job, I suppose."

He opened the door and they started down the path in the darkness. At the end of the path they turned and started across the road. A twig snapped. There was movement off on his left side. Suddenly a mass of floodlights came on, like a night game for the World Series, blinding Zank. He shielded his eyes with his arm momentarily. Goddamn. His hand reached into his coat and he grabbed hold of the hilt of the Ruger Blackhawk .44, but he didn't pull it out. Now he could see shapes. Two men standing in front of him came into focus, blocking his way. Zank turned around and there were two more behind him. All four were dressed in white. Zank held onto Cleomona tightly. She was trying to pull away from him. "Let go of me, asshole!" She kicked him, but it didn't hurt.

One of the men standing in front of him was one of the two who'd gone to Cleomona's—not the one who had gone inside. He was about Zank's height, six feet even, but thinner, and had shoulder-length golden hair and a beard. It was the guy he'd seen earlier walking around like the king of the place. His face, up close, looked like the painting of Christ in Cleomona's cottage, except this man's eyes were small and black and sharp. He was smiling a snake charmer's smile.

"I'm Vernon Cole, and who, sir, be you?"

"I'm the guy who's gonna take Cleomona home to her mama."

Cole stretched his arms out, like he was really surprised. "Cleomona belongs to us."

Zank was still looking around, making sure nobody was sneaking up on him. "Cleomona don't belong to no one," he said. "But her mother needs her. She's going home."

Cole said, "She is, of course, perfectly free to go if she wishes. Do you want to leave, Cleomona?"

"I was playing this chump along, Vern. You know I want to stay. I'm never leaving you."

"You heard her," Cole said, as if the matter were settled.

Zank said, "She's a minor. That means her mama decides where she lives."

Cole put his hands in his pockets. Zank thought he looked relaxed. Just having a chat. "Her mother is mentally unstable, sir, not equipped to handle the child. Cleomona is far better off with us, who love and care for her and are preparing her to cope with the harsh realities of modern times."

Zank wasn't sure what the hell that meant, if it meant anything. He said, "Still, her mama's got the right. She can get a writ anytime she wants and the cops will pick her up."

Vernon Cole shook his head slowly. "Cleomona is merely visiting, my friend, just for today. If the police want to check, she'll probably be gone like the wind. You know how rootless young people are these days. In fact, you may even have a problem finding a collaborating witness who will support your wild story that she's been here at all. Now then, over here, Cleomona."

More of the little band was gathering around them, with makeshift clubs and kitchen knives. Zank spread his gaze over the little crowd. By the awkward way they held their weapons, he figured most of them had never attacked anything more dangerous than a mashed potato. "She can come back later if she wants and her mother says it's okay," Zank said, "but she's leaving with me now. That's the way it's got to be."

"You must have been asking around about me in town today," Cole said. "Were you out to see Mrs. Fisk? Have you got a phony police badge in the name of Sergio Veracruz? The San Francisco police never heard of Sergio Veracruz. Who is paying you? And don't tell me it's Cleomona's mother."

"I do this for the fun of it. I used to grow pumpkins, but this is better exercise."

Cole laughed. "I certainly enjoy having guests with a sense of humor. But seeing how egregiously outnumbered you are, I would say the chances of you taking Cleomona away tonight are slim."

Zank pulled out his Ruger Blackhawk, cocked it, and pointed it at Cole. "You mind repeating that for my friend here?"

Cole's sharp black eyes blazed in the light of the floodlights. He put his hands behind his back and spread his legs like a soldier at parade rest, then motioned to his men to move in closer. They nodded, and as each raised his club or knife, Zank saw fierce determination pour into their eyes, as if they were willing to die to prove something. Zank had seen the same thing in the eyes of men he'd fought in the ring. Men he'd pulverized but still kept coming. He kept the Ruger leveled at Cole. "Back off!" Zank hollered. "Get back, all of you!"

They stepped even closer, raising their weapons higher.

"Tell them to back off," Zank said, holding the Ruger steady, aiming at Cole's head. "I'm taking Cleomona home to mama. I got a hotload 250-grain slug in here that will make a pizza-to-go out of an African elephant, and before anybody gets about one foot closer I'm going to give a demonstration."

Cole turned to the man on his right, a big-boned redhead holding a meat cleaver. "If he kills me, be sure my remains are given a proper burial, and *his* remains are fed to the dog."

The man with the meat cleaver smiled and nodded and stepped closer. The look on his face said he'd enjoy feeding

Zank to the dog, and unlike the others, he seemed like he knew what he was doing. If things go down bad and physical, Zank thought, Meat Cleaver gets bullet #2. He tightened his grip on both Cleomona and the Ruger Blackhawk.

He swung around, pointing the gun at each of them in turn. None of them flinched. Goddamn. Might just as well be pointing a chicken leg. They were in a tight circle around Zank now, no more than two quick steps away. Zank's heart pounded in his ears and sweat rolled down his neck. Goddamn crazy sons of bitches must wanna die.

Zank jerked the gun upward and fired into the air. The flash and boom rent the night like lightning splitting a tree. The suddenness surprised Cole's men; two of them jumped back, the other froze. The woods momentarily sprang alive with fleeing animals and birds. Zank's ears rang.

"Back! Back! Back!" Zank shouted, swinging the gun around. "Talking time is over!" He pointed the gun at the earth in front of Meat Cleaver and fired. Meat Cleaver leapt backward five feet in one hop.

They were all backing up, their fearful eyes darting between Zank's gun and Cole's face.

"Hold it!" Cole yelled. "I tell you when to move, nobody else!"

They stopped moving like kids playing Simon Says. Zank thought it looked as if they had strings tied to them and Cole had jerked on them. They seemed more afraid of Cole than of a .44 magnum.

"Let's go, Cleomona," Zank said, dragging her toward the path. The little crowd moved with him, circled around. He kept the gun pointed at Cole. "I take out you and Meat Cleaver here, and I think the rest, seeing all that blood splatter might just decide they'd rather give at the blood bank than here. Want to bet on it? Tell Meat Cleaver here to step up and get his first."

Meat Cleaver was holding his cleaver back now, like he was getting ready to throw it. He flicks his wrist, Zank thought, he gets blown to hell.

"He's chicken," Cleomona said. "Look at him sweat. He ain't gonna shoot nobody. Make him let go of me!"

Cole circled around and stopped in front of Zank. Zank kept the gun pointed at him.

"Okay, my friend," Cole said to Zank, "I've decided you definitely may not take her with you. Now, do you shoot, or what do you do? We are not going to be cowered by a bully."

Zank pulled the gun's hammer back. He held his aim steady, sighting down the barrel at Cole. Cole smiled. "Well, shoot if you're going to, but let's not stand here getting eaten by mosquitoes all night." Zank didn't move. No one moved. It was suddenly quiet and still. No one spoke. Zank felt the sweat rolling down his back now. The gun in his hand weighed ten times its two and a half pounds.

Then Cole said, "Come over here, Cleomona." He said it soothingly and slowly.

Cleomona jerked herself loose from Zank's grasp. Zank didn't try to stop her. She darted to Cole's side, grabbing hold of his arm. Everyone held their positions. Zank lowered his sights. "You've won, Cole. I'll leave. Just tell everybody to move back and give me some space."

"By all means," Cole said with a sweep of his arm. The men retreated, lowering their weapons. A couple laughed in nervous relief. Zank turned around and backed away from them, keeping his gun aimed at Cole. Then he turned again when he was a few yards down the trail and jogged down the path toward the main road, glancing back over his shoulder every few seconds. A half dozen of Cole's men were following him, perhaps fifty yards behind.

He jogged the two or three miles back to the main road, turned south, and ran back to his car. There were headlights following him back through Eagleston and a couple of miles past. When whoever it was turned around, he pulled off onto a side road, stopped, and turned on the interior light. He took out a map, studied it for a few moments, then turned off the light, started the car, and headed back toward Eagleston.

A light rain fell for most of the morning. After the rain a heavy mist hung in the air above the trees. In the afternoon it rained again, heavily, for an hour, and the mist disappeared. The pine smell was strong in the air, clean and fresh.

Zank, wearing a camouflage poncho, sat on a hill behind the small collection of buildings and watched with binoculars. He'd had a few hours' sleep in the LTD, which he'd left on a small ranch road east of the Bright Horizons camp. He'd walked eleven miles along a creek bed in the predawn and had been in position when the sun came up. Now he was cold, tired, and miserable.

This time he figured to do it differently. He was going to make sure they weren't looking out for him. Then maybe he'd get his car, drive close, and take her out quick.

In the morning Zank had spotted a yellow Hertz pickup. Three men loaded a few dozen boxes in the back of it, covered them with a tarp and drove off. He didn't see anyone else until two-thirty in the afternoon, when a Winnebago appeared during the heaviest part of the downpour and four men and two women came out of the big house, got in, and drove off. A few minutes later a woman came out of a cottage with a newspaper over her head as protection from the rain and went into the big house. After the rain had all but stopped, she came out with Vernon Cole and together they walked up the road toward the parking area. Zank heard a car start up and drive off.

Now where the hell was Cleomona?

Zank sat under a tree and waited. There was no other activity during the day. No sign of anyone. When nightfall came, no lights came on in any of the cottages or in the big house. Zank made his way down the hill. No dog barked. He went from one cottage to another listening for voices at closed windows and doors. He heard none. He saw no one.

He checked the cottage where he'd met Cleomona the night before, and found the door unlocked. He went in and shined his flashlight around. Nothing. Nobody. The picture of Christ on the wall was gone. The closet was empty. He looked in the bureau drawers and found them all empty. He found nothing in the five other cottages either. None of them were locked. But the door to the main house was. He tried to pick the lock, but the tumblers inside were too small and numerous and he soon lost patience. He kicked it in.

Inside he found the furnishings were modern and probably expensive. There was a stereo, a huge air conditioner, and a color TV with a screen a yard-and-a-half wide. The kitchen was modern and spotless, with a lot of Formica and stainless steel. He made a cursory check to make sure he was alone, then started searching the place thoroughly. He began upstairs in the bedrooms and bathrooms. Everything had been cleaned out except the furniture, two towels, and six rolls of toilet paper.

Downstairs, he went through the closets, a desk, the kitchen cupboards. He found two old fishing reels, assorted nuts, bolts and screws, and a pair of old rubber boots with a hole in the right toe. And he found a door off the living room with a padlock on it. He tried kicking it in, but it wouldn't go, so he went outside and found a piece of iron pipe under the porch. He used it to pry the lock off. It was a darkroom, complete with chemicals, enlargers, and printers. That was it. Not a clue to where they'd gone.

So, he thought, they want to play hide and seek. Okay, we'll play. But they're gonna find out pretty goddamn quick, the planet ain't big enough to hide her, even though it's the fifth goddamn largest planet in the solar system.

5

"Extension 225."

"Hi, Ruby, honey."

"Who this?"

"Joe Zanca."

"Ah don't know no Zanca, 'cept Babe Zanca who fixes my car. And he call me *Miss* Hazeltine 'cause he have nice manners."

"I'm the other Zanca. No manners."

"Don't know no other Zanca."

"Ruby, honey, how can you say that after all we've meant to each other?"

"What we meant to each other? You snake! You been sweet talkin' me all these years and ah been listenin', and for what? Ah thought you an honest man who jus' wanted a wholesome hunk of my beautiful black ass, and all the time all you interested in is my files."

"Ruby, Ruby, bitter words."

"Zanca, you a loathsome piece of small change. What you callin' me for?"

"I got to have some license checks in a hurry, Ruby."

"Noooooooooo way!"

"Ruby, please listen, lovely lady, there's a young girl in the hands of a sex cult and her mama is desperate to get her back. The girl's being used as a sex slave, Ruby. She's just a kid. I've got to find her and save her."

"You makin' this up?"

"I swear it, Ruby. The cops won't help me because of my record. The cult's supposed to be a corporation, but they ain't even in the phone book. I checked all the phone books in the Bay Area. And the California Department of Corporations says they are owned by some outfit in the Bahamas, but no local address. I called the Bahamas, got a phone number, but nobody answers. They ain't anyplace. All I got is a couple of license numbers that may be a lead. Please, Ruby, she's just a little kid."

"When you comin' over?"

"Soon, I promise—Ruby, she's only nine!"

There was silence on the line for a moment.

"How come The Agency don't get them for you?"

"I can't ask."

"Why not? You always did before."

"Just can't this time—I missed the snatch and I don't want The Agency to know, okay?"

"Zanca, if you lyin' to me, Ah hope yo private parts turn to cement. You know Ah ain't supposed to give this info out to the public. The sheriff's office is an official place, we got strict rules."

"I wouldn't ask if it weren't for the girl. And her so young and helpless."

"Ah ever find you lyin' to me, Zanca, Ah'm gonna have you arrested and beat with rubber hoses. Ah can do it too—Ah know some mean-ass deputies."

"Take these numbers down, Ruby."

He gave her the numbers he got off the cars he'd seen at the camp in Eagleston. She was back on the line in less than a minute.

"Ah got 'em, Zanca. The Winnebago and the Datsun is registered to Bright Horizons Inc. at Post Office Box 7427, Berkeley. The Continental's registered to Franklyn Dix, 1111 California Park Drive, San Francisco. You know him?"

"He on the Board of Supervisors?"

"You got it. He's one big shot, Mr. Zanca. You best be watchin' yo'self."

"I'll be in touch, Ruby."

"Rather you jus' don't bother, Mr. Phonybaloney."

*   *   *

The Electronic Marvel Shop fronted on Clement Street. The red-lettered sign in the window said: GIGANTIC SALE, EVERYTHING IN THE STORE AT HUGE SAVINGS. The sign had been there for six years that Zank knew of, and probably a lot longer than that. There were no customers in the store taking advantage of the huge savings. The shelves were packed with every kind of electronic gadget imaginable: from amp meters to video tape machines to kits to make your own lie detector. Zank went in and found Wendy Chow, Harry's wife, behind the counter.

"When you gonna take that sign down?" he asked.

"You say that every time you come in." Wendy smiled a bright, easy smile that lit up her small China-doll face.

"Where's that Fu Manchu you're married to?"

"In the office—thinking."

"Ah, but what's he thinking *with*?"

"Come on, Zank, don't pick on him—are you here on a social call or business?"

"Maybe a little of both."

Her eyes widened. "Please don't get him into any trouble, Zank. Please."

"No trouble, Wendy. Piece of cake."

She scowled.

"I mean it, Wendy. I wouldn't ask, except I'm in a terrible bind."

"Zank, you were born in a terrible bind." She lifted a folding section of the counter to let him pass through to a small door that led to a storeroom. On the other side of the storeroom another door led into a small, overcrowded office. There were a couple of chairs, a small desk piled high with papers, boxes of electronic parts, and stacks of files and catalogues.

Harry Chow sat behind the desk with his feet up, reading a comic book. He looked up. "Morning, Tank. Your face looks much better. Ready to take on Kid Swan again?"

"Some things you shouldn't joke about, Harry."

"You want to go for a workout? Wendy'll watch the store."

"Work day, Harry," Zank said. "Still got a snatch to

make.'' He sat in a chair and put one leg up on Harry's desk. He wanted it to look like he wasn't being pushed.

Harry twisted the ends of his thin mustache, which made him look slightly sinister. Zank figured he liked to look sinister. Harry lit a cigarette. ''How'd my little telephone device work out?''

''Okay.''

''So now what can I do for you?''

''A small favor.''

''What's it pay?''

Zank shrugged. ''Twenty an hour.''

''Business is bad, but not *that* bad.''

''Okay, I'll make it twenty-five. But the job is a piece of cake and ain't worth no more than twenty-five.''

''If that Radio Shack hadn't gone in up the block, I wouldn't even be talking to you. What do I have to do?'' He leaned forward as if he expected Zank to whisper, even though there was no reason. Goddamn Harry likes intrigue, Zank thought, more than he loves money. And he loves money the way a career virgin loves not getting laid.

Zank played along. He whispered: ''There's this P.O. box number. Watch it, and when somebody picks up the mail, find out where they go. No cowboy stuff, Harry. I don't want you taking no chances.''

''Where's the box?''

''Berkeley.''

''You never said it was Berkeley. Make it thirty an hour.'' Harry looked suddenly serious.

Zank was puzzled. ''Okay, but what the hell's wrong with Berkeley?''

''I don't like Berkeley. Too many yuppies.''

''What the hell's wrong with yuppies?''

''I see them, I break out in a strawberry rash.''

''That sounds like strawberry bullshit to me.''

Harry Chow's face exploded with a wide grin. ''You went for the thirty, didn't you?''

''Look, Harry, let's not screw around.'' He stood up and gave him the number of the Post Office box. ''I want to find this girl and get her out of there, okay?''

"Hey, I'll watch that box like it was full of gold. Worry not, old pugilist."

The doughnut glaze stuck to Detective Sgt. Leslie Donaldson's mustache like frost. He slurped his coffee and gulped it down with the rest of his doughnut. Leslie Donaldson ate doughnuts like an addict.

He said, "Yeah, we did an investigation of Bright Horizons, so what you want to know for?"

"Just asking," Zank said. He sipped his orange juice, trying to act like he was just mildly curious. Donaldson licked some glaze off his thumb. Zank noticed a little glint of pleasure in Donaldson's eyes. Zank never saw it except when Donaldson was here at Happy Donuts, sitting in the back booth eating his way through a couple of giant old-fashioned glazed.

Donaldson said, "Doing a piece for *People* magazine or what?"

"I'm just a curious citizen," Zank said.

"You still working for The Agency?"

"What agency?" He tried to look genuinely perplexed.

"You know damn well *what* agency, don't play smartass."

"Never even heard of no agency."

Donaldson stuffed his mouth full of doughnut and said, "You got no visible means of support, Zank the Rank, and that makes you a damn suspicious character."

"I'm mooching off my sister."

"Why do I even talk with you? If you're mooching off your sister, I'm Ayatollah Khomeini. Your sister's a nun and took a vow of poverty, for Christ's sake. Go bother some other cop, would ya?"

"Didn't I hand you Fats Mercurio on a silver platter last year?" He emphasized the point by thumping his chest. "You owe me, Donaldson."

"You haven't done bird turd for me lately."

"Maybe I'm getting ready to give you the bust of the century."

"What bust?" His eyes flickered with mild interest.

"I just said maybe." Zank tossed his empty Styrofoam cup into a nearby trash can. The can had a worn picture of

Daffy Duck on it with the caption, *We aim to keep Happy Donuts happily clean. Your aim will help*. "So tell me about Bright Horizons."

Donaldson glanced around as if he were suddenly worried they might be overheard. Then he said, "Why is it with you *I* feel like the snitch?"

"Goddamn it, Donaldson, I got to know what's with these people."

"Why?"

"I just do." Zank sat back against the wall. "I just do, that's all."

Donaldson eyed him suspiciously. "You trying to extricate someone from Vernon Cole's sphere of influence?"

Zank nodded. "She's just a kid, Donaldson. Her mother's dying of cancer."

"Well, hell's bells, ain't you the soft-hearted slob."

"Maybe I am." Zank sat up and handed him a napkin out of a napkin holder. "Your mustache is clogged."

"Thanks." Donaldson rubbed his mustache with the napkin, but the glaze didn't come off. "How's that?"

"Terrific."

Donaldson slurped some more coffee. "They're all fucked up, these kids today. Ever listen to their music? Listen, Zanca, you find this kid, get a signed authorization from the parent or guardian, I'll have her picked up."

"Yeah, then by the time you get a warrant and send a squad car, she'll take off and nobody'll ever see her again. There are what, twenty-five thousand runaways in this town? What the fuck the cops doing about it? They ain't doing shit. This is my deal, Donaldson, I'll handle it."

"So what do you want from me?"

"She's with Vernon Cole. I was hoping you could tell me where to find him." Donaldson's eyes softened. A sucker for a kid in trouble, Zank thought.

Donaldson stuffed the last of his doughnut into his mouth and started wiping his fingers on a napkin. "Since he folded his seminar business, he's laying low, I hear. He don't exactly let on to where he's hanging out. Thinks people are after him."

Zank said, "Is this Bright Horizons a cult?"

"Cult, shmult. What's a cult? They live together and pass the broads around, that make them a cult? They used to make a lot of money by making a lot of dummies think they can get their intelligence raised and that kind of crap. They ran these weekend seminars, used to be big a while back. Then seminars went out of style, but a few hearty souls stuck with Cole because they think he's the answer to all the weighty problems of the universe. I don't know what the hell they're up to, but I wouldn't call them a cult."

"They do a lot of dope?"

"Everybody does a lot of dope." He stopped wiping his fingers. "You want another doughnut?"

"No."

"I shouldn't have one either, but they got a strawberry jellyball here as good as a screw."

"Have one then."

"I'm thinking about it." Zank noticed his eyes were pointed at the glass doughnut case like a bird dog's at a downed duck.

"Bright Horizons into any criminal activity?" Zank asked.

"Probably. But who isn't?"

"You know Supervisor Dix? He's connected to them."

"How connected?" He seemed suddenly intently interested.

"He's screwing one of the women. I saw his car up at their country place."

"You see *him*?"

"No, not that I'd know him again."

"Then it could have been his chauffeur or his garage mechanic on a test drive. He might have loaned his car to his brother-in-law. I loan my car to my brother-in-law all the time."

"I think it was him."

"Don't mess with Dix, okay? Just leave him the hell alone." Donaldson said nothing for a moment, then shrugged. "I'm having one of those jellyballs." He got up and went to the counter, bought a jellyball, came back and sat down.

Zank said, "I don't get it, you guys got this Cole figured for a flimflam man and you don't even know what he's doing?"

"Hey, the CIA we ain't. We need a complaint before we

go out and investigate something. We don't spy on citizens just because we don't like the way their dong dangles."

"Who is this Vernon Cole, Donaldson? Why do people think he's got the answers to the weightier problems of the universe?"

"Vernon Cole was a Stanford psychologist or philosopher, or some damn thing." Donaldson's cheeks bulged with jellyball. "Don't you read the papers? He has some wild-eyed theory about the superior man and how to develop him. Stanford thought he'd gone around the bend. Cole eventually got himself canned. He went out on his own and started a self-improvement fad. The fad made him rich. The fad passed. He spent a hell of a lot of money trying to keep it going, and, from what I hear, went belly up." He swallowed a mass of doughnut and took a few quick sips of coffee, then jammed some more doughnut in his mouth.

"Belly up, you mean he went broke?"

"Yeah. Bankrupt. Kaput. Must have been rough on him, because for a while there he was something. Dinner parties with the mayor, the governor. Then all of a sudden he was pretty much a nobody. May have made him a little wizzo in the bean. Bright Horizons is paranoid city from what I hear." His eyes narrowed suddenly and he leaned over the table toward Zank. "Listen, Zanca, whenever you got people worshiping somebody like they were a god, you got a dangerous situation. He had maybe two hundred fifty thousand people take those seminars. Out of that many people you're sure to have a few very fanatical followers that will kiss his butt every time it itches. Vernon Cole's little band does *everything* he says. And he's got it in for a lot of people, starting with Stanford. He thinks his fellow shrinks are out to get him too. Hey, the pattern is here. He's as paranoid as Nixon. You got the makings here, my friend. He need only say to one of his dip-shit followers, kill that pesky Joe Zanca, and the next thing you know you're finding bombs in your bloomers. Look, you want to know about Vernon Cole? All you got to do is go to the library and read his book, it'll tell you more than you ever want to know."

*   *   *

"Excuse me, ma'am, are you the librarian?"

"I'm *one* of the librarians." She had a half smile on her thin lips. It looked like a decal glued onto her face. She was a medium tall, medium old, medium stout, black woman wearing oversized glasses.

Zank said, "I'm interested in finding out about a guy. His name is Vernon Cole."

"*Freedom and Self*?"

"Pardon?"

"A Stanford professor named Vernon Cole wrote a book called *Freedom and Self*. Very, very controversial. A work of true genius. Heavily influenced by Nietzsche."

"Friedrich Wilhelm Nietzsche. German philosopher, 1844 to 1900. He was opposed to Christianity and was a follower of a guy name of Schopenhauer. Friedrich Wilhelm Nietzsche died insane. He had the—you know—the pox."

She was gaping at him through her large glasses. "However did you know all that?"

"I read at home a lot. I have my own *World Book*. I'm all the way to Q. Seven years I've been reading it."

She said, "Then you know Nietzsche formulated the doctrine of the *Ubermensch*."

"Of course—what was it again?"

"The *Ubermensch*—the super man, the higher form of life through which culture can be uniquely expressed and interpreted. Vernon Cole based his phenomenological psychological model on *Ubermensch*."

"Yeah? Sounds like it ought to be good reading."

She smiled politely. "The card catalogue is right over there. Look under C for Cole in the author section."

He turned away from her desk, then stopped. "You ever hear of Zank the Tank?" he asked.

"What? Who?"

"Joe Zanca, the boxer. Zank the Tank. He knocked out Salvatore Pedrone, the Argentine light-heavyweight champ, in the eighth round. Happened right here in San Francisco at the Cow Palace. A right cross. Ended Pedrone's career at twenty-six."

"Oh, my."

"That was me. I was the 'Tank.' "

"You don't say." Her smile faded, but being glued on, it didn't disappear completely. "The card catalogue is still over there, Mr. Tank."

He found the catalogue with no trouble at all, found the card, and found the book in the stacks. The sticker in front indicated that it had been checked out a dozen times so far that year.

The opening paragraph read:

A civilization of free men is not possible. Civilization itself *means* slavery. It means that men of great will and great talent must be subjugated to the collective will of the masses. Great thinkers of the past such as Marx and Hegel have observed and even embraced the concept as an *a priori* requisite to human life. The Western democracies' veneer of freedom, they knew, was nothing more than empty rhetoric. Civilization, from the moment the individual is born, inculcates *woulds, shoulds, mays,* and *don'ts,* often beating the hapless young individualist who dares risk nonconformity. The process is called *socialization.* Only the strongest and most brilliant men, the Galileos, the Martin Luthers, the Marquis de Sades, the Jesus Christs and Adolf Hitlers, can withstand such a process and bend the culture to their will. Freedom cannot exist within the confines of conformity to culture and civilization, it must exist in opposition to it. . . .

A sign on the wall said: RIDE THE UNICORN NOW! There was a picture of a white unicorn and a nude woman with long hair riding it. Zank didn't ask what it meant to ride the unicorn. The woman seated at the desk beneath the unicorn sign was small-breasted and braless. The faded T-shirt she was wearing said: GO BAARF!—THE BAY AREA ANTI-REAGAN FESTIVAL.

"You Martha Manning?" Zank asked her.

She said: "Where'd you get my name?"

"You are Martha Manning?"

"I asked you where you got my name."

"Okay, a guy name of Vernon Cole who used to teach at

Stanford University wrote a book called *Freedom and Self*. I got the book out of the library. It's dedicated to Martha Manning. I called Stanford and asked the secretary in the Philosophy department if she knew where I could find you. I told her I was Joe Manning, a cousin, who just got out of prison in Oregon and was passing through and needed a place to sleep.'' He grinned. ''Worked like a charm. She felt sorry for me, so she gave me the name of the center here and told me you were on the staff. I read some of Dr. Cole's book, but I still have a lot of questions and I can't find Dr. Cole.''

Martha Manning had a steel-hard look in her eyes, and her long, chestnut hair was cut in bangs across her forehead. It didn't look right on a woman in her thirties, Zank thought.

''What's your interest in Vernon? It can't be just because you read a book.'' She spoke through clenched teeth. ''Who are you?''

''Okay, my name is Rick Conrad. It's on account of my sister. She's a secretary. She's thinking about going to work for Bright Horizons.''

Her narrow eyes were full of suspicion, Zank thought. There was a chair for visitors, but she hadn't offered it to him. He didn't ask. He thought maybe she liked sitting there and looking up at him, maybe it made her feel important.''

She said, ''I don't like to talk about Vernon.''

''I can understand that, sure. I wouldn't ask except on account of my sister. I figured you'd know. I mean, you must have been close for him to dedicate his book to you.''

''Vernon Cole and I had a relationship.''

''I see. The lady I talked to at Stanford said you'd broken up.'' He said it softly, trying to sound sympathetic.

''I had a bad time, so big deal. I was young and in love, it went bust. Crap like that happens to everybody.'' She said it matter-of-factly, but Zank could sense the bitterness.

''If you could just give me a lead on where I might find him . . .''

''Doesn't your sister know?'' She said it, Zank thought, with a sly smile. She ain't buying the sister razzmatazz.

He said: ''She tells me to mind my own damn business, but I worry. Please, just tell me: Is Vernon Cole an okay guy or ain't he? I can't find out anything about him. I can't even find *him*.''

''God can't find Vernon Cole unless he wants to be found. I don't know what to tell you. If he doesn't want people to know where he is, that's his business. I've got work to do.''' She shuffled some papers around on her desk. She seemed to be doing it to let him know she wanted him to leave.

But he didn't leave. He just stood there for a few moments watching her move papers around. Then he said, ''You counsel women who get beat up by their husbands?''

''That's right.'' Her eyes said: Want to make something of it?

''Must be a good job,'' Zank said. ''Helping people.''

''What's your business with Vernon Cole? Don't give me that shit about your sister.''

''You know Cleomona Fisk?''

''Heard of her.'' She laughed. Zank didn't know why.

He said, ''Her mother thinks she should come home. She's just a kid, only sixteen.''

''Cleomona Fisk was never a kid, mister, believe me.'' She shuffled the papers around on her desk again. ''Christ, we're busy around here. There must be a million battered women in this fricken city.''

''You think Vernon Cole is a genius? I talked to a librarian today who thinks he is.''

''He's a genius at manipulating people. He makes you think you're scum if you don't do what he says you should do. But you know, he works miracles with kids.''

''What miracles?''

''You really don't know what's going on with Vernon Cole, do you?''

''Not got the foggiest. What is going on with him?''

''I'll never talk about it.''

''I ain't the law.''

She arched an eyebrow. ''I really don't know who you are, now do I?''

''Why'd you leave him?''

''None of your business.''

''Why won't he let Cleomona go home to her mama?''

"That's the way he is. He has something, he hangs on to it. He won't let her go, not in a million years."

"Maybe if I ask nice."

She smiled at him. For a moment she looked like a happy kid. But just for a moment, then the hardness returned.

"Where can I find him? Give me a clue. *Please.*"

She leaned back and shook her head. "I don't know, okay? Nobody knows. He keeps on the move. He wants you, he finds you. You call his office, leave a message."

"You got that number?"

"Sorry, I don't. Really." She went back to her paperwork. Her fingers were trembling.

Goddamn, Zank thought, she's really shook up just talking about this Cole creep. "Hey," he said, "I'm sorry, I didn't mean to rattle your cage. I know how it is to get burned in the love game. My wife waltzed me to the judge, so I know all about it. Anyway, you don't want to talk, okay. Thank for your time." He took out his wallet and put a hundred dollar bill in front of her. "Here, take it."

"What's this for?"

"For your center here. My old man used to bat my mother around. I know what you people are talking about."

She looked at Zank, then at the bill, then at Zank again.

"Maybe you're for real."

"I'm going to get Cleomona and take her home. If that's what you mean by being real, I'm for real."

Martha Manning sucked on her lower lip, thinking for a moment. "Close the door," she said. "I want to show you something."

He closed the door. She stood up and pulled down the shades.

"You don't know what you're dealing with when you go up against Vernon Cole. The power he has over people. You want to know what he's saying in his book? He's saying he's a special person and he has the right to do any damn thing he wants." She turned sideways and lifted her T-shirt, exposing her left breast. "See that?"

Zank turned away. "That's okay, I believe you."

"No, I want you to see what he did to me."

He took a quick look. There were two initials above the

nipple: V.C. They were deep brown in color, rough edged, the size of quarters. "Geeezus," Zank said.

She pulled her shirt down and sat behind the desk again. Her face turned gray and her eyes were far away.

"One day Vernon got this weird idea. He got hold of this branding iron. He heated it up in a charcoal fire till it was white hot. He put some acid rock music on the stereo, real loud. I stood still and let him do it—proud to prove my love for him. Fifteen people watched. They cheered."

Zank said, "I—I can't imagine it."

Her mouth got tight again. "I've since had my consciousness raised. I don't let men fuck me over anymore. Period."

Zank parked the LTD in front of the emergency room of Walker Memorial and went in through the glass doors marked EMERGENCY ROOM PERSONNEL ONLY and up the stairs to the trauma center nurses' station. He was wearing a sport jacket and tie, and had had his shoes shined. The nurse's aide looked up at him. "Yes?" she said.

"Miss Jill Stanyan, please."

"Nurse Stanyan isn't here at the moment."

"I phoned earlier, she's scheduled to work this afternoon."

"Perhaps you should see the supervisor, Mrs. Radcliffe, right down the hall."

Zank went down the hall to a small office. Two supervisors shared a large table with nameplates propped up on it. Mrs. Radcliffe was on the phone. She was a big-boned woman with short gray hair combed in a part. She had a long, serious face, and deep-set, no-nonsense eyes. When she finished talking, she turned to him. "Are you here to see a patient?"

"I'm looking for Jill Stanyan."

"I'm sorry, she's gone home for the day—ill. Are you a friend of Jill's?"

"Police matter," Zank said, displaying his Sgt. Veracruz ID.

She gestured for him to follow her down the hall, past dozens of glass-paneled rooms, one patient to a room. Most of the patients were hooked up to machines. Many of the rooms were marked: "Sterile area, masks and gowns required." They went into the nurses' coffee room. It was small and cluttered. A sign on the wall said: KEEP THIS ROOM CLEAN OR YOU'LL GET HEMORRHOIDS. Two nurses were finishing their coffee from Styrofoam cups. When they saw their boss come in with Zank, they left. Mrs. Radcliffe closed the door and offered Zank a seat. She pulled up a chair next to him. "Is Jill in any trouble?" she asked.

"No, no. I'm looking for a man who she may know. His name is Vernon Cole."

"Why, yes. She met him right here. He was a patient. Snakebite. Jill may have saved his life. If he'd had a lackluster nurse that first day, he'd have been gone."

"You know where I can find him?"

"You could check with records downstairs."

"Would you mind giving them a call?"

"Not at all."

She phoned the records office and asked them for Vernon Cole's address. She wrote it down and handed it to him. It was the same P.O. box in Berkeley. Zank put the paper in his pocket.

She said, "I take it you already had that."

"Yes, we did. Can you tell me something about Jill Stanyan?"

"Jill is the best nurse we've got. She's not only good technically, she's also extraordinarily compassionate and can handle the relatives and friends like a real diplomat."

"Do you know anything about her personal life? It may be important."

"Can't you tell me what this is all about?" Worry lines were deep in her forehead.

"We aren't after her. She's being taken advantage of. It would help us a great deal if we knew more about her."

She seemed relieved. She thought for a moment, then began: "Her husband deserted her, oh, maybe three, four years ago—before she came to Walker. She came to work here about two years ago and, because of her husband, her self-esteem was down to nothing."

"She was drinking a lot?"

She studied Zank's face for a moment, then nodded. "She did drink perhaps a little too much, yes."

"And then she met Vernon Cole."

"Yes. At first Cole was great for her. She stopped drinking altogether. She looked younger, happier. He was living with his group someplace out in the Mission, I think. She was transformed. It was great for six months, maybe a little longer. Then something happened about a year ago. She wouldn't talk about it. One day she came to work crying. She said she had left the group, and she wouldn't tell me why. Ever since, it's been tearing Jill apart."

"Where can I get in touch with her? I already tried her apartment. Please believe me, Mrs. Radcliffe, I want to help her."

Mrs. Radcliffe sighed. She lowered her eyes and said in a hushed voice, "She wasn't feeling well. We're not super busy today, so I told her we could cover for her. I doubt she went home. Check over at Gunther's on Polk Street. She usually starts there when she's going on a tilt."

Gunther, the owner-bartender of Gunther's Place, was standing behind the bar under an old-fashioned reclining-nude painting. He was making entries from his racing form into a gray IBM PC. It was three in the afternoon, and the place wasn't busy. A brittle-faced woman in a business suit sat at the bar drinking a martini. A couple of old-timers were shooting a game of nine ball. Jill Stanyan was sitting in a corner booth shuffling empty glasses around in front of her.

Zank walked up to the bar. "Hello, Gunther."

Gunther looked at Zank over the top of his square Ben Franklin glasses and said, "Well, well, well, Zank the Tank. Long time no see."

"Draft beer, Gunther, please."

Gunther poured a beer from a spigot and slid it across the bar. Zank motioned for Gunther to come closer, and whispered, "I want to talk to that girl over there, but I don't want her to know who I am, okay?"

"Whatever you say, Zank."

"She thinks I'm a cop. Somebody told her I was a detective name of Sergio Veracruz. She's got the hots for cops, so why disappoint her?" Zank winked. Gunther smiled.

"Let me have one of what she's drinking, Gunther." Gunther made up a screwdriver. Zank left a ten dollar bill.

When he put the screwdriver down in front of her, she looked up at him. Her eyes were dull. She looked, Zank thought, like she was lost in a fog in her head. It gave him a pang of sadness.

"Go away."

"Just relax, I ain't gonna hurt you." He slid into the seat across from her.

"You got a lot of brass, mister." She brushed some hair off her forehead.

"Answer a few questions, I'll be gone."

"You can ask, I don't guarantee I'll answer." She rotated the glasses in front of her. "I'm playing a game. The object is, you move the glasses around the table. You try to make a nice design. That's all. Nobody wins, nobody loses. Simple game, eh?"

"I know you called Vernon Cole up at his place in Eagleston after I was out at your apartment."

"How the hell could you possibly know that?"

"I have a recording of the call. Would you like to hear it?" He put the small recording device on the table between them.

"I don't think so. . . ." She changed the pattern of the glasses. Zank sipped some more beer. "There now," she said, "doesn't that look like the Washington Monument?"

Zank didn't look at it. "He's taken Cleomona from the place up in Eagleston. Where did they go?"

She looked at him and shrugged. "You ever seen the Washington Monument? It's a huge phallus."

"I asked you a question, Miss Stanyan. I still don't have an answer."

"The question was what again?" She grinned a drunk's grin. Zank figured she was retreating into the fog in her head.

"Where has Vernon Cole taken Cleomona Fisk?"

"Don't know. Don't care."

Zank leaned across the table toward her. "Aiding and abetting a criminal activity can carry an equal penalty to the crime itself."

"What are you talking about?"

"Child stealing, Miss Stanyan. Vernon Cole has stolen Cleomona Fisk, who's a minor, and you are just as guilty as he is, unless you cooperate."

"I can't tell you where they took her."

"Do you know?"

"No."

He took a sip of beer, studying her. Through the fog he thought he could sense the fear. "You tell me, we'll protect you."

"Who's 'we'?"

"The San Francisco Police Department."

"If you're a cop, I'm the Queen of England. Vernon Cole didn't steal Cleomona Fisk from her mother. Cleomona Fisk isn't Vernon Cole's captive, he's hers."

"Highly unlikely."

She took down the rest of her drink. "You don't screw around with the Vernon Coles of this world, mister, whoever you are."

"Want to see my badge?"

"What for? You got it at Woolworth's. Leave me alone, would you please? I have only one ambition in life, and that is to be a harmless drunk." She downed the rest of her screwdriver and turned the glass upside down on the table, spilling the ice.

Zank said, "I'm trying to keep you out of trouble."

She was sloshing the ice chips around. "I'm trying to keep me out of trouble, you're trying to get me into trouble." She slid out of the booth and got to her feet. She was a bit unsteady.

He said, "Can I give you a lift?"

"I make it a policy never to accept rides from phony cops."

"Okay, okay. I'm not a cop. My name's Rick Conrad and I've been hired by Cleomona's mother to bring her home."

She stared at him. "You could get decisively hurt trying something stupid like that."

"Can I drive you home?"

"Nope. Double nope. Vernon may be keeping an eye on

me, and I'd just as soon not be seen with you, if you know what I mean.''

She slid out of the booth and headed out the door, weaving, he thought, like a punch-drunk boxer.

6

Zank walked outside into the night air. It was misting and cold. Jill Stanyan was crossing California Street. He followed her. He figured if she was being watched, he wanted to find out who was doing it.

She weaved down Polk Street. He thought she might be looking for a cab because she was in no shape to drive. A couple of Norwegian sailors spoke to her. She ignored them. They persisted, walking along beside her, talking and gesturing wildly with their hands, but she just kept on walking. They keep it up, Zank thought, they're gonna get a boxing lesson from an old fisticuffer. They finally reversed course and went into an adult bookstore, laughing and slapping each other on the back. Zank crossed the street, staying back half a block. No one seemed to be following her.

She went into the White Stag Tavern. Zank waited patiently in the doorway of a vacant store across the street for an hour. The mist soon turned to rain. People were on their way home from work, stopping in the stores along Polk Street to get groceries for dinner. Jill Stanyan didn't come out of the White Stag. He went up the block to where he'd parked the LTD, got in, and drove it back down and parked across the street from the White Stag. He listened to the Giants play the Pittsburgh Pirates on the car radio. The Giants were losing, 6 to 2. Another hour passed. No sign of her.

It was after seven o'clock. He figured she had to have enough booze in her to be legally dead. He went to the front door of the White Stag and looked inside. He didn't see her. He went in and ordered a Dos Equis at the bar. The place was packed with the after-work crowd, the air fogged with cigarette smoke. He turned around and there she was, hanging onto a cigarette machine, talking to some joker in a three-piece suit. He had a lot of gray hair, razor cut. Styled. Guy must be on the make, Zank thought. She was nodding to what he was saying, and her eyes looked like a couple of shot glasses full of milk. She didn't notice Zank. She ain't gonna notice it, Zank thought, if a lizard gives her a kiss on the lips.

Zank drank the beer straight down and went back out to his car. On the radio they were interviewing the unhappy Giants in the clubhouse. Nobody was making alibis. It was their fifth straight loss and they were clean out of alibis. Zank turned it off. He felt angry and didn't know why. His old man had been a boozer, and maybe that was why he didn't like to see somebody waste their life like that. And he didn't like Mr. Three-Piece Suit talking to her either. What was he after? Pretty damn obvious. What kind of a jerk would take advantage of a drunken woman who didn't know what she was doing? He felt like just taking her out of there. But where the hell would that get him? What he needed was for her to tell him where he could find Cleomona. So the drunker she got, the better. If she got real stinko, she wouldn't know what she was saying and then he'd find out real easy. The fighter who waits, wins. Mole Allen had taught him that. He couldn't be concerned about her personally. He was on a case. So she was a lush—let her do her lush thing.

Ten minutes later she came out of the place alone. She stood under the striped awning over the door and looked first one way and then the other, like she was trying to get her bearings. But she didn't start walking. She was waiting for Mr. Three-Piece Suit. He came out a moment later. Zank could see his face now. He was pudgy and had bushy eyebrows. Mid-fifties, Zank figured. Maybe. Lecherous bastard. Probably married, with thirteen kids. The two of them were having an animated discussion about something, with a lot of pointing. They finally settled it and started walking south toward Gunther's Place. Zank waited for them to get halfway down the block before he started the car and pulled out into the street. He thought they might be going bar-hopping, but they kept going past Gunther's and got into a gray Toyota down the block. She drove.

Zank thought for a moment he might have lost her and was following the wrong person. The woman could hardly stand up, and here she was behind the wheel of a car! Zank figured he didn't have to stay back, she wouldn't be looking to see whether anyone was following her. She'd have to use her full attention just to keep the wheels on the pavement.

She went up Sacramento, made a left on Van Ness, and headed for the Excelsior District. Her car wove slightly, but stayed in the right lane. She kept the speed at twenty-five or less. It was raining hard now. Zank's wipers streaked across the window. He was tempted to just head on home. It was a fifty-to-one shot that this was going to net him anything. Still, he told himself, fifty to one was better than none at all.

The Toyota stopped at a liquor store and Mr. Three-Piece Suit went in and bought something, came out, and got back in the car. They continued up Mission, turned up Cedarwood, and pulled into the driveway that ran alongside Jill Stanyan's apartment house. Zank parked in front and turned off the engine. He saw them go in the side door.

It was ten minutes to eight. He hadn't eaten since breakfast and his stomach was complaining. He looked around to see whether there was any interest in her arrival. He didn't see any. He figured to give it a few more minutes and then he saw three guys get out of a yellow Dodge down the block and head for the front door of the apartment building. Someone on the inside let them in, Zank couldn't see who. Maybe the manager. Maybe Jill Stanyan. A couple of minutes later Mr. Three-Piece Suit came out, hurrying down the block, looking back over his shoulder.

Zank got out of his car. Ladies and gentlemen, he thought, for the main event this evening . . .

He sprinted across the street, up the front steps of the apartment building, and rang the manager's bell. When the manager answered, Zank said, "Open up, Nostrum, it's me, Sergeant Veracruz."

The front door buzzed and Zank stepped in. Down the hall the door opened and Nostrum stuck his head out. Zank waved at him to get back inside. Nostrum's head disappeared. Zank listened at Jill Stanyan's door. Inside, he heard her say, "I haven't said anything to anybody." A man said something, then another said, "Come on, Vernon wants to see you." She said, "I don't want to see him." A man said, "Take her." Then he heard what sounded like a slap.

Zank had a sudden stupid impulse to smash the door in, but held himself in check. All he had to do was follow these clowns and they'd take him right to Vernon Cole, and Vernon Cole would lead him to Cleomona Fisk. So they beat Jill Stanyan to a pulp, so what? Life in the big city. It was none of his business.

The conversation started up again: "Move it, Jill."

"Fucking asshole. I'm not going anywhere with you."

Another slap, this one louder. A muffled cry.

Suddenly the door in front of Zank flew open at about the same time he realized it was his foot that had blasted it.

The three men were trying to get Jill up off the floor. The men turned to Zank with surprise imprinted on their faces. Zank grabbed the nearest man by the back of his collar: a slight young man in a leather jacket. Zank spun him around and slammed him into the wall, face first; he bounced back, stumbled, and crashed on the floor.

The next closest took a swing at Zank that glanced off his cheek. This one was big, clumsy, dull-eyed. Zank counterpunched with a shot to the man's soft, voluminous belly that dropped him to the floor with an oomph.

Number three was not going to be so easy. He'd drawn a knife and was holding it in the classic knife-fighter's stance, feet spread, arms outstretched. The knife had a blade at least eight inches long and looked as sharp as a scalpel. Zank recognized the man as the redhead at Cole's country place, the guy with the meat cleaver. The redhead said to Zank, "Step right up, motherfucker, let's see what your liver looks like."

"You better put that thing away, sport," Zank said, "or you might have to have it removed from your ass." He reached in his sport coat as if he were reaching for his gun, which was at the moment under Nolan's sink so he wouldn't be caught carrying it.

The redhead's two partners were up off the floor now. The kid in the leather jacket said, "We don't need none of this action." Blood was gushing from his nose. The big guy with the soft belly was already halfway out the door. The kid with the leather jacket swung around and followed him. The redhead said to Zank, "Some other time, sport." Then he backed out the door, keeping his knife between them.

Zank turned to Jill Stanyan. She was still on the floor, but was sitting up. He said, "Where were they gonna take you?"

"I have no idea."

"I've got to follow them."

"Take me with you—I don't want to stay here alone."

"Okay, but we gotta get moving."

They hurried out to Zank's car. The yellow Dodge was already making the turn at the end of the block. Zank fired up the LTD and took off with tires screaming. "Just hang on, Miss Stanyan, this old sled can fly." They caught up with the yellow Dodge two blocks away. Zank slowed down, stayed way back, and followed them onto the freeway. If they knew they were being followed, they didn't seem to care. Jill sat silently by the door. Zank kept his attention on the Dodge. It headed for the Bay Bridge, but at the last San Francisco exit it crossed four lanes of traffic and turned off toward Broadway. Zank stayed with them.

Back on the city streets the Dodge headed for Fisherman's Wharf. The streets were full of people. The Dodge came to a stop near the Wax Museum and the three men got out and in a moment had melted into the crowd. Zank ran after them, but they'd disappeared. Goddamn.

He checked out the Dodge. The ignition had been punched out. The registration said it belonged to Vemal Paris in Oxnard. Zank got back in the LTD. "Stolen car," he said to Jill.

"Now Vernon's got his people stealing cars." She started shivering.

Zank put his arm around her. "Hey, it's okay. They're gone."

She leaned her head on his shoulder for a moment. Gradually she stopped shivering. Then she looked at him and said, "I'm all right."

"You want to go get a coffee or something?"

"No, thanks. Can you drop me at a motel? I don't want to go home."

"You can stay at my place tonight," he said. "I'm a gentleman, you don't have to worry about nothing."

At eight-thirty the following morning he came into the living room wearing his best herringbone tweed sport coat and his too-fat striped tie; he was carrying a tray with a mug of coffee, orange juice, and toast. Jill was asleep under a pile of blankets on the hide-a-bed. He stood and looked at her for a moment. Goddamn nice looking woman, he thought. Her hair was down over her face so she looked like a kid. Her cheeks glowed pink. He nudged her. "Humph?" she said.

"Sorry to wake you, Miss Stanyan, but I got to go out."

She blinked and rubbed her red eyes. "Good morning, cruel world."

"Here," Zank said. "I made some coffee." He put the tray down on the coffee table and passed her the mug of coffee.

She sat up. It looked as if it was painful for her to move her head. There was a little blue-black swelling around her left eye where she'd been slapped.

"Sugar, cream?" he asked.

"Just black." She took a gulp from the steaming mug and rolled her eyes back in gratitude. She was wearing a pair of his pajamas, safety pinned at the collar. She looked great in them, he thought.

Zank said, "I got a friend, lives across the hall, name of Nolan. He's a sculptor. I asked him to look in on you while I'm gone, see if you need anything."

"Thank you, but I can't stay here."

"Sure you can. Why not?" He stood back from her and gestured with the sweep of his hand that the place was hers. "The place is rented under a phony name. Maurice Garcone. Nobody can trace me here, even if your friends find out my real name."

"Which is?"

"Joe."

"Nice to meet you, Joe. I'm Jill. Joe what?"

"Zanca."

"Italian?"

He shuddered. "If God made me Italian, I'd drink battery acid. I'm Sicilian."

"Aren't Sicilians Italian?"

"Not even close. We're stronger, smarter, better looking— better everything."

"It's very apparent," she said with a grin.

"I would like to spend the morning telling you how wonderful Sicilian men are, but I have a job to do."

"Cleomona?"

He nodded. She lowered her eyes. "I don't know anything— honestly. I'd really like to help."

She seemed sincere. She was looking right at him now with a sort of apologetic smile on her lips. Nice lips, he thought. Not too thin, not too fat. Just right. Eyes just right. Shoulders just right. Just right about all over.

"Do you have any idea where she might be, Miss Stanyan?"

"Please call me Jill. Isn't she up in Eagleston?"

"No, Jill, the whole gang split."

"Then I don't know where they are—really."

"I believe you. You got any idea where she *might* be?"

"If they aren't at Eagleston, I don't know where they could be. Cole used to have a house up in Pacific Heights, but he sold it last year some time. He changed his phone in the City a long time ago. Vernon Cole doesn't like to have his whereabouts known."

"So everybody keeps telling me. He got a family?"

"Not that he ever told me about."

"Were you and he . . . you know . . ." He felt his cheeks getting warm. And she seemed to notice, which made them get even hotter.

"Are you asking if we were romantically involved?"

He cleared his throat, and tried to act like he didn't care one way or the other. "I'm just trying to get a picture of things, is all."

"I'd rather not answer that. We had a unique relationship, that's all I'll say."

"Okay. Can you tell me a little something about him? He

must have some good in him. Tell me what you liked about him. Everybody tells me what they don't like." He smiled at her. He didn't want her to think he was pushing her.

She sipped some coffee, staring out into space. Then she said, "When I first knew him, he was wonderful. Inspirational. That's the only way I can describe him. After things with his seminars went sour, he just changed. Before that he used to rage at people who didn't understand him or wrote bad things about him. And he got angry when some of his people didn't get what he was talking about, or they left him. After, he raged all the time." She shook her head sadly. "He had so much to teach, so much to give. He had a way of opening up your mind and getting you to see things about yourself and the world that you never saw before. Beautiful things, like how orange the morning sun is. How good cold clear water can taste. How much your mind could hold. There is no limit. There is no limit except what others have put on you . . . that was the way he was at first. He had the seminars, and the people who took the seminars loved him. When he no longer had that he just became different somehow. He started doing things . . . things that he wouldn't have done before. Maybe something exploded in his brain."

"Why did you leave exactly, Jill?" He liked saying her name. Jill. Joe and Jill. They sort of went together. Joe and Jill went up the hill.

"Why I left is something I don't talk about."

He remembered what Martha Manning said when he'd asked what Vernon Cole was up to. *I'll never talk about it,* she said.

"Where does Cleomona Fisk fit in?"

"She's one of his . . . people."

"She's sleeping with Franklyn Dix, isn't she?"

"I don't know, is she?" She said it with a blank look, but her cheeks colored. She knew Cleomona was sleeping with him.

"Can you tell me just one thing—how often does Dix see Cleomona?"

"Please don't ask me things like that."

"All I want to know is how often. Just an estimate."

She lowered her eyes. "Almost every day—from what I hear."

Zank smiled. "Then finding Cleomona ought to be E-Z."

The rain was steady all that morning. The weather service had said a ten percent chance of showers, and now it was raining a hundred percent. April had been a wet month and now May was even wetter. Zank waited in the LTD down the block from Franklyn Dix's home for thirty-five minutes before he saw the chauffeur back the Continental out of the garage and wait for Dix to come out. Zank followed the Lincoln to City Hall and saw Dix go into his office at nine-fifteen.

San Francisco's City Hall is a stately Greco-Roman affair with columns and marble halls. Like every city hall in America, it's full of officious bureaucrats, bored secretaries, and citizens petitioning for everything from building permits and zoning exceptions to a spot on the arts commission. Unlike other city halls in America, the citizens might be men dressed as nuns or women in crew cuts with lightning bolts tattooed on their arms. Goddamn city's got more crazies than there are Jews in Jerusalem.

Zank waited in the hall, trying to look like he belonged. A citizen's group with placards and lapel buttons showed up at ten. They were tenants' rights advocates lobbying for stricter rent control. The placards read: NO MORE RENT RIP-OFF, HUMAN RIGHTS, NOT PROPERTY RIGHTS! TENANTS, SI, SLUMLORDS NO! Zank was pleased to see them because they made him invisible, but he worried that they would bring reporters and TV cameras. He had no desire to be on TV.

Dix came out of his office at ten and crossed the hall to a committee hearing room. He was about fifty, immaculately dressed, with wavy gray hair, and appeared fit and tanned. Zank thought he looked like something you'd see in a men's store window. Dix told the tenants' rights people he'd do what he could and he'd let them know the outcome. Then he went into the committee room. The tenants' rights activists clapped and hooted.

A young woman carrying a clipboard approached Zank. She looked like what he would call the Berkeley type: long hair, jeans, flannel shirt, oversized glasses, and the stern, steady stare of the truly committed.

"You here for the hearings?" she asked.

"Sure."

"You don't have a button."

"You're right about that."

She pinned one on him. The button read: PERSON POWER.

"Which group you from?" she asked.

"Wops for Social Justice."

Her face turned from copper brown to burnt orange. "I don't find ethnic jokes funny."

"What do you find funny?"

"Your dick."

She did an about-face and stormed off.

Reporters showed up at noon. And a mobile TV crew. Zank maneuvered himself to the far edge of the crowd and kept his face away from the cameras. Ten minutes later the doors to the hearing room opened and Supervisor Dix came out. The protesters and reporters swarmed around him. A broad grin flashed across his face. Dix said, "We've done it, ladies and gentlemen, the committee voted unanimously in favor of every single change in the law recommended by the Tenants' Rights Committee!"

A cheer went up from the crowd. The reporters pressed in close for questioning. The cameras panned the group to get the happy, smiling faces for the six o'clock news. Zank didn't want any part of that, so he slipped down the back stairs and went across the street and had a hot dog and a cup of coffee at the Piccadilly Circus Café. The café was run by a recent arrival from Hong Kong by the name of Hu, and featured bean and cheese burritos, and pizza by the slice. The place was packed. A plaque on the wall said that in the days of the Barbary Coast the place was once a front for a gambling den, which Zank thought was funny because there was a bookie operating out of the back room, name of Maude Weibel. The rain had stopped, but it was heavily overcast and looked as if it would start up again at any moment. Somebody nudged him.

"Hey, man, yo' Zank the Tank?"

Zank turned and faced a shabby man. His eyes were

rheumy and his nose as flat as the tongue on a pair of old hiking boots. No front teeth. "Yo' is the Tank, ain't ya?"

"Used to be," Zank said.

The man smiled. His teeth were brown and gapped. "Don't remember me, do ya?" he said slowly, a smile on his puffy lips.

"Can't say as I do."

"Bill Kincade—'Wild Bill' they used to call me. We fought—you and me—once, in seventy-four or -five. Down in L. A. The Great White Hope they was callin' me then."

"A long time ago."

"Three rounds, amateur, I think."

"Who won?" Zank asked.

"Don't remember now," Bill Kincade said, shaking his head. "You got cut up bad, I remember that."

"I was always a bleeder."

"I had what they call slow feet, or I be right now livin' big."

"You had to have the luck too," Zank said.

"That's the righteous truth." He rolled his eyes. "Them was good days, though, hey?"

"You bet."

"Heard you went to the joint, Tank."

"Twice."

"I been in too. Me and another fool name'a Kid Gomez tried to take a bank. We got about ten feet out the door. Had a sackful of hundreds, though."

"You wouldn't need a few bucks, would you?" Zank said, taking some money out of his pocket.

"Me? Shit, I got plenty. The state takes care'a me good." Zank tried to pass him a twenty, but he wouldn't take it. "I'm okay. See you around, Tank."

Zank watched him shuffle off down the street.

He looked back toward City Hall. The protesters were coming out the doors and down the front steps. He ran across the street and into the building where he met two TV cameramen coming down the broad central stairway in the rotunda.

"Where's Dix?" he asked one of them.

"Supervisor Dix? He went down in the elevator, I think."

Zank ran down the stairs, and out the front door, down

the front steps, and around the corner to where the Continental was parked. It was just pulling out of the parking space. Dix had a splashy smile on his face.

Zank hurriedly crossed the street to the LTD, started it up and sped after the Continental. He had no trouble finding it on the freeway heading south. He stayed two lanes over and six cars behind. The Continental remained in the slow lane, behind a truck. Zank kept back a quarter of a mile. Be a good time to visit your girl friend, Dix. Celebrate your victory. Zank clicked on the radio and listened to some old Johnny Cash.

The Continental exited at Third Street, and pulled over to the side of the road and stopped. Zank pulled ahead half a block and stopped too. He waited. Barbara Mandrel sang "I Was Country when Country Wasn't Cool." He watched in the rearview mirror as the Continental suddenly pulled out, made a U-turn, and headed back onto the freeway again.

Zank spun the LTD around and went after it, but before he got to the freeway there was a powder-blue San Francisco police car behind him with a red light flashing. Zank pulled over and rolled down his window. The cop was tall, with an olive complexion and a mustache. That was all Zank noticed about him; that, and the fact that he had drawn what looked like a Colt Python .357 magnum and was pointing it through Zank's window.

7

Zank lay on one of the top bunks in the eight-man cell and looked at the ceiling where someone had drawn a circle with a woman's crotch in the middle of it, an oblique line drawn across it. A skinny Mexican kid on the bunk next to Zank said, "Whoever do that could draw good, you think?"

"Yeah," Zank said.

"If I could draw like that, I draw the most beautiful woman you ever see in your life—with me in the saddle." The Mexican kid laughed in a sharp, staccato burst. He stopped laughing as suddenly as he started, turned on his side, and said, "You got a smoke, amigo?"

"Nope," Zank said.

The Mexican yawned and put his arms behind his head. "I kill a fat nobody last year, April. A no-good pig name of Fernandez. He say bad things to my friends about me. He cheat us on a deal for some very good coke. I do it with a knife. I been to Tijuana, they no find me. Now I come back. They get me in one day. You believe that? *One* day."

"Why'd you come back?" Zank was flexing his fingers. They seemed stiff.

"A woman, what else make a man do a crazy thing? Such a woman! Breasts like I don't know what. Eyes as black as the devil's soul. She turn me in, I think."

"They gonna hit you with first degree?"

"That what they talking about. They give me gas. It no hurt, what you think?"

"I guess not."

The Mexican kid crossed his legs. "Dying is *de nada*. I hate the suffering. I never in my life make anyone suffer. Not even an animal. Even with Fernandez, I do it quick. And he was a no-good pig. If they kill me with a whip or something, I would never let them take me. But gas, what is that? You go to sleep."

The cell door opened. The jailer said: "Zanca."

Zank rolled off the bunk. "Right here." The jailer motioned for Zank to come out.

The Mexican kid said, "You come back, my friend, bring me a cigarette?"

"If I remember."

"Remember, *please*, I go crazy with nothing to smoke."

"What's going down?" Zank asked the jailer.

The jailer shrugged. He had white hair and a pot belly, and no expression on his flat face. Even if he knew, Zank thought, he wouldn't say. Jailers were the same as cops, Zank figured, only dumber and lazier. To them prisoners were like orangutans in a zoo, and the jailers were the zookeepers. Keep the orangutans fed, keep 'em from killing the zookeepers, and don't let them get out. Simple job for the simpleminded.

"Ever hear of Zank the Tank?" he asked the jailer.

"That you?" the jailer asked.

"Yeah."

"We got a lot of has-been boxers in here."

Zank didn't say any more after that. Goddamn, he thought, you're in the slam, you're an orangutan.

He walked with the jailer to the end of the cell block, through a door, down another corridor, through another door and into a small office. It didn't look to Zank as if the office was used much. It had a desk, a couple of chairs, one small window, and nothing but cracks and smudges on the pale blue walls. Sitting behind the desk was Detective Sgt. Leslie Donaldson, leaning on his elbows. Zank thought he looked about as happy as a five-year-old whose birthday party had been rained out.

The jailer shut the door and left them alone.

"Sit down," Donaldson said, stabbing his finger in the direction of the empty chair.

Zank sat. Donaldson folded his hands on the desk. He said, "Zanca, you really are a dumb fuck."

"Sister Mary Joseph in third grade used to tell me the same damn thing. 'Joe Zanca,' she would say, 'you are nothing but a great big dumb fuck.' "

"You think that's funny, don't you? I don't." Donaldson scowled to emphasize how much he didn't like it. Then he said, "Franklyn Dix is one of the most important men in this town."

"He's tied to Bright Horizons."

Donaldson sighed. "Bright Horizons is *not* a criminal organization."

"So everybody's been telling me." Zank ran his hand across the top of the desk; it had a million cigarette burns in it. The tile floor had two million. Zank got up and went over to the window. He looked out past the wire mesh to the traffic on the freeway heading for the Bay Bridge. Then he said, "Maybe they ain't a criminal organization, but their leader, Vernon Cole, is a bad actor, and loony as they come."

"He's a college professor. They're all a little loony."

"The guy is a hell of a lot more than just a little loony, Donaldson. He's a tree frog if ever there was one."

"Then you ought to steer clear of him, right?"

"I ain't exactly his best pal."

"Why did you give them my name when they busted you? Huh? Tell me that, why? I don't want to have anything to do with you. I don't even like you." Donaldson's cheeks flushed red.

Zank threw his arms up. "I gave you Fats Mercurio, remember? You loved me then more than Sister Mary Joseph loved pure thoughts and good deeds." He paced to the wall and back again.

"You turned in Fats because he was trying to kill your ass," Donaldson said. "Listen, this city, you may recall, had a supervisor and a mayor gunned down. The powers that be are understandably touchy when an ex-con, twice convicted of assault on police officers, is following a supervisor."

"I was *not* convicted twice of assault on a police officer. The first time the charge was reduced to felonious assault. We plea bargained—you got any idea what they're charging me with?"

Donaldson grinned. "They haven't decided yet. Dix wants you kept on ice until you cop to why you were following him."

Zank stopped pacing. "I like Continentals, so I follow them. That's legal, ain't it?"

"Zanca, honest to God, I wish I never met you."

"They can't hold me, can they?"

Donaldson said, "You've been through the system enough times to know they can do whatever they damn well please— why were you following Dix? Especially since I told you to leave him the hell alone."

"I'm with Wops for Social Justice. We want him to lead the fight."

"Here we go with the comedy again. You want out of here or not? You better make it good, Zanca, or they will find thirty-one reasons to hold you, and I'll give them reason thirty-two."

"All right, all right." Zank resumed pacing. "I was following him because I thought he was a guy I know, name of Peabody, who owes me money. Tell them that. Peabody's a pimp. He owns a car just like Dix's. A big Continental."

"So why didn't you tell that to the cop who stopped you?"

"He never asked me. He had me with my arms stretched out before I had time to inhale. Tell me what you know about Dix, Donaldson, and why he's so touchy about being followed."

"Why should I tell you anything?"

"How about I give you a good bust, hand it to you on a platter?"

"What kind of a bust?"

"The biggest auto-theft ring in the state is working out of a body shop in Hunter's Point. They get Mercedes and Porsches from L.A. and San Diego and everybody thinks they go over the border to Mexico, but they don't. They come north. They get papers on wrecks, change numbers, and whamo, they're resold right here in the city by the bay.''

"How you know about this?"

"They tried to sell me a hot car. Give me a piece of paper, I'll write it down for you—come on, you're gonna be a star, Donaldson.'' Donaldson gave him a pen and a page out of a notebook.

Zank wrote something on it, folded it, and passed him back his pen, but kept the piece of paper in his hand. He said: "Okay, I got the name of the place and the address right here. You tell me about Dix, I give you the bust of the year. You may even make Captain out of it.''

Donaldson half smiled. "Lieutenant first,'' he said. Zank thought he meant it as a joke, but he was half serious. His eyes became cop eyes again. "Listen, turdball, I tell you about Dix, it doesn't go any further than the inside of your cranium.''

"You got my sportsman's word.''

"This car racket better be a crime in progress.''

"You can rely on me, Donaldson. Come on, what's with Dix?'' He wiggled the piece of paper in his hand.

Donaldson tucked his thumbs in his belt. "I used to work bunko,'' he said. "There's a sleazebag contractor in this town named Melinkoff.''

"Melinkoff? Yeah, I know him. Used to play pool pretty good.''

"That's him. Melinkoff got investigated for some shit he was pulling with phony mortgages on nonexistent properties. Anyway, our boy Dix went to bat for him and got the DA to let him cop to a couple of misdemeanors.''

"Half the politicians in this town are playing footsy with sleazebags, so what?''

"There's more: Dix has a lot of bread. Lives high. Ever ask yourself where'd he get it all?''

"Tell me.''

"Nobody knows. He heads a company called Ideocom-X International. Supposedly made him rich in real estate. He buys scrub land for nothing and somehow always manages to resell it for millions. He pays taxes out the bunghole, so it all looks good on paper. But I ask myself, how can a guy get so lucky?''

"How *does* he get so lucky?"

"That's just it, I don't know. I can't open a file on this guy, he's a city supervisor for Christ's sake."

Zank nodded that he understood. ''You're a good cop, as cops go, Donaldson.''

"Part of being a good cop is to know what's possible and what's pie in the sky. Nailing Dix is like nailing lemon meringue in orbit around the moon."

"What's his connection to Bright Horizons?"

"They can turn out a few hundred precinct workers, show up with placards for the TV cameras anytime he wants them. Vernon Cole may not be what he was once, but he still has some juice.''

"Where do these few hundred come from?"

"From the thousands who have taken the Bright Horizons raise-your-intelligence bullshit courses. After they take the classes, some of them love this guy Vernon Cole and think he's the new Messiah. My brother-in-law took one of the courses and thinks he *himself* is Einstein. He would kiss Vernon Cole's tush if Cole asked him to.''

"What does Cole get outta being chummy with Dix?"

"Figure it out for yourself, dummy. Franklyn Dix is the biggest supporter of the police force on the Board of Supervisors. The chief would do anything Dix asked him, just about. Dix has got a lot of schwack, get what I'm saying? How'd you like to have him for a pal?''

Zank said, "It stinks, Donaldson. He's dirty, go get him."

"I got a career that could go down the crapper real fast, I don't watch where I put my nose."

"I got to find Vernon Cole, Donaldson. Can you help me?"

"Okay, you're looking for Vernon Cole and that's why you were following Dix. Vernon Cole is paranoid and doesn't let it out where he's camped, but you figure sooner or later Dix is going to stop by—because you think he's banging this Bright Horizons bimbo.''

"Her name is Cleomona, and she's sixteen years old."

Donaldson's face lit up. "Dix is banging a minor?"

"Yeah."

He thought for a moment, shook his head, and said, "I don't want to hear about it."

"Okay, forget it. I want to find Cole, that's all. Dix can bang Saint Simon the Pious for all I care. Just tell me where I can find Vernon Cole."

"Vernon Cole doesn't exactly report his whereabouts, and finding him is not part of my caseload. Okay, Zanca, enough chitchat. Give me that piece of paper."

Zank handed it to him. Donaldson opened the paper and read it.

"You're sure about this?"

"They grab most of the cars over the weekend, so Monday or Tuesday would be a good time to come down on them. The guy who's running things keeps a Mauser machine pistol in his desk, so watch your ass."

"This doesn't work out, we aren't going to be friends any more, Zanca, you get my meaning?"

"Is that all we are, friends?" Zank smiled at him. "I thought we were going steady."

"Zanca, I wouldn't walk the surface of the same planet with a puke like you if it weren't in the line of duty."

"When can you get me out of here?"

"You gonna behave yourself and be a good boy from now on? Promise you'll never give my name again to anyone at any time for any reason?"

"You have my word as a sportsman and one-time contender for the title of Heavyweight Champion of the World."

"Fuck your word as a sportsman. You going to be on your best behavior of your scuzbag life or not?"

"Good enough to please Sister Mary Joseph, and she was very strict."

Harry Chow answered on the first ring.

"How'd it go, Harry?"

" 'Lo, Mistah Zanca."

"Cut that Charlie Chan crap, what you got?"

"Number one son bettah?" Harry Chow chuckled.

"They come to get the mail or not?"

"I went to Berkeley. Yuk. Worse than I remember it. You leave San Francisco, you're really in a foreign country, know that? I got Berkeley yuppie crud on me and it don't wash off."

"Look, Harry, I been in the can all afternoon and you know how much I hate being in the can."

"What'd you do, piss on another cop?"

"This time I was just minding my own business."

"I believe that like I believe in the Great Pumpkin. But leave us not debate it." His voice turned businesslike. "Your friends picked up the mail."

"Where'd they take it?"

"You want a full report or just the highlights?"

"Highlights."

"The suspect was a white Caucasian male—"

"All whites are Caucasian."

"A white Caucasian male, six-foot-two to six-foot-four, two hundred fifty to two hundred seventy-five pounds—get this—wearing all white. White shoes, white socks, white shirt, white belt, white hat. The guy was *really* Caucasian."

"That's the way these guys dress."

"Snappy. I followed said suspect to a hardware store, a supermarket, a gas station, a stationery store. You want to know what he bought? A screwdriver, three light bulbs, a lot of canned goods, five loaves of bread—"

"Okay, Harry, where'd he end up?"

"In San Francisco—606 New York Avenue. I put a homing device in his car—anytime we want, we should be able to pick him up."

"What's at 606 New York?"

"Used to be a beer-bottling company."

"What's it now?"

"You aren't going to believe it, Zank, when I tell you what these bad guys are running over there."

"Come on, Harry, what? Some kind of pill factory? A marijuana farm? A fuck factory, what?"

"Nope. They're running—get this—a nursery school. Golden Sunrise. Isn't that a chuckle and a half?"

*　　*　　*

Zank called his home number. The answering service got it. They told him he'd gotten no calls. He hung up and called Nolan.

"Where's Jill?"

"Went out maybe two hours ago. Seemed a little worried about you."

"Where'd she go?"

"Shopping, she said."

"Christ, Nolan!"

"What was I supposed to do, chain her up?"

"No, I guess not . . . sorry I snapped. If she shows up, tell her please not to go out again."

"I'll tell her, but I can't stop her if she wants to go. She's a nice girl, Joseph. She's kind. You don't find many kind people these days. We had a long talk."

"She drinks, Nolan."

"I know."

"My old man was a drinker. I know what that's about."

"There are drinkers and there are drinkers, Joseph."

"Yeah, and there are *drinkers*."

"You get to know her, you might find yourself overlooking her faults."

"She's part of my case, that's all, Nolan."

"Oh, just another customer, is she? That's not the idea *she* gave me."

Zanca cleared his throat. "She say anything about me, did she?"

"I never reveal a confidence."

"Goddamn it, Nolan. Tell me."

"Sorry, you're just going to have to find out for yourself."

Zank drove over to New York Avenue and checked out number 606. It said GOLDEN SUNRISE over the door, with a rainbow over a sunburst. It was a white three-story square building with a railroad siding along one side and a parking lot and playground along the other. Zank took a walk around the building. Sure don't look like it was ever a goddamn brewery, he thought. At least not in the dark. It was clean and modern-looking and had a little flower garden in front between the sidewalk and the street. Large windows overlooked the front and sides, but there were none around back. There were two doors in front, two to the playground, one to the railroad siding. The one to the railroad siding looked permanently shut. The station wagon Harry Chow had followed from the Post Office was parked nearby.

He checked out the burglar alarm. It was an infrared and ultrasound affair. Goddamn high tech. Monkey proof except by somebody who knows what's what. The doors all had deadbolts. He sat in his car and watched the place for two hours. There were lights on inside; occasionally a shadow crossed a drawn curtain or shade, but no one came or left. No sign of Cleomona. The lights went off at ten-ten.

He got home at ten-thirty. Jill was still gone. He went over to Nolan's. Nolan told him she'd come back but went out again.

"Where'd she go?"

"Didn't say. I don't think she had anything to drink. She just seemed bored and nervous."

Nolan was sculpting, wearing the same blue smock he always wore, an unlit cigarette dangling from his mouth. The piece he was working on now looked like a fist.

"She say what time she'd be back?"

"Nope." Nolan stopped pushing clay around with his fingers. He lit his cigarette, coughed, and inhaled. "Have some coffee, Joseph?"

"No thanks. Tell me something, Nolan, you're a smart guy." He put his hands in his pockets like he was just hanging around, making small talk. Like he really didn't care one way or the other.

"Shoot."

"Why does somebody like Jill drink so much?"

Nolan took the cigarette out of his mouth and dropped it into an ashtray. He thought for a moment, then said, "Don't know, but something's bothering her a lot. She wouldn't say what it is."

"She could find some guy, some businessman or a dentist, somebody solid, and marry him, have kids, that kind of thing."

"Businessman or dentist, huh?" He cocked one eyebrow. "How about an ex-boxer?"

"Come on, Nolan, don't kid around. She's got an education, and she ain't that bad looking. She's a nurse for Christ's sake. What'd she want with a used-up fisticuffer like me?"

"I don't know, Joseph. I have no idea." Nolan took another drag on his cigarette, keeping one eye on his sculpture, the other on Zank.

Zank was still puzzling over why she drank. Then he said, "How come people join these cults, Nolan?"

"People sometimes lose hope," Nolan said, working in some clay. "They feel lost. They feel they have no place on earth where they fit in. My nephew was a member of the People's Temple. The Reverend Jim Jones, as far as he could see, had the answers to life's mysteries. When my nephew joined he felt love, not only from this wonderful Jim Jones who had all the answers, but from the rest of the members. I went up there once. Everyone loved each other so much in the People's Temple that even I could feel it. It was something. Hugging all over the place. You get involved with something like that, suddenly the rest of the world doesn't seem to matter. It's us, the folks who have the truth, against them, everyone else on earth who is living a lie. But it's just a dream. My nephew never woke up from the dream. He died in the Jonestown massacre."

"I'm sorry about your nephew, Nolan."

"It was a long time ago. He was a fool."

"Jill must have woke up. She's out of it, so why is she still protecting this Cole character?"

Nolan wiped his hands and stepped back to admire his work. He said, "You don't get over an experience like that overnight."

"You think she will get over it eventually?"

"If she finds somebody to love her, it's possible."

Zank opened the freezer and found a Chinese-style TV dinner Jill must have bought. He put it in the oven and sat down to study his encyclopedia—quantum theory. He'd been trying to figure it out for a month. The Planck constant, photons, the uncertainty principle. Goddamn uncertain, all right. So far he hadn't made any sense of it at all, and was considering going on to quarks. But quarks looked just as mysterious as quantum theory. He put the book down and paced around. Where the hell could she be? Pretty stupid question. She was out getting smashed. Well, what was that to him? Nothing. Why should he give a goddamn? She hadn't told him one damn thing he didn't know already. She was no doubt playing footsy with Mr. Three-Piece Suit.

He made himself a screwdriver and sat on the couch. He had to get his mind off Jill and on to Cleomona. An assignment was like training for a fight, he thought. First rule of training: don't pay no attention to anything but the fight. Vernon Cole was the opponent and Cleomona the prize. Keep it simple. He gulped down the screwdriver. He couldn't take sitting, so he got up and paced around some more. Then he took a shower. He put on a robe and a pair of clean sweatpants and lay in bed. He read some more about quantum theory, but it just gave him a headache. He stared at the ceiling and tried to think of anything but Jill Stanyan.

He was still trying half an hour later when he heard the door open. He got up and went down the hall. She was taking off her coat and she looked sober, standing straight. She looked good, he thought. Goddamn good, except for the worry lines.

"Hello," she said.

"Hello."

"Nolan gave me the key to your apartment."

"Sure, that's all right. I've been worried about you." He sat down on the couch, leaning forward, like he was anxious to hear her out.

"I was just out walking, thinking."

"Come to any conclusions?"

"Just one. I can't stay here. Really."

"How come?"

"It isn't fair to you."

"I got the room, don't cost me nothing."

She shook her head as if to indicate he hadn't understood her. "I'm poison."

He said nothing. She stood in the middle of the room for a few moments just looking at him. Then she said, "Did you locate Cleomona?"

"Not yet. Would you care for something hot? Tea? Coffee?"

"You have any decaffeinated?"

"Sure. It's instant, okay?"

"That'd be fine."

They went into the kitchen and he turned on the burner under the pot. They sat at the table. He looked at her eyes closely. Clear. She ain't been drinking, he thought. She ain't a total lush.

"I hear you've been talking to Nolan," Zank said. "He's about the best friend I got. Him and this nut I know name of Harry Chow."

"Don't you have a girlfriend?"

"No. Not at the moment. You have a boyfriend?"

She shook her head.

"We've got something in common." He winced. That sounded dumb, he told himself. But she smiled at him like she was letting him know it was okay.

He cleared his throat. "Where you from, Jill?"

"The midwest. I was born in Chadwick, Nebraska."

"I fought once in Omaha. Lost a close decision. Guy outpointed me with a wimpy little jab. Omaha was okay. It was in autumn. Lots of leaves turning color . . . What did your folks do?"

"My father sold used cars at the Chevy dealer. My mother worked in a café. I didn't have any brothers or sisters."

"Too bad," Zank said.

"Where are you from?" she asked.

"Oakland, originally. My old man was a longshoreman. Real mean son of a bitch."

"My father was like a big kid. He liked to play cards, go drinking with the boys, that kind of thing. He cheated on my mother."

"These things happen."

"Yeah, I guess they do." She was quiet for a moment; something was going through her mind, he figured. He waited. "I don't usually like to talk about myself," she said.

"I talk about myself all the time." he smiled.

"I wish to hell I'd never met Vernon Cole," she said, as

if that was what they'd been talking about. Why she said that just then, he had no idea.

"Pretend you didn't," he said. "What the hell. Let's you forget Vernon Cole, I'll forget I was ever married to Arlene Rotelli."

She nodded and smiled. "Okay, it's a deal." He put out his hand and she shook it. Now that that was settled, he said, "How'd you happen to land in California?" She seemed to settle back. Goddamn nice, Zank thought, sitting here in the kitchen, just chatting.

She said, "When my mother found out my father was fooling around, she left him. We moved to Los Angeles. I don't know why. I think she had dreams of getting into the movies. We bounced around lot. One little apartment after another. I never had any friends."

"That's too bad. Friends are important."

"I think I wanted to be a nurse so people would need me. I got married to Johnny Stanyan when I was twenty-one. He was a med student at UCLA. I was already a nurse. He had three years to go, then his residency. After he finished up, he became a cardiologist. Nine years we were married. Nine pretty good years, really. When you're working hard for something, life is good."

"Goddamn right," he said. "That's why I got plans in the works for a training camp up in the Sierras."

The water was hot and the kettle started to whistle. He poured them two cups of coffee and sat down again. "You were telling me about this guy you were married to before I interrupted."

She stirred some sugar into her coffee. "After a while he didn't want to be married to just a nurse any longer. There was this woman, she lived in Beverly Hills. You know. I don't think he really loved her, he just wanted out of our marriage. It was a combination of factors."

"I think my wife thought our marriage was temporary right from the start." He said it with a smile, so she wouldn't think he was feeling sorry for himself.

"I guess most marriages are temporary these days," she said. She lit a cigarette, blowing the smoke toward the ceiling. For a moment he could see pain in her eyes, then it passed. "God, why can't I just forget this shit?"

"It's okay, Jill. Then what happened?"

"I came to San Francisco three, four years ago, right after it happened. When I met Vernon Cole I thought life was going to be good again. And it was—for a while. I felt he could make my life worth something. I thought I could help him really change the world for the better— Look, Joe, I got to get out of here. This is crazy, me sitting here talking to you like this." She pulled back her chair and started to get up.

"Hey, I'm a good listener, don't go, please."

"Yeah, until you get what you want—Cleomona."

"You think that's why I want you here? Just because of Cleomona?"

She looked at him for a long moment. "No. No, I don't." She eased back down into her chair.

Zank said, "I like you." Goddamn if his tongue didn't feel thick. Like a goddamn pimply kid on his first date with a girl.

"Don't like me," she said. "I'm a basket case."

"I like basket cases."

"You're a dope."

"It's a free country, I can be a dope if I want to be."

"You don't know what I've done." Her eyes were as cold as snow when she said it, he thought.

"I don't care what you've done. You don't think I got all my lumps being a knight in shining armor, do you?"

"I'll end up hurting you."

"I'll take the chance."

She looked away from him, staring off into the room. She took a long drag on her cigarette, then said, "Let me at least tell you this. I'm trying to get over Vernon Cole. I was completely gone on him in a very special way I don't think I could ever explain. He was sort of a god to me. It was easy. I just made one decision, and that was to let him make all the rest of my decisions. I was so sick and tired of thinking! He was so soothing. So confident. Trust him, and he'd make me over, and then he'd make the world over, he said. All I had to do was let go of self, he said, and become one with him, and I'd never want for anything again. I'd never feel alone or afraid. And for a while I just rode along with it and it was beautiful. I worshiped him." She paused for a moment, then continued. "Maybe what I'm trying to say, Joe, is that I want you to know that I'm damaged goods." Tears started down her face. She didn't do anything to stop them.

Zank said nothing. His mouth was dry as volcanic ash.

She took three quick puffs on her cigarette, then crushed it out. She held her head in her hands, her elbows propped up on the table. She was sobbing now. Then she got up and started down the hall, but suddenly turned and came back to him, put her arms around his neck and eased onto his lap. She said, "I want him out of me so bad. I want to have myself back. Help me, Joe. I want to forget everything. I want to feel something. Hold onto me, please. You don't have to even like me, just hold me. Hold me tight. I hate being me. I'm tired of wanting to die. I want to live. Hold me, Joe. Please. Tighter. Tighter!"

Zank had his arms around her tight, her tears soaking through his shirt. "When people get rescued by other people," he said, "they naturally start having feelings, and it usually wears off. A friend of mine, a fireman, says it happens to him every time he saves a woman."

"Stop talking."

"Listen, Jill, I ain't nothing but a washed-up boxer that quit high school in the ninth grade. Just because I knocked around those birds in your kitchen don't mean I'm anything special. Look at my face. Scars like the craters on the moon. Nose is bent. I've been trying for seven years to get some knowledge into my head with my *World Book*, and I'm only up to Q—"

"Shut up, damn it!"

She put her arms around his neck and kissed him on the mouth. A meteor shower flashed in his head. He picked her up in his arms and spun her gently around. Amazing. Goddamn, if she ain't light as air. . . .

He loved waking to her woman smell.

"The alarm go off, Joey?" she asked.

"It's about to."

"You mind if I call you Joey?"

He kissed her. "It's better than 'Hey stupid,' which is what Arlene used to call me. That was, of course, before things started going sour. When things started going sour, she started calling her lawyer." He kissed her again and cupped his hand over her breast.

She slid her arms around his neck and kissed him. She said, "Promise when you get tired of me you'll tell me."

"Promise me you'll never hit me on the head with a potted geranium."

"Arlene do that?"

"We had a lot of fun." He kissed her again. "I got to go to work."

"After you finish your business with Vernon, are you going to get rid of me?"

"Sicilians don't get rid of people like that. We get rid of things. We keep people."

"You look like you're busting this morning, Zank," Harry Chow said.

"Yeah, well, some days just seem rosier than others." They were in his office at the back of Harry's store. Harry had been working over his ledgers.

"What can I do for you, Zank?"

"I want you to call Golden Sunrise and make an appointment to have a look around. Tell them you got a kid and you'd like to sign him up for the nursery school."

"It's got to cost you."

"How much, Harry? Be reasonable."

He considered for a moment. "Five hundred—dollars, not fortune cookies." He tapped his pencil on his accounts payable.

"Geezus, Harry, that's a lot of baked goods."

"Then get some other fool."

Zank sighed. "Okay, Harry . . . five hundred."

"You got the number?"

"I memorized it." Zank picked up Harry's phone and dialed. He handed the receiver to Harry. Harry smoothed out his thin mustache. "Good morning, this is Mr. Chin. My wife Henrietta and I are interested in a top-notch— Oh . . . oh, I see . . . yes. Good-bye.'' He hung up.

Harry went back to his account books. "They have no openings. And they don't expect to have any in the foreseeable future. No charge for the phone call—don't say I never gave you anything.''

Zank circled the tiny office with his hands in his pockets. "That's odd, now, ain't it? A nursery school that isn't going to have any openings?''

"I'm just telling you what she said.''

"Some way or other I got to find out if Cleomona is in there, and I don't know any other way than to go in and have a look-see.''

"How about asking your friend Sergeant Donaldson to get a warrant and go in and look around for you?''

"He ain't that good a friend.''

Harry toyed with his mustache. "If I get you in, it's gonna cost you.''

"How much?''

"Two grand.''

"Goddamn.''

"Sorry, friend, but I got a lot of expenses and there's a lot of risk.''

"Look, Harry, I want to get that girl out of there, and I got to do it fast so I can get on with some other important business I got cooking. So give me a break, will ya?''

"The price is two thousand.''

"Maybe I'll think of something cheaper.''

"Like what?''

"Like a disguise or something.''

"And you'll just walk in and ask them to show you around and they'll fully cooperate?''

"Depends on the disguise, don't it?''

8

Zank walked into Gunther's at ten A.M. Gunther was cleaning glassware and setting up the bar. The only customer in the place was an old-timer nursing an Irish whiskey and reading the sports page of the *Chronicle*.

Zank walked up to the bar. "Morning, Gunther."

"Good morning. Hey, nice to see you again, Zank. Hope things went well with Jill Stanyan." He smiled a grandfatherly smile.

"If anyone asks, Gunther, please say you never seen us together, okay?"

"Right. I don't even know either of you. Now what can I do for you, who is a perfect stranger to me?"

"I need a tip on a horse. I've been getting tips from Freddy the Moocher, but he's in the can."

Gunther's eyes became suspicious. "Never knew you to like the ponies."

"A guy I know does me favors if I give him a good tip now and then. And I need a favor. Give me a good pick, okay, Gunther? Something with long odds. This guy dreams of instant riches."

Gunther reached behind the bar and took out his racing form. He looked it over, then turned on his IBM PC and put in a disc. The monitor flickered green, then a list of horses and numbers appeared.

"I spend a lot of time trying to figure this out, Zank, just to give it away free."

"I ain't trying to beat the odds, I just need a horse that looks like he could have a little magic in him."

Gunther looked at him over the top of his glasses. Then he looked at his screen, scrolled it, and said, "There's a horse in the Cal-Stakes I saw run last week. My grandma in a wheelchair could beat him, but a lot of the cards are picking him as hopeful."

"What's the nag's name?"

"Sweet Something."

"Sounds like a winner."

Zank walked into the Union Square parking garage and took the elevator down to the bottom level. He was wearing black pants, a black pullover sweater, and a black jacket. A stocking cap covered his ears. He got off the elevator and walked down the rows of cars, careful to keep his back to the surveillance camera—even though he had it on the very best authority that the camera hadn't worked in over a year—until he'd found a new Chevrolet Caprice Classic. He walked up to it, removed a small flat bar from the kit he was carrying, and slipped it between the window glass and the door skin, then slid it forward until it caught on the locking arm. He snapped it upward and the door opened, as quickly and nicely as if he'd had a key. He got in, took a pry bar with two claws on the end out of his kit, and sprang the locking device on the steering wheel, then stuck a screwdriver into a slot, twisted it, and cranked the engine over. It took no more than fifteen seconds and he was happily on his way.

He drove his new Chevy up to the exit line. The ticket was on the dash. He paid the attendant the two dollars forty cents and drove into the bright light of day. Twenty minutes later he parked the Chevy in a small parking lot behind A.G. Nichols Body Shop on Valencia. There were two other cars in the lot, both with bashed-up right front fenders.

Zank went in through the back door and into the shop. A young Latino was working on an old Packard, getting it ready to paint. The place was dusty. A.G. was in his office on the phone when Zank walked in. A.G. was sixtyish, unshaven, with pale cheeks and tobacco-stained teeth. He was wearing a Yankees baseball cap and talking into the phone. ". . . What the fuck you mean, you can't get me none today? What the fuck I'm going to do without reducer? Spit shine 'em? Yeah, okay, four o'clock. I'll be waiting. Yeah. Okay.'' He hung up, looked at Zank and said: "Fuck you.''

"I didn't even ask yet.''

"I seen you drive up in that thing, I know what you want. I'm not fucking around with no more fake cop cars.''

"I don't need a cop car.''

"Is it hot?''

"A little warm, maybe.''

"I don't want nothing to do with it, absolutely nothing!'' He picked up the phone as if he had to make another call.

"Come on, A.G., you do me a favor, I do you a favor.''

"I don't want no favors from you.''

Zank leaned over the desk and whispered, "I know a guy who knows a guy who knows who's gonna win the Cal-Stakes at Bay Meadows next Saturday. The morning line is gonna be sixty to one.''

"Shit, how's he know?''

Zank shrugged. "It's a setup. One of the jocks is retiring, so they're gonna let him win a sockful.''

"You shittin' me? Sixty to one?'' His eyes blazed. He put the phone back down. Got him, Zank thought. "Righteous stuff, A.G., no shit.''

"Last thing you give me wasn't worth doggy piddle.'' He was suspicious now.

"I gave you Easter Wind at Golden Gate Fields not one month ago, and it paid twenty to one.''

"Yeah, so big fucking deal. I put the whole wad on Tasmanian Devil—which you said was as sure as the national debt—and the fucker fell down coming out of the chute.''

"Accidents happen. That's why they call it gambling. Look, A.G., all you got to do to my new Chevy is hose it red with quick-dry enamel, slap the Fire Department logo on the side, and give it a couple of red lights on top. And get me a set of government-type plates.''

"Fucking-A, I knew it was something like that.''

The Latino worker put his head in the door: "You want me to wet-sand it first?'' He jerked a thumb in the direction of the Packard.

"Sure," A.G. said.

"Got a lot of web, take some time."

"Give it a once over."

"Okay."

The Latino went back to work. A.G. said, "That kid can really crank out the work. No green card, so I get him for five bucks an hour. He works as hard as a fucking one-legged whore."

"Can you have my car done by tomorrow morning?"

A.G. wanted to say no, it was in his eyes. Zank knew he had a healthy respect for the law and hated courts, lawyers, and jails. He rubbed his chin. He also wanted a winner in the Cal-Stakes. "Sixty to one, you say?"

"It's as sure as sin in San Francisco."

A.G.'s lips were tight as his greed wrestled with his conscience. Conscience, Zank figured, was losing two out of three falls. A.G. said, "It'll cost you one thousand plus the horse."

"Fair enough." Zank counted out ten one-hundred-dollar bills onto the desk.

A.G. looked at him with one eye cocked. "What's this hayburner's name?"

"Sweet Something."

"Sweet Something? What's that, a fag name? Turns out to be a sweet nothing, I'm going to drive that car right up your ass."

"Hey, that horse don't come in, I stand still while you do it. It's a sure thing."

A.G. leaned over the wastepaper basket and spit. "The only sure thing around here is I'm a turkey."

At one o'clock the following afternoon Zank marched into the first-floor office of Golden Sunrise wearing a fire captain's uniform, a full raven-black beard, and thick-rimmed glasses. He carried a clipboard and a flashlight. Children's voices and laughter drifted out to him from the room behind the reception area. One was crying. A woman's voice said, "Give him back his jump rope." A boy yelled, "Runyon hit me!"

A receptionist with curly brown hair hung up the phone and said: "May I help you, sir?"

"Routine fire inspection, ma'am," Zank said, "under city code 40-4053 as amended 6-20-82."

The receptionist swallowed and smiled simultaneously. "You'll have to speak with Miss Hill. Just one moment, please." She disappeared through a doorway.

While she was gone, Zank made a cursory inspection of the lobby just in case the mirror behind the receptionist's desk was a two-way job. Got to be official. Then he went through the door the receptionist had used and found himself in a hallway. The receptionist and another woman were coming toward him. The other woman had a long face and wore a stylish tweed business suit and heavy makeup. She puckered and smiled a plastic smile at Zank.

"You wanted what now?" she asked.

"Fire inspection, ma'am."

"Might I see some identification?"

Zank pulled out his wallet and showed her a badge and a green-and-white identity card, an almost perfect forgery. It had cost him five hundred dollars from a craftsman he knew in the Tenderloin named "Benny the Pen," the Picasso of California forgers.

"Captain Feltcher?"

"Yes, ma'am."

"I don't understand this. A Captain Martinez was here not one month ago. We were cited for a minor wiring problem, had the electrician in; he repaired the problem and gouged us, but we got the clearance."

"I'm here on another program, ma'am. It's a special inspection. The uniform fire code in and for the County of San Francisco states that unannounced inspections of facilities designated for use as a school may occur at any time and without prior notice." He pointed at his clipboard as if it were the sacred code itself.

She sighed heavily. "See to it you don't bother the children."

"We never do, ma'am. Won't take but fifteen minutes. We'll start with the upper rooms."

"Take him upstairs, Maggie," she said to the receptionist. The receptionist smiled a receptionist's smile.

Zank followed her down a thickly carpeted hallway and up a metal staircase. Fancy goddamn place for a nursery school. The noises of the children playing grew softer. The top floor was quiet. The smell of fresh paint filled the hallways. They walked through half a dozen offices where secretaries clacked away at typewriters and word processors. Why in a nursery school? Zank wondered, but didn't ask. He checked the electrical outlets and the pressure in the fire extinguishers, asked about inflammables, and looked inside the photocopy machine. He made notes and checked boxes on sheets of paper on his clipboard. He kept humming to himself like a man doing a routine he'd done a million times before. At the end of the hall was a large green door. He said, "What's through there?"

"That door is always locked."

"I have to inspect every room."

"I'm sorry, I don't have a key."

"Can you get one, please?"

She went off down the hall and into the office. He tried the door handle. It was locked tight with a deadbolt. The receptionist came out of an office. Vernon Cole was with her. He glanced at Zank apparently without recognizing him, then nodded to the receptionist. She went downstairs and came back a minute later with Miss Hill. Miss Hill was carrying a large key ring. She said something to Vernon Cole, who shrugged and nodded, then went back into his office. A visit from the Fire Department didn't seem to bother him any, Zank thought. Miss Hill approached Zank.

"We don't use this room much," she said, fumbling around to find the right key.

She found a key, tried it, it didn't work. She tried another, then another. "Has to be here someplace," she said.

"I can wait," Zank said.

"I brought the wrong key ring," she said with irritation. "I'll be right back."

She went back down the hall to Vernon Cole's office. Zank waited a couple minutes. She didn't return. Zank drifted down to the second floor, where he found a long narrow hall with many doors. The first one said, POSITIVELY NO ADMITTANCE. If there's positively no admittance, Zank thought, why have a door? He tried turning the knob. It was locked. No problem. He pried it open with a small bar he had in his jacket.

It was a small room with locked cabinets lining both walls. No window. On the far wall was a small workbench, very clean, neat, and orderly. The cabinets were double-locked. In the crack between the workbench and the wall he found small flecks of what looked like clay. Under the bench he found a few fragments of wire and tape. The Agency had trained him to make plastic bombs. The plastic was just like clay. Like this clay. What the hell would they want bombs for? Naw. Gotta be kiddie clay. They ain't into bombs. It's a goddamn nursery school.

He went back into the hall and checked some more doors. Most of them were storerooms or offices, a few bedrooms. In one of the bedrooms there was a double bed, a dresser, a desk and a TV. On the wall was the picture of Christ and the Sacred Heart he had seen in the cabin in Mendocino. Cleomona's room? Goddamn. Had to be. Now where was she? He stepped back into the hallway. A woman wearing all white walked past. She took a look at his uniform and nodded without asking what he was up to.

Down the hall he found another open room, an office of some kind, full of file folders, ledgers, and records of the kids' progress. He looked out the wide window and saw the kids playing in the yard, supervised by a woman leaning against the fence. He waited for her to turn so he could see her face. She didn't. He slid the window open and tore a piece of paper off his clipboard and let it drift out the window to catch her attention. It floated down into the play yard. She noticed it and looked up. It wasn't Cleomona. Damn.

He checked the next room. An empty office, with a desk and a phone. The next room was locked, and so was the one after. At the front of the building was a narrow room. He went in. It was a lounge of some sort. He glanced out the front window. Down below, where he had left his phony fireman's car with the lights on top, he saw Miss Hill. And two cops. The three of them were looking over the red Chevy, and she was saying something and pointing to the top floor. Even the dumbest of dumb cops, he figured, would be able to tell in about three seconds that the red Chevy wasn't an official Fire Department vehicle.

He turned quickly, went down the hall to a back stairway, and flew down the stairs and through a door to the outside, to the rear parking area. He started around the building, and as he made the turn, found himself face to face with a cop. He was young, blond, lantern-jawed, and large. Zank tried to juke around him.

"Hold it!" the cop ordered, reaching for his service revolver.

"Ah, shit," Zank said, dropping his clipboard and throwing a punch at the cop's lantern jaw, a slow, looping left the cop blocked easily. Despite his size, he was agile and quick. But not quick enough to block the hard right cross Zank unleashed on him. It hit him high on the side of the head and rocked him.

"Motherfuck," he said, blood and spittle running down his chin.

Zank kicked him in the stomach, then dropped him with a crashing left, a straight shot that hit him on the chin. One knee buckled before the other, so he went down like a corkscrew drilling into a wine bottle cork.

Zank sprinted down the railroad siding that ran along the building and around the next building, climbed over a Cyclone fence and ran down an alley. He threw his beard, glasses, and uniform jacket into a trashcan. He continued out to the street and into a residential neighborhood. Five minutes later he caught a number 62 bus at the corner of Alabama and Twenty-fourth.

A young black man with an open shirt and two earrings in each ear sat across from him. He looked at Zank and said: "Been joggin'?"

"Beating up a cop."

"Yo' jivin'?"

Zank grinned. "Took him out."

"Right on, man!"

"Harry?"

"Hello, Mr. Z."

"Remember the deal we talked about yesterday morning? You were going to get me access to a certain place."

"I remember."

"I'd like to give you the green light on that, only . . . only I think two thousand was a bit heavy on your bid."

"What did you have in mind?" He sounded, Zank thought, like he was in a mood to negotiate.

"Fifteen slam."

"That's a big no go."

"Hey, Harry, this whole thing is coming out of my bag."

"Unfortunate." His voice was toneless. "You can seek further remuneration from your principals."

"That ain't possible. Harry, come on, give me a break."

"Sorry, Mr. Z, but I have my standards."

"Shit, standards! Harry, you are one greedy prick."

"My only fault. The one blemish on an otherwise perfect human specimen. The price is two big ones and that's that."

After a pause Zank said, "Okay, okay."

"When do you want to go in?" He sounded cheerful now.

"A.S.A.P. I had a little problem out there today. They might be looking for me soon. My apartment is safe, but they might have a warrant out on me, so I got to be careful until I can cook a deal with Donaldson, help him bag some big ones."

"What did you do?"

"Me and a cop collided by accident. And then there was this car I borrowed—you know how these things go."

"When do I get my two thousand?"

"I'll have Charlotte transfer it from my operations account to yours."

"Stay close to your phone, I'll check things out and get back to you."

Zank hung up the phone and went into the kitchen. Jill was cooking something on the stove.

"You look worried," she said.

"I'm on a case, I worry till it's over."

"What happened today?"

"What makes you think something happened?"

"I don't know, you came in looking upset. Would you

like a drink?'' She threw some sliced onions into the pan; they sizzled.

"No drinking allowed in this house." He looked into the skillet. "What're you making?"

"I don't know, I never really learned to cook. I just throw things together and hope for the best."

He sniffed it. He looked at her and wrinkled his nose. Picking up a wooden spoon, he tasted it. He put the spoon down. "How about we call Pasquale's and get a pizza sent over?"

"Coward." She threw some sliced mushrooms at him. He laughed, retreating. "Hey, watch out. I'm Luca Brasi, from da Godfadduh." He held his breath and flexed his muscles, making his face and neck thicken and turn red and his eyes bulge. He stomped on the floor and grunted.

"You look more like a little boy who has to go to the bathroom!" she said, and burst out laughing. He laughed too. "Face it, Joey, you just don't have it in you to be a monster."

"For a Sicilian, what a disgrace." He shook his head and started washing the mushrooms in the sink. "A wimp Sicilian," he said.

She kissed him. "Can we get serious for a minute, I want to tell you something, okay?"

"Okay. What?"

"I went out this morning."

"Oh?"

"I wore a kerchief tied tight to my chin and had my collar turned up. Nobody could have recognized me. I went over and saw Mrs. Radcliffe, my boss, and explained that I'd had it with Vernon Cole, that I had met a very nice man and was getting my life together, and she said they'd still have a job for me when I got it all together. She's good people."

"I know. I talked to her. She said you were a great nurse."

"You know, I feel better than I have in a long, long time."

"You don't look too bad neither."

"Let's take a trip somewhere. I've always wanted to travel. See Spain. The Taj Mahal."

"The Taj Mahal is in Uttar Pradesh, India. It was begun

in 1630 and completed in 1648. A guy name of Shah Jehan built it for his bride, Mumtaz Mahal.''

"That's absolutely amazing," she said.

"Naw, I got it out of my *World Book*.''

"I thought you were only up to Q.''

"I jump ahead sometimes when I get curious.''

After dinner they sat on the couch listening to country and western records, drinking hot chocolate. She loved Tammy Wynette. He had all her records, he said.

Zank was feeling mellow. Goddamn, if they didn't seem to like the same things. Goddamn. He poured her some more hot chocolate. "Maybe I told you before, but do you know what I always wanted to do? Go up to the Sierras and build myself a training camp—you know, for boxers. Young Olympians. A lot of fresh air, good food. I could teach them a lot. You know, not charge much. Be good for them.''

"Sounds like a wonderful idea.''

"Yeah, I've been thinking, the work I've been doing, you know, is okay, but it ain't something with a future. My friend Harry wants to put in with me. He's got this idea of building cabins with hot tubs and stuff for people who want to get away, relax. We'd maybe be on a lake, too, have canoeing.''

"Could work," she said, nodding.

"I got a little saved, enough to get it off the ground.''

"You should really do it.''

He wasn't looking at her. He was looking down, trying to be casual. "Well, I was thinking something else. You know, boxers get banged up. I mean, you run them through the woods, they get poison oak. They spar, they get their noses busted sometimes. A lot of sprains, things like that.''

"And?''

"Well, I was thinking we might be needing a nurse. You know, somebody who knew how to take care of those things.''

"You probably would." She was smiling. He figured she knew what he was leading up to.

"That's what I was thinking. We probably would." He cleared his throat. "I was thinking, you know, since you're a nurse and all, well, you know, maybe you'd like to come up, see what you thought of the setup and all.''

She kissed him on the cheek.

"That mean yes?"

She kissed him on the lips.

"You have a very nice way of putting things." He put his arms around her.

There was a knock at the door. "Must be Nolan, nobody else knows where I live." Zank went to the door. "Yeah?"

"It's me, Zanca, you fucking creep. Open the goddamn door."

Donaldson. Zank froze. For a moment he thought about taking the fire escape, but decided against it. If Donaldson had come to take him in, he'd have brought an army. Zank opened the door. "How'd you find where I live?"

"I'm a detective, remember?"

"You ain't that good a detective."

"Ever hear of clairvoyance, Zanca? I got it." He pointed to the middle of his forehead. "Cop's third eye, they call it."

"Gee, I'm impressed," Zank said. "This is my sister, Jill Zanca, who used to be a nun. Jill, Sergeant Donaldson."

Donaldson said, "Not much of a family resemblance, is there?"

"Different mothers," Zank said. He turned off the stereo.

"And fathers, too, looks like," Donaldson said. He turned to Zank. "We got to talk about the dangerous games you've been playing."

"I'll go see Nolan," Jill said.

"This won't take long," Zank said.

Donaldson circled the living room, looking at everything. He stopped circling and stood in the center of the room with his thumbs tucked in his belt.

Zank said, "You think I was doing something today I shouldn't ought to have done?"

"You're sharp tonight, Zanca."

Donaldson dropped onto the couch and put his feet up on the coffee table, folded his arms, and stared at Zank through squinted eyes. Zank stood in the middle of the living room with his hands in his pockets.

"Got any cookies or anything?" Donaldson asked.

"Sorry, I'm all out."

"You should always have cookies around in case a pal stops by."

"My pals don't eat cookies."

"I'm your pal and I eat cookies." Donaldson's eyes were fixed. "If I wasn't your pal, I'd have you in the cooler this very minute. And believe me, old bone, they would put you in the hamper forever for what you did today."

"What is it you think I did today?"

Donaldson's feet came down off the coffee table. He leaned forward, glaring at Zank. "You struck a policeman. Naughty, naughty." His finger wagged back and forth.

Zank said, "Ain't you gonna warn me of my rights?"

"You know your goddamn rights better than I do."

"Look, Donaldson—"

"No, you look, turdball! You knocked a policeman on his keester today. You loosened his incisor tooth and cut his cheek on the inside. That is a *very* painful injury. Not only did you injure that man physically, you injured that man's dignity and the dignity of the department."

"You ain't talking about me," Zank said, trying to sound amazed and astounded. "I've been shooting pool all day with a couple of sports down at Nelson Pea's Pool Parlor. You want me to get a couple of people who saw me down there on the phone?"

Donaldson didn't answer. He was looking at Zank top to bottom and shaking his head. Then he said, "How come you always got to be punching cops, Zanca? Four years of your life in the can for hitting cops. One, you pissed on." He shook his head violently. "You *pissed* on an officer of the law!"

"He rousted me for no fucking reason!" He could feel his neck swelling.

"Maybe he didn't like your stink."

"Look," Zank said, trying to calm himself. "I was nineteen years old. Me and a bunch of guys were having a few beers out by Lake Merritt. This jerkoff tenderfoot cop is looking for some guys that were fag bashing down on Polk Street. Hey, we're mellow as hell. Beer, that's all we were doing and this goddamn rookie gets it into his peanut that we're big bad fag bashers and we maybe killed a guy. We told him, hey, you don't kill some guy and then just go and sit and drink beer. Anyway, he pulls his gun on us. Frankie

Marshall—he's a kid I used to hang out with—he don't like guns. Frankie is drunk. Frankie starts to run. This punk cop starts shooting at him. What the hell was I supposed to do? Just let him shoot?''

''You weren't supposed to put him in the fucking hospital!''

''I told you, I was nineteen. I hit him exactly twice. We all peed on him, thought it would humanize him a bit. Give him a little humility.''

''In some civilized countries of the Islamic faith they'd have chopped your joint off for that.''

''Donaldson, get out of here, will you?''

Donaldson leaned back and folded his arms across his chest. ''Not until I find out what the hell you were doing in a nursery school.''

''I wasn't there, I told you, I was shooting pool all day and I got witnesses.''

Donaldson drew a small notebook from his sport-coat pocket and flipped it open. ''You stole an almost brand-spanking-new Chevrolet Caprice from the Union Square Parking Garage at approximately eleven A.M. yesterday and had it painted bright red and decked out with lights and a siren.''

Zank drifted over to the window. There was a black kid standing in front of the apartment building across the street, just hanging around with his hands in his pockets. A lookout for a burglar, Zank thought. Maybe. Or maybe a purse snatcher.

''Well, Zanca?''

''Steal a car, paint it red? Why would I do a thing like that?''

''Because you work for a kind of private dirty-deeds company called The Agency and they paid you to go into Golden Sunrise and snatch somebody named Cleomona.''

Zank turned to Donaldson. ''That would be a heavy-duty rap, Donaldson—a very serious kidnapping beef could be leveled against me for doing something like that. Except, of course, if she was a minor out of parental control. That would be a different story then.''

''Car stealing is a violation almost as bad. Have you been so informed?''

"Car stealing? What you've described is more like car borrowing. I mean it's only stealing if you intend to *keep* it."

"You, Zanca, are totally and hopelessly corrupt. Your value system is ruptured." He put the notebook away and got to his feet. He seemed jittery. Zank couldn't figure why. Zank said, "Did you get out to Hunters Point? Find a lot of Mercedes Benz automobiles?"

"One good bust does not a career make."

"Ah, but you did go!" Zank pointed at him.

"It's going to be on the news tomorrow morning. We got fifty-five cars. Twenty-two suspects."

"And so you must be thankful."

"A tiny bit." Donaldson was standing next to Zank at the window now, looking down on the street. The black kid was facing the building, writing on the wall with a spray can.

Zank said, "What do you want from me now, Donaldson?"

"What's going on at Golden Sunrise?"

"It's just a goddamn nursery school, far as I could see—you find any prints on the car?"

"No."

"No prints, no case."

Donaldson shook his head and made a gurgling little laugh deep in his throat. "Zanca, you have a mind like a thirty-foot trench, deep and straight, but you don't see much side to side. Vernon Cole has been a very bad boy—we think."

"Who's we?"

"Me and maybe an assistant DA."

"Yeah?"

"But we got a problem."

"Supervisor Dix."

Donaldson turned back toward the window again. The kid had written "Death to Police." Donaldson didn't seem to notice, or if he did, he didn't seem to care. He said, "You're smarter than you look, Zanca."

"You want to use me to get Vernon Cole."

"Vernon Cole's bird turd."

"You're after Dix!"

"Listen, Zanca," Donaldson said. "That fucking rookie

you punched out today deserved to get punched out if he had no better sense than to butt heads with you.''

"Had I been there.''

"Yeah, had you been there. And since we haven't got any fingerprints on the stolen car, we can't have you for that because the dumbass rookie can't recognize you. Now, should you go back to that place again, there's a room on the third floor. Has a heavy door, painted green I hear. It's always locked.''

"What about it?''

"I want to know what they're doing in there and I don't want anybody to know I've been asking. Got it?''

"Yeah, I got it. Why don't you just get a warrant?''

"We don't want Cole to know we think he's up to something.''

"How come you're interested now when yesterday you acted like you'd rather be canoeing in a sewer?''

"We didn't know how deeply Dix was involved, but I checked out his bank and his deposits match your pal Vernon Cole's withdrawals, and what do you know, we find a very nice flow of gold.''

"Why not get a building inspector, somebody like that?''

"Because I'd have to go through the chain of command and the chain of command is wired in parallel to Dix. You don't know beans about how things work in real life, Zanca. The real world is just like the fight game, *the fix is in.*''

"If I go in there and risk life and limb to get you this information, what you gonna pay me for it?''

"Zanca, you can't fucking squeeze me. I'm letting you walk, that's pay enough.''

"You aren't letting me walk on anything,'' Zank said with a smile. "You haven't got one damn thing you can take to a jury. No prints, nothing.''

Donaldson smiled right back. It was a theatrical smile, the kind that could be seen in the third balcony. He said, "How about A.G. Nichols, the body and fender man, eh? How about I take him by the fucking ears and drag him down to the Hall of Justice? How long you think I got to sweat him before he cops to painting that damn car for you?''

Zank said nothing. He just stared straight ahead. Then he

swallowed. "You know something, Donaldson, you ain't a bad detective. I'll be letting you know what they got in there, you can count on it."

"Make it soon."

Donaldson opened the door and stood there for a moment, then turned to Zank and said, "Something you ought to know."

"Yeah, what?"

"When I was down at the jail seeing if I could get a home address on you, the records guy told me somebody else was looking too."

"The address I gave them belongs to a church. The priest forwards my mail and wouldn't rat on me if you nailed him to the floor."

"I know, but there was somebody else looking and I just wanted you to know."

"Who?"

"An assistant of Supervisor Dix, the records guy thought."

"You think I might be having company?"

"The San Francisco Police Department recommends that all citizens keep their doors and windows locked at all times."

"Next time you come, Donaldson, I'll have cookies."

Zank was standing by the window watching Donaldson get into his car and drive away when Jill came back in.

"What'd he want?" she asked. She looked frightened.

"He wants to know what goes on in the room with the green door." She stared at him, her mouth open. "What does go on in there?"

"What green door, where?"

"At Golden Sunrise."

"I don't know what you're talking about."

"You never heard of Golden Sunrise?"

"No, what is it?"

He searched her eyes. "Who are you afraid of, Cole or me?"

She turned away from him. "Both," she said.

"I never hurt a woman in my life."

"Please don't ask me anything more about Vernon Cole, okay?"

"What's he doing there that Donaldson would give a damn about?"

She shook her head. She looked frightened. "I wish we could just go away and never come back."

She went into the kitchen. He didn't follow her. He paced around the living room. A few minutes later the phone rang. It was Harry. "Mr. Z, all is ready, I've rolled out the red carpet for you."

Zank hung up the phone. "I got to go out. A friend of mine's got a buzz on. The cops got him, I gotta make bail for the jerk."

"Should I wait dinner?"

"Go ahead and eat. I'll heat mine up when I get back."

She kissed him good-bye at the door. The lie was still on his lips, so the kiss wasn't good.

9

A stiff wind gusted from the southwest as Zank made his way across the roof of the building next to the nursery school behind Harry Chow. Goddamn cold night for it, Zank thought. They both wore black pants and jackets and black rubber-soled shoes. Real pro stuff they'd been issued by The Agency. Harry stopped next to the wall at the top of the building. He turned to Zank and whispered, "Who are these guys that run this nursery?"

"A guy named Vernon Cole leads them."

"Weird, huh? When I was checking them out, I saw one of them go down by the underpass and bury something. I figure that's weird, so I went and dug it up. Guess what it was?"

"Got no idea."

"Dead rabbits. Four of them. All with their heads cut off."

"Why would they cut the heads off rabbits?"

"That's what I'm asking you."

Zank shrugged. "Beats the hell out of me. Goddamn strange though, ain't it?"

"You got a gun, Zank?"

"No. If I get caught with a gun, I get nailed. I've been to the joint twice, for Chrissake. Every damn cop in San Francisco has my name engraved in his arrest book just waiting for me to scratch my ass where I ain't supposed to. I only take along heat where I'm not known and I can get away with a good fake ID. We go in here, it's simple breaking and entering without malice, a misdemeanor. Since we're doing it for her mother, we couldn't catch a kidnap rap—the jury would stand up and applaud. But we go in there with a gun, it's heavy-duty felony time.''

"Hey, what the hell you going to do in there, ask 'em nice to give you the girl?''

"I figure I snatch her and get out before they're even wise we're in there.''

"Man, that's planning.''

"Look, Harry, I got two grand worth of services coming from you. You been paid, now unless you want to refund it all, show me the way in.''

Harry Chow groaned. "Okay,'' he said, "follow me.''

"Wait, Harry. I don't want you to go with me, just show me.''

"You go in there alone, I know you'll just get into trouble. I studied karate. If you have to punch your way out, you're going to need me.''

"Goddamn it, Harry, I ain't gonna figure you out if I live to be a hundred fucking years old. You stuff it to me in the ear for two grand, then you turn right around and volunteer to put your ass on the line.''

"The oriental mind is well known for its inscrutability.''

"I don't even know what that means.''

"It means I'm your friend. I hit you for the two grand because I'm in business and you can afford it. I'm going in because you and me are partners.''

"Okay. But we get in there, you got to do what I say, Harry.''

"It's your show, Zank. Worry not.''

Zank followed Harry over the roof to the fire escape and down to a point level with the roof of the nursery school. They both carried knapsacks, and on the way they smeared their faces with lampblack. Goddamn, Zank thought, they looked like Marine commandos. Looking at Harry the commando, he felt a jolt of fear. He remembered the knives and axes up at Eagleston. Then he had a gun. Now all he had was Harry.

He didn't like taking Harry along, but what could he do? The goddamn guy wanted to help out. Prove something. What the hell, it was a nursery school, not a Hell's Angels training camp.

The buildings were twenty feet apart. Below them was the alley with the railroad tracks where Zank had hit the cop.

At the edge of the roof Harry whispered, "You ready?"

"Piece of cake."

Harry took a small rope out of his knapsack. On the end was a metal hook encased in rubber and painted black. Harry swung it over his head and tossed it to the roof across the way; it hooked, and he pulled the rope tight and tied his end to the fire escape.

"How come we got to do this Batman routine?" Zank asked in a whisper.

"I'm a trapeze artist in my soul."

Zank lowered himself over the side and went hand over hand quickly across the alley and onto the roof next door, quietly slipping down behind an airshaft. He was breathing a little hard. He decided he better get over to Murray's as soon as he could and work on his wind. Harry followed, his movements quick and spiderlike. He brought the other end of the rope with him, jerked on it, and the knot on the fire escape fell open; the rope dropped, gently slapping the side of the nursery school building.

"Geeeeeezus," Zank said under his breath.

"Nobody heard it," Harry whispered, reeling in the rope. Then he tapped Zank and motioned him to follow. They stayed at the outer perimeter of the roof, where the roof beams joined with the walls, to lessen the chance of making creaking sounds. On the far side of the building Harry tied the rope to a pipe and lowered it over the side.

"You sure the alarm is out, Harry?" Zank whispered.

"They no longer have an alarm system, but they think they do. They can push any test button they want and it'll show it's in working order. I know my shit, concern thyself not."

"What's inside that window?"

"An office. I already checked."

"You know what, Harry? You might just be worth your money."

"I'm the Leonardo da Vinci of burglars."

"Okay, Leo. You first."

Harry picked up the rope, said something that was lost in the wind, and lowered himself over the side. Zank took a

look around. In the distance he could see the car lights going
along the freeway. The buildings around were all dark. An
occasional car went by in front. Okay, everything's copasetic. He looked down and could just barely make out Harry
slipping into the building. Zank took hold of the rope, lowered himself down, and stepped inside after him.

He found himself in a small office. Harry, standing by the
door in the shadows, motioned to him. A trickle of light bled
from under the door. Zank crossed the room, gingerly feeling
his way around the furniture. Harry handed him an electronic
gadget that worked like a high-power stethoscope; Zank used
it to listen to the sounds in the hall outside. Two men were
talking.

"Those little bastards are going to drive me right out of
my skull."

"Yeah, I know what you mean. They finally get to
sleep?"

"That, or they're faking it real good."

"Don't put nothing past them."

"I've had it, I'm going to hit the sheets."

"I'll be down in a bit."

Footsteps. Then, from the floor below, Zank heard a door
close. Silence for a moment. A door opened. A woman's
voice: "Who's the asshole that uses up the last of the toilet
paper and never puts it back?"

A man said: "Not me, Rose."

"Yeah, sure, must be Mr. Nobody."

A door slammed. A toilet flushed. A door opened. A door
closed. Footsteps. A door opened. "You got any action for
tomorrow, Cleo?"

"Maybe."

"We got two sessions with the kids."

"I'm not *it*."

"Who is?"

"Sandy."

"Okay."

Silence. Then from the hallway near Zank a door opened
and closed. A light switch clicked and the light coming in
under the door vanished. Footsteps on the stairs. Quiet. No-

body giving any warnings. Good. Maybe it was going to be a piece of cake.

Zank handed the stethoscope back to Harry. "She's here," he whispered, giving the thumbs-up sign. "First we got to check on the green room."

Zank opened the door and stepped into the hallway. A dim night-light shone over the stairway at the end of the hall. He moved down the hall to the stairs and looked up and down. No one in sight.

He went back down the hall toward the green door and motioned to Harry to follow him. Harry glided down the hall, silent as a shadow. When he got to the green door, Zank clicked on a small penlight and made a gesture to Harry to open it. Harry tried the handle, then reached into his bag and took out a small case; he opened it and removed a couple of lock picks. He inserted one in the deadbolt lock, made a few twists, and listened to the click. Okay, way to go. Then he tried the lower lock. In a few seconds it was open.

Zank pushed the door back slowly and stepped into the darkness of the room. It was empty and cool. He flicked on his penlight. Harry came in behind him and shut the door. Covered with lampblack, Harry's face looked as round as a basketball. The soft glow of the penlight made eerie shadows on the wall. They started looking around. Large, colorful cushions were scattered about. A bright yellow area carpet with green star designs covered the center of the floor. Murals adorned the walls: a train full of clowns, a tugboat, a woods full of bad wolves, little pigs; and the Mama Bear, the Papa Bear, and the Baby Bear wearing straw hats. There were no windows, closets, cupboards, or toys. What the hell, he thought. Ain't nothing here Donaldson would be interested in. Then he looked up. Overhead there were rows of small, black spotlights.

Zank whispered, "What d'ya make of this?"

Harry shrugged. "Reminds me of my dentist's waiting room when I was a kid."

Zank whispered, "Picture studio, looks like."

"Yeah, could be."

"What'd they want it for?"

"Beats me."

Zank took a camera with an infrared lens out of his pocket and shot a roll of film, then gestured toward the door.

The night-light in the stairway at the end of the hall was still on. They went down the darkened hall and stopped at the top of the stairs. Down below, a television was on, and someplace else a radio or stereo was playing softly. Zank and Harry stood still and listened. A phone rang twice. Someone answered it, mumbled something, and hung up. Someone else coughed. Nothing out of the ordinary. *Still ain't figured they got guests,* Zank thought.

Zank signaled Harry to wait at the top of the stairs on the third floor, then he started down the stairs slowly. At the first landing he stretched out and looked around the corner to see down the hallway of the second floor. The music was louder now. It sounded like Gershwin's "Rhapsody in Blue." The noise from the TV was coming from the first floor. Laughter. A woman said, "Goddamn Steve Martin is *fun-nay!*"

Zank inched his way down the hallway on the second floor. He passed a room with the door open. It was dark inside, and someone was snoring. Zank could feel his heart pounding behind his ears, but he was feeling high. It was going down right. The rest of the doors were closed and the hallway dim, lit only by the night-light over the stairway. Zank made his way in the semidarkness to the room where he'd seen the picture of Jesus the day before. He took a large roll of duct tape from his knapsack and tore off a long piece. Then he tried the handle to Cleomona's door. Locked. He heard someone coming on the stairs. Someone mumbling and carrying a flashlight.

Zank backed down the hall and waited. The man on the stairs was making his way slowly up the stairs, humming. *Come on, just keep going, sport.* The man passed the landing and continued up the stairs a short way, then stopped as if he forgot something. He paused for a moment, then went back downstairs. A door opened. Muffled voices. Zank waited. He could still hear the radio and TV. Three or four minutes passed; nothing happened. *Okay, just stay put, sport.* He went back to Cleomona's door. He took a knife out of his pack and opened it, then slid the blade into the wood stop along the door until he came to the tongue of the lock. He twisted and pushed; the lock sprung. He slipped inside the darkened room, closing the door behind him.

"What the hell?" Cleomona said, clicking on the light. Before she could scream, Zank had hold of her, his hand over her mouth. He forced her down on the bed and put tape on her mouth, then taped her hands behind her. She was making noise through her nose and wiggled like mad.

"Quit making a fuss or I give you a needle," Zank whispered. She stopped struggling and looked at him. "It's me, Conrad. I'm taking you home to Mama. You gonna come like a good girl, or do I put you to sleep? Your choice."

She nodded. He let her get up. She was wearing a short, blue lace nightie. He found a robe and wrapped it around her.

"Okay," he said softly, "Mama waits."

He opened the door and looked down the hall. The music and the TV had stopped. That was the only change. What the hell's going down now? He stood in the doorway and listened intently. It was quiet now. No sound of movement anywhere in the building. Goddamn strange.

He pulled her along behind him down the hall to the stairs. He looked up and down. He didn't see Harry. That didn't mean anything, he really didn't expect to see him. He motioned with a jerk of his head for Cleomona to go up the stairs ahead of him. She obeyed. He followed her closely. The stairs squeaked under their feet and echoed in the stairwell. They went down the hallway on the third floor and into the empty office. Zank clicked on his penlight and looked around. No Harry. Damn. Zank checked out the window. No rope. Sticking his head out the window, he looked up and called in a loud whisper: "Harry!" No answer. Maybe the fucker turned chicken. Naw. Not possible. It ain't in Harry to turn chicken.

Zank pulled his head in and turned to Cleomona. "We'll use the back stairway. This way." He took her by the arm and led her into the hallway and down the hall to a door at the end. He tried it; it opened. It was a darkened stairwell. There was a strong smell of fresh paint. Zank shut the door quietly behind them and turned on the penlight. Nobody around. Okay. He descended cautiously, holding tightly to Cleomona's arm.

When they got down two flights, they found themselves faced with another door. He tried the handle. It opened. They stepped into a darkened room. He shined the penlight around. It looked like some kind of storeroom, full of shelves and boxes. There was a side door that he figured must lead to the alley with the railroad siding. "Come on," he whispered to Cleomona. They started across the room; Zank kept his penlight on the door ahead of them.

Someone said: "Welcome to Golden Sunrise."

Zank swung around. The light clicked on. Two men faced him. One was the redhead he had met up with at Eagleston and at Jill's apartment, the one who had been so eager to use the meat cleaver on Zank's cranium; the other was short and round and had deep-set black eyes. They both had guns in their hands. Black Eyes had a small-bore automatic, probably a .32, Zank figured. The redhead had a Smith and Wesson snub-nose .38. Black Eyes looked nervous and held the gun high, sighting down the barrel at Zank's nose. The redhead was cool. He liked holding a gun. They quickly freed Cleomona.

"Can you believe it," Cleomona said excitedly as soon as her gag was off, "he came right into my fucking bedroom! Where the hell's our security!"

"We got him didn't we?" the redhead said. "Cool down."

The redhead patted Zank down for weapons, took his knapsack, and tied his hands behind his back; then they marched him back up the stairs. Before a big fight, he always went into a kind of dream state. He could never explain it. All he could say was that his *feeling* increased about a hundred times. Zank's mind was clear, his every muscle tense. Goddamn. Jake La Motta creamed fifty guys by feigning weakness, then coming on like a raging bull. Good goddamn strategy when the other guy's got you on the ropes.

At the top of the stairs Zank stopped, as if to get his breath. They jammed a gun barrel into his back and told him to keep moving. "Wait a minute," Zank said. "Ten thousand bucks each if you guys let me walk."

The redhead laughed.

Cleomona said, "My mother would hire a ninny like this."

10

They took him into a posh office about the size of a three-car garage. Nine Bright Horizons members were standing along the walls: five men, four women. They looked excited, Zank thought, like dorks at a bullfight just before the bull comes out and picadors start to stick him. Goddamn thirsty for blood. Zank recognized more of them from the camp at Eagleston. Vernon Cole sat behind a broad, gleaming, mahogany desk, his black eyes blazing. He wore a flaming-red silk robe with a black Chinese dragon embroidered on it. Cocky bastard, Zank thought. A regular Claudius Caesar Nero, Roman Emperor. 54–68 A.D.

The two guys with the guns stood behind Zank on either side of the door. Zank watched Cleomona slide into a chair; she was tugging on a strand of hair, sliding it over her lips. She looked pleased, Zank thought.

Cole said, "I give you credit, Mr. Zanca, you're certainly determined to deprive us of Cleomona's company."

"Name's Richard Conrad."

"Oh? It was Joseph Zanca when they put you in the lockup." He grinned. "Surprised? I know all about you. You're a former boxer. A number-one contender for a while. You served two prison terms for assault on police officers. Your wife divorced you. You work for a group of neo-fascists called The Agency."

"Never heard of no agency."

"Why bother to deny it? You should be proud of it, Mr.

Zanca." His tiny dark eyes became dots. "Where's Jill Stanyan?"

"Have no idea."

"If you cooperate with me, Mr. Zanca, you might find me a little more generous. She must have told you where to find this place. We have kept my affiliation with Golden Sunrise a closely guarded secret."

"She wouldn't tell me jack about you—mind untying my hands, Dr. Cole? The ropes are cutting off my blood."

"Sorry about that, but you are, after all, a captured knight."

Cole rocked back and forth in his chair. He ran his fingers up and down the lapels of his flaming-red robe like he was pondering a weighty question. Then he got to his feet. "Maybe you don't understand, Mr. Zanca. You have invaded my world. I decide who comes and who leaves from here, nobody else." He said it calmly, but there was an edge to his voice.

"Cleomona's mother is dying," Zank said, as sadly as he could. "I just want to get Cleomona home for one last visit. It'd mean a lot to the poor woman."

"Everyone is dying, Mr. Zanca," Cole said. "It's only a matter of time." He leaned against the edge of his desk and pulled his robe tighter.

"I told him Mama hates my guts," Cleomona said.

"I say we give him the black box treatment," the redhead said. "He's got it coming."

Cole smiled and shrugged the kind of shrug, Zank thought, that Pontius Pilate must have shrugged. Cole said, "I don't believe in violence, but you are a violent man, Mr. Zanca, and must, I suppose, learn the lesson of violence the hard way." Cole's smile faded as he pushed a button on his desk.

A voice answered: "Yes?"

"We have the malefactor up here." Cole's voice had a strange, hollow ring to it. "Anyone who's still awake and not on watch should come up and witness punishment. Tell Maria to bring the box."

"Yessir."

"Zank glanced at Cleomona. She was glaring at him with

a strange look on her face. Hate maybe. Then again, maybe not.

Cole leveled his eyes on Zank. "Now then, Mr. Zanca, let me tell you how things are with me." He was looking at Zank, but it was apparent that what he was saying was for the rest of them. "I live in a small world. I have a certain number of very loyal friends who believe in me. For that I am grateful. I need all the friends I can get because I have set out a very big goal in life. That goal is to change the very nature of the human psyche."

"How you gonna do that?" Gotta keep this joker talking, Zank thought.

Cole flexed his fingers. "By systematically taking off the controlling mechanisms that society puts on it." His voice had dipped into a lower register now, solemn. "Society fears the free man, Mr. Zanca. And the free man of genius it fears to the point of labeling him either a criminal or insane, and locking him up or killing him."

"Depends on what he does, doesn't it, Dr. Cole?"

"Yes! Yes! Exactly! He's safe so long as he does their bidding and bends to the will of others."

"I figure a man has to do what he sees is right, and everybody else be damned. I got a thing about cops. I figure society is kind of like the weather, you can't do much about it." Zank tried to look relaxed. Show Cole how friendly he was, how much they had in common.

Cole cocked an eyebrow. "I like your philosophy, Mr. Zanca. You are truly a rare man. I admire men who act out of their own inner voice and don't bother with the constraints of society. And I appreciate a man of courage. I think you are a genuinely brave man. It's truly quite remarkable, I see no fear in you at the moment."

"I got plenty of fear. Two guns pointed at me, you'd have to be a tree stump not to feel fear." He could feel the river of sweat rolling down his back, but he decided not to mention it.

"How much are you being paid to get Cleomona back to her mother?"

"A lot."

"So you're risking your life for mere money."

"A window washer risks his life for twelve bucks an hour."

Cole made a fist, then unmade it, as if fascinated by how his hand worked. Then he said, "Let me show you something." He rolled up his sleeve. "See these two tiny scars?" He stretched his arm out and leaned across the desk so Zank could see. There were two dots just above his watchband.

Zank said, "Yeah, I see them."

"I let a rattlesnake bite me. A Texas diamondback, six inches around. A test for myself, a test of my courage. I've passed many such tests. I know what I am capable of. I know exactly how much fear I can face."

"Tell you what, Dr. Cole, why don't you let me and Cleomona go visit her mama and I'll bring her back when the visit's over. I give you my word on it. Fair enough?"

Vernon Cole smiled and shook his head. "No, Mr. Zanca, we need Cleomona here. A certain very important person we both know appreciates the services she can perform." He turned to Cleomona. "Do you wish to go home and see your poor dying mother, Cleomona?"

"I don't give a damn what happens to the old bat. What the hell she ever do for me?"

The door opened and a man and a woman came in. The woman was dark, with large, brown, curious eyes. The man was balding and tall. They said nothing as they positioned themselves along the walls.

"Anybody else coming?" Cole asked.

"Cheryl and Tom are both asleep," the man said.

"Maria's getting the box out of the safe," the woman said. "She's coming."

"Good," Cole said. "We shouldn't keep our guest waiting for his treat."

Zank saw something flash in Vernon Cole's eyes that he'd seen before. He'd seen it in the eyes of a heavyweight from Puerto Rico named De Vega the night he pounded a black guy from L.A. into a six-day coma. Zank felt the taste of panic begin to rise in the back of his throat. Where the hell was Harry? If he was waiting for a good time to come to his rescue, Zank thought, he could stop waiting and start rescuing.

Cole sat back down, glowering. He's working himself up,

Zank thought, so he can go through with what he's got planned.

A woman came in carrying a black bag with a small electronic gadget with dials and wires attached. She put it down on the desk. Zank's stomach knotted.

Zank felt a bead of sweat roll down his cheek. He glanced behind him. Both of the men guarding him had their guns trained on Zank from less than eight feet away. No way to get past the bastards. He looked at the faces of Cole's people along the walls. Some were eager, some tense. Some were looking away. One young woman had tears in her eyes. Whatever was coming his way, he figured it was going to be gruesome.

Cole came around the side of the desk. He said: "On your knees, Mr. Zanca."

The young woman started sobbing.

Zank didn't move. Cole turned to the two men with guns and said, "If he doesn't get on his knees in ten seconds, shoot his legs out from under him."

Zank knelt down. His eyes were fixed on Cole, who was leaning back against the desk and stroking his beard, a thin smile on his face. The silence seemed long. No one moved. Like just before the matador kills the bull. The only sound was a slight whimper from the young woman behind him.

"This is for the good of our movement," Cole said to her. "It has to be done, Julia. He came here, we didn't ask him to come."

"I know . . ." she said with a choked voice.

The knot in Zank's stomach cramped up. Cole motioned to one of the armed men, the black-eyed one, to give him his gun. Cole checked it to be sure it was loaded, then walked slowly behind Zank and pressed the barrel of the gun into the nape of Zank's neck. The gun felt cold and hard against Zank's skin, and a prickling sensation radiated across his scalp. He began to feel strangely removed, like he was watching a movie from the back row of the balcony.

"Relax, we aren't going to kill you, Mr. Zanca," Cole said. "Maria?" Maria came and stood with him behind Zank. Cole now pressed the gun against the back of Zank's head.

"Maria is going to give an injection to relax you, Mr.

Zanca. Do not resist. If you do resist, I will not hesitate to shoot you.''

Maria came around in front of Zank, stuck a hypodermic needle into an ampule of something, and drew it into a syringe. The expression on her face was cold and detached. She didn't let her eyes wander in Zank's direction. Zank glanced to his right and left; everyone was watching with the same morbid curiosity that he had seen at a bullfight in Mexicali. Some were white with fear. Their eyes were fixed on Cole. They were all tense. Cleomona was holding her head in her hands. Zank looked at the box on the desk and a wave of nausea washed over him.

Cole said, ''Where is Jill Stanyan? I want to speak with her.''

''I-I put her on a bus to Reno,'' Zank said. His mouth was dry as sand.

''Too bad you don't know where she is. I bet she could talk me out of going ahead with this.''

''Honest, I don't know where she is, but you let me just walk out of here, I give Cleomona's mother her money back and I'll never bother Cleomona or you again.''

''Sorry.''

''Lieutenant Leslie Donaldson of the SFPD is waiting outside.''

''You're really reaching now, Mr. Zanca.''

Zank's mind was alive with wild schemes now. He could duck his head and kick out a leg behind him and maybe be able to deflect Cole's gun. But it didn't seem plausible. He was trying hard to weigh the risks. If they were going to kill him, why drug him? What if he just ran for the window? Two floors to the alley. The gravel alongside the tracks would cushion the fall. Chances were good. Once he was on the ground, if no one fired on him he could run for it. But there was every reason to believe they would fire. Besides, it was ten feet to the window. They could shoot him half a dozen times in that distance.

He felt the sharp prick of the needle. Maria pushed the fluid in. The gun against the back of Zank's skull held him frozen. The needle came out. Nothing happened for a moment. No one made a sound. Then the drug hit him. His muscles started to relax. He felt warm. Serene. Everything in the room glowed pink. Like a nice drunk. He told himself to fight it. In the ring he had often stayed on his feet for round after round, fending off punches, conserving his strength until his power came back and his mind would clear.

For a moment he fixed his eyes on Cole, filling himself with hate. He imagined Cole hitting Jill, whipping her, stabbing her. He felt the adrenaline surge through him. Now he deliberately let his head flop to one side, magnifying the apparent effects of the drug. Half of being a good fighter was being a good actor, Mole Allen had told him. You had to be an Academy Award winner to be a champ.

"How much did you give him?" Cole asked.

"Twenty cc," Maria said.

"He's big, it might not be enough."

She pulled down Zank's eyelid and moved his head around.

"He has little tolerance, it is enough. Any more and he sleeps."

Cole patted Zank's cheeks. "We wouldn't want that. We want him to know what's happening. Can you hear me, Mr. Zanca?"

Zank didn't answer him. He was busy squeezing his toes inside his shoes, trying to make pain; pain would fight the drug. Cole stuck a small piece of wood in Zank's mouth. "We don't want you to bite your tongue, do we? Bite down now."

Zank spit it out.

"Suit yourself," Cole said.

Zank sensed people moving behind him. Cole had his hands on the small electronic machine.

"Wait'll you see this," someone said.

The young woman who was crying burst into loud sobs and left the room.

Cole said, "You've heard of electroshock therapy, haven't you, Mr. Zanca? I know you have. It's wonderfully effective. It makes you forget. You froth at the mouth. You have convulsions. If the treatment is strong enough, you're disoriented for days. This box has been modified. We can go beyond ordinary treatment levels. We can actually serve you up a cooked brain."

Despite the drug, a jolt of panic hit Zank in the top of the head and sent a shudder through him. The pinkness of the room faded. He looked around to see where the guns were pointing. Black Eyes had his in his belt. Cole must have given it back to him. The redhead was leaning on the desk in front of Zank now, holding his gun down at his side. Okay, just keep it pointing to the floor.

Zank was breathing in short, choppy breaths now.

Cole said, "Watch now, everyone, the professor will show you how it is done. Gather around. First, you must lubricate the temple area to get a good conduction of electricity. That is most important."

Someone standing behind Zank rubbed grease onto his temples. Vomit rose in Zank's throat. Cole suddenly had something in his hands. Zank didn't see who gave it to him. It looked like a radio headset attached to a small wire. The wire went to a small machine with lights and dials on it.

"This will straighten you out, Mr. Zanca, and take the fight out of you." The headset touched Zank's temples and Cole's hand reached for the switch. Zank heard someone gag, and thought, it's goddamn now or never. He sucked in as much air as he could and looked at the redhead. The redhead's eyes were following Cole's hand to the control switch. Zank reared back and stumbled to his feet, jerking violently from side to side, smashing into people and furniture, butting people with his head, kicking wildly and clumsily. Black Eyes fell back and jerked the gun out of his belt. Zank kicked him in the chest and knocked him back over a chair. The redhead grabbed Zank from behind. Zank butted him full in the face with the back of his head. Sparks danced through Zank's brain. He butted him again. How's that, asshole?

"Stop him!" Cole yelled. "Grab him!"

They were on him now, dozens of hands. Zank put his head down and charged them, kicked them, threw his shoulders into them, stomped on their feet. He dropped one with a kick to the groin.

"Yeow!" someone screamed.

A chair crashed against Zank's shoulder, and something else broke over his head. Geezus. He gasped for air. Kicking wildly, taking blows and kicks. Everything seemed blurred and out of focus. The goddamn drug. His legs wobbled. Got to get out of here. And then he saw Cole in front of him waving his arms, encouraging the others to attack.

Zank charged forward, head down, directly at Cole, like the bull going for the matador. Cole yelled and spun away, but Zank put his shoulder into his midsection, and with a powerful thrust of his legs pushed Cole toward the window. Cole put his foot behind him under the window to stop himself, but Zank was thrusting forward with all his weight and all his strength.

A woman's long, shrill, terror-filled scream swelled the night as Zank and Cole went out the window together in a spray of glass, tumbling through the air. Buildings, ground, sky, light and shadow, Cole, the sound of yelling filled Zank's head. Zank hit the gravel more on his right foot than his left and rolled across the railroad track. He lay there for a moment with the world spinning around him in the darkness. Geezus, still in one piece. Cole moaned softly near him. Someone in the window above shouted, "Don't shoot, you might hit Vernon!"

A moment later Zank heard voices at the end of the alley. He staggered to his feet. His head was cloudy and his legs unsteady, like a beaten fighter at the bell in the fifteenth round.

A voice in his head said: Run! Run!

11

Zank cut the cord that bound his hands behind his back on the corner of a building, then climbed over the gate at a power company substation and watched the street through the slats of the redwood fence. He was dizzy, his foot hurt, his face bled, his hands were numb. He had to concentrate hard to stay awake.

Cole's people, in groups of twos and threes, were combing the alleys and looking under parked cars in a frantic, disorganized way. A small group came to the substation and shined a light through the fence, but Zank crawled behind a transformer and they moved on without seeing him. Fifteen minutes later they came down the street again talking excitedly to each other, turned the corner, and disappeared.

Zank sat on the cement behind the transformer for a long while, pinching himself and breathing deeply, trying to keep himself stimulated until the effects of the drug wore off. He stood up and did clumsy jumping jacks and jogged in place. Sharp pains shot up his right leg. His ankle throbbed. After a while his head cleared, then he climbed back over the fence and headed for home.

When he came up the stairs to the apartment, Jill was waiting at the door. She'd been sleeping on the couch, her hair and clothes were messed.

She said, "What the hell happened to you?"

"Just a misunderstanding with your old friend Cole, nothing to get hot and bothered about."

"You should see a doctor."

"Ain't you a nurse?" He bent down for her to take a look at the top of his head.

"Those cuts are deep." They went into the bathroom. He looked in the mirror. His right eye was swollen almost shut, and dark cakes of blood plastered the side of his face from a cut above the temple. It was still oozing.

"Can you sew it up?" he asked.

"Bend down, let me see." She probed it with a Q-tip. "You need sterile thread to sew. There's pieces of glass in here."

"I got bandages in the medicine chest, I ain't got time to go to the hospital."

He sat on a small stool in front of the sink while she shaved part of his head, then started cleaning the wounds and putting cold compresses on his face.

Zank said, "Harry Chow, a friend of mine, went in with me, but he finked out. I get my hands on the little bastard, I'm gonna french fry him good. First he begs me to let him go along, and then he finks out and takes the rope with him. How's my head?"

"I think I might be able to stop the bleeding if you don't touch it." She opened a bottle of antiseptic and started dabbing it.

Zank said, "Cole was positive you must have told me about Golden Sunrise."

"So he's mad at me for that now."

"Yeah, well, couldn't be helped—zow! That stuff stings."

"Sorry. Maybe it would be best if you left Vernon Cole alone. There's dirt in with the glass. Do you have tweezers?"

"Medicine chest, top shelf. How can I leave him alone as long as he's got Cleomona?"

"That's her business and his business."

"Geezus, Jill, she's just a kid."

She was gingerly pulling out tiny pieces of glass and debris and dumping them in the sink. "Vernon Cole has done some remarkable things, Joe. He took in a supposedly retarded kid a few years back and now that kid is going to Harvard. I'm not kidding. His name's Randy Hess, look him up. Cleomona is better off with him, maybe, than with that crazy mother of hers. You ever think of that?"

"He was going to fry my brains."

"He was probably just trying to scare you."

"If that's what he was trying to do, it worked— Ouch!"

"Hold still! I'm trying to get out the glass."

"My hand hurts like hell."

She took hold of his hand and looked at it. "Busted knuckle." She went back to removing the glass.

"How can you tell?" He looked at his hand, making a fist.

"I'm a nurse, remember?"

"You ain't seen no X ray."

"I can see it's blue. They don't turn blue if they aren't broken."

"Damn. That's four times I've busted that son of a bitch. Did you know about Golden Sunrise?"

"Here we go again."

"Come on, Jill, level with me. Cole knew that you knew. I'll protect you. You don't have to be scared."

"I don't know what you're talking about. Just look at you. What a sorry mess. What's wrong with your eyes? You drunk? Your pupils are big as quarters."

"They injected me with something."

"Vernon did?"

"Yeah. Wait till you see Harry Chow when I get through with him. You finished?"

"In a minute."

"My ankle hurts like hell too."

"Let me see it."

He lifted his right foot. She took off his shoe. The ankle was swollen and blue.

"Did I break the son of a bitch?"

"Maybe."

"Can you wrap it?"

"It's got to have ice."

She headed for the kitchen and came back after a minute with a plastic bag, an ice-cube tray, and his bathrobe.

He took his clothes off and put on the robe. She packed

the ice in the plastic bag, then wrapped it tightly to his ankle with an Ace bandage. "How's that?" she asked.

"Numb. Feels better. Thanks." He stood up and put some weight on it. "Cole was sure you knew about that place. What is it you don't want to tell me and why don't you want to tell me?"

"I don't know what he thinks or why. Nobody does. He's crazy." Zank sat back down; she went back to work on the cuts.

Zank said, "Vernon Cole's crazy, but not stupid."

"Certainly not stupid," she said. She put the last Band-Aid on a cut on his nose. "God, what an awful mess." She had a tear in her eye. She brushed it away. Zank gave her a pat on the arm to let her know that everything was going to be okay.

He didn't say anything for a while, while she finished bandaging him up. Then he thanked her, kissed her, and limped into the living room, where he picked up the phone and dialed Harry's number. Wendy answered.

"Wendy? I didn't wake you, did I?"

"Who's this?"

"Joe Zanca."

"Where's Harry?"

"Ain't he home?"

"He said he had to do a deal. He got a call about seven, eight o'clock, and off he went. Said I wasn't to wait up." Her voice had a sharp edge to it.

"I'm sure he's okay, Wendy, don't worry. Go back to bed."

"How can I sleep with him out doing who knows what?"

"Have a little wine or something."

"Call me, Zank, if you find out where he is."

"Sure, Wendy."

He hung up the phone. Jill was standing by the couch.

Zank said, "The little twerp's hiding out from me. He's probably home sucking on some French wine and making Wendy lie to me. He knows I'm gonna kick his ass from here to Colorado."

"Can we talk a minute?" Jill said.

"Sure, shoot."

"I'm scared, Joey. We should get out of here, now. Vernon's capable of anything. I mean it, *anything*. We've got to get as far away from here as fast as we can."

"No, Jill. You can't run away from trouble. I know that for a fact. And I didn't even have to study the *World Book* to know it."

The dawn was gray and still. Zank climbed the fire escape at the rear of the paper box company across the street from Golden Sunrise and crept along the roof. The air was moist and chill. His ankle throbbed. He had a headache. He looked over the rim of the building and down on to the nursery school. A uniformed security guard walked back and forth in front, taking sips from a thermos of coffee.

A feeling of nausea and dread came over him. It was in that nursery school he'd almost had his brains fried. Goddamn Vernon Cole. Goddamn crazy fuck. He leaned against a chimney and rubbed his temples. The dawn grew brighter and the sun showed orange and liquid beyond the hills of Oakland. Now he could see that there was a plywood sheet over the window above the railroad tracks where he'd made his exit.

At ten after six a powder-blue police car came by and stopped in front of the building. The security guard spoke to the driver, who then circled the building and went down the street. Ten minutes later the police car returned and the guard waved. Everything A-Okay. The cop drove on. A piece of machinery started up in the paper box warehouse beneath Zank. On the bay a large Japanese cargo ship was leaving the Oakland Estuary on its way out the Golden Gate. Business as usual. The sun was fully up now and it was getting warmer. A salt-scented breeze blew steadily from the south. Zank fought off fatigue by slapping himself on the face and pinching his arms. His ankle ached maddeningly.

At 6:45 the receptionist showed up, parked her blue Volkswagen Rabbit in front of the building, and knocked on the front door. The security guard tipped his hat to her. Someone on the inside let her in, Zank couldn't see who. At seven o'clock a second security man came out and said something to the first. They laughed about something and then went around the side of the building together. At seven-ten they came back, carrying lunch buckets, and stood by the corner of the building. One lit a cigarette. A Dodge van drove up and two more security men got out. The four spoke for a few minutes, then the two who had been waiting got into a yellow Pinto and drove off. The changing of the guard, Zank thought. Both of the new security men went inside.

A few minutes later the first mother arrived with her two small boys. They went inside. Then a father dropped off his little girl. A station wagon brought six more little kids. One, resisting, was carried in crying. No sign of Cleomona, Cole, or Harry.

He knocked on the door.

"Who is it?"

"Joe Zanca."

The door opened. Wendy Chow stood in the doorway. She looked small. She'd been crying. "Every time I see you, you look worse than last time," she said. "Somebody take a beer bottle to your face?"

"I fell in some bushes. I was driving my motorcycle and a guy forced me off the road."

"Where the hell is Harry, Zank?"

"You *sure* he ain't here?"

"He's not here. He hasn't been here. What the hell you think I'm doing, playing some stupid game? Where'd you two go last night, Zank? And I don't want to hear any bull about falling into the bushes."

"I ain't sure." He looked around the living room, at nothing in particular, not wanting his eyes to meet hers. There were a bunch of balled-up Kleenexes on the coffee table.

"I thought maybe the cops got him," she said. "But if the cops get you, you get to make a phone call, don't you?"

"Sometimes you do, sometimes you don't," he said, trying to make it sound as if he believed it. "He's bound to show up, Wendy, don't get disturbed."

"We got a baby on the way, he tell you that?"

"Hey, no, that's good news!"

"You got him into something, didn't you?"

"No way, Wendy, honest."

"Yeah, shit, honest! You don't know the meaning of the word. Get out of here, would you please?"

"Okay, Wendy, listen. I'll level with you." He looked away from her. "We had a bag job last night."

"Christ!"

"Listen to me, will ya?" He turned to her. "It went down okay. His part didn't have a hitch. I had to fight my way out. That's how I screwed up my ankle and got all these cuts. But just before that, I discovered Harry took off—disappeared. It's me he's hiding from. He thinks I'm gonna pulverize him for splitting. But you tell him enough is enough, okay? I ain't going to hurt him—honest."

She didn't move, she didn't say anything, she just stared at him. He could see she was reading his face for the truth. After a moment she nodded. "When he gets in touch," she said, "I'll tell him. You're sure about this?"

"We came in a window with a rope. I went back to the window a couple of minutes later and he was gone, and so was the rope. I'm telling you, Wendy, he must have heard something and just decided to split."

"I'm glad you told me, Zank." She smiled faintly.

Zank said, "Can I use your phone?"

"Right there."

Zank called the police station and asked for Sgt. Donaldson. They put him through to the Metro squad.

"Donaldson's out, this is Inspector McGivy."

"Where's Donaldson?"

"Out, like I said, O-U-T."

"Out where?"

"None of your business."

"Tell him Harry Chow's missing."

"Okay, Harry Chow is missing. Who should I tell him called?"

"Zanca."

"Right." He hung up.

Wendy Chow said, "What were you two up to?"

"There's this girl, we were trying to free her from a cult."

"And you think Harry ran out on you?"

"Yeah."

She bit her lower lip. "Zank, Harry wouldn't ever run out on anybody. He had this stupid code."

Zank felt something sharp forming in his gut and drawing tight around his throat. He said, "Maybe he did this once."

Zank went downstairs, got into his car, and headed over to the south of Market area. She was right, he thought. Harry and his goddamn code. Harry Chow would never fink out on a buddy in a million years.

Zank drove down Twenty-fourth Street, up Alabama to Twenty-eighth, around the block to Utah, and then back down Twenty-seventh, looping back to Rhode Island, looking for Harry's Toyota. No luck. Goddamn, it's got to be someplace. He turned east on Rhode Island and drove back to Twenty-fourth and around again to Mississippi. Still no luck. He was beginning to feel that Harry must have driven it away, and that made him feel better. But still he searched the alleys between Twenty-fifth and Twenty-sixth. He found it parked behind a printing plant at the corner of Twenty-fifth and Bryant.

It was locked up tight.

Zank stood on the sidewalk staring at it for a long moment. Maybe he got hurt and couldn't drive. Maybe the car wouldn't start. Then again, maybe he never got out.

On the way back to stake out Golden Sunrise, the pager on Zank's belt sounded. He stopped at a gas station and phoned his answering service. The operator said, "Charlotte wants to see you, pronto."

"Okay, I'm on my way."

Zank limped up the familiar stairs and through the eternally empty waiting room. The *Time* magazine with the missiles on the cover was still on the coffee table. He pushed the button in the thermostat and went up the stairs and into the inner office, where a surprise was waiting: sitting in one of the chairs in front of the desk was a familiar face, Sgt. Leslie Donaldson, SFPD.

Donaldson said, "Pick your jaw up off the floor, Zanca."

Charlotte smothered a laugh. It was the first time Zank had ever heard her laugh.

"What gives?" Zank asked.

"So you never heard of any Agency, eh?" Donaldson said.

"Listen, Donaldson, if this is a bust, I want an attorney, and I mean right now."

"No bust, relax. What happened to you? You look like you went a few rounds with King Kong."

"My necktie got caught in an orange juice-blender."

"Sure it did."

"Sit down," Charlotte said. "We're working with Donaldson on this one."

Zank eased into a chair. "I never heard of us working with the police."

"We'll keep it a secret, Zanca," Donaldson said. "Don't worry about your reputation."

"The department know you're here?" Zank asked.

"I'll ask the questions, Zanca, you do the answering."

"Okay, ask away."

"You went into Golden Sunrise last night, didn't you?"

Zank glanced at Charlotte. She nodded. Zank said, "I might have been there, yeah."

"You take a look inside the room with the green door?"

"For a minute or two. I gave you a promise, didn't I?"

"What's in there?"

"You ain't gonna like it when I tell you, Donaldson. There was no dope-processing plant, no stolen artworks, no counterfeiting shop. Nothing in there but a lot of cushions on the floor and choo-choo trains on the walls. Kiddie stuff. They must use the place for putting on plays or something. They had spotlights on the ceiling. That's it, just a big goddamn empty room."

Donaldson nodded and flexed his fingers.

"Now I got it figured how you got my home address," Zank said. "You got it right here."

"You ought to be a detective," Donaldson said.

Charlotte laughed again. This time she didn't try to suppress it. Zank suspected she was laughing to flatter Donaldson, and he seemed to like it. She stopped laughing and stroked the jade cat on her desk. Donaldson reached into his sport-coat pocket and took out a thick envelope and handed it to Zank. "Take a look at these."

Zank opened the envelope and took out a stack of photos. He started going through them and felt his blood run cold. "Jesus H . . ." he murmured.

"Look at the background, Zanca, the walls. The little train, the clowns. That's where these were taken. Right there in that room."

The photos showed children and adults. Mostly they were naked. There were close-ups of male children having oral sex with men and women. Everyone was wearing masks. Sometimes the kids were in costume—a princess, a soldier, a vampire. In most the kids had no expression, but one little girl's face was twisted with pain as a big guy was mounting her. The pictures made Zank nauseous and he leafed through them quickly. Even with a white mask over her eyes, he could tell that one of them was Cleomona Fisk. "Ah, Christ," he said. He handed them back to Donaldson. "I've seen enough."

"Child porn is a multimillion-dollar business in California," Charlotte said.

Zank said, "What kind of perverted asshole would pay for something like that?"

"Who the hell knows?" Donaldson said.

"How can they get away with something like this?" Zank asked. "Don't the parents know?"

"The pornographers intimidate the kids. Kill a pet, show them what could happen to the parents if they talk."

"Like pet rabbits. I get it. But that ain't gonna work all the time. How long can they keep this shit up before some kid yaps?"

"A gang of pornographers in L.A. went on for seventeen years," Donaldson said. "Cole must be careful about which kids they pick. They tell the parents they want their kids for an accelerated program to develop their minds and they move the kid in. They terrorize the kid. Brainwash him. Fuck his head all up. The parents figure Cole's a genius, he must know best. The kid seems pushed out of shape, Cole explains it away with some gobbledygook. They're glad to have the kid out of the way. These are people married to careers and kids just make their lives messy. If the parents catch on, a couple of Cole's people lean on them a little. They don't want their kids hurt, they don't want to look stupid in the newspaper, so they shut up. People are assholes, it's a fact.''

''He's got to know it can't last.''

''Sure, he knows it can't last. When it sours, he'll take the dough and split, let his followers take the heat.''

Zank got to his feet. ''Listen, Donaldson. Harry Chow went in there with me last night. We went over the roof and dropped down the side and went through a window. He was supposed to wait for me and didn't. Either he chickened out or they got him. I think they got him. I found his car parked a couple of blocks away. That guy Cole is crazy, Donaldson. He was going to fry my brains with some electro-shock machine.''

Donaldson arched his eyebrows. ''Like, for real?''

''Yeah, like for real. I got my face cheese grated coming out the window, but Harry's still in there. Get a warrant, Donaldson. You got to get in there, see what the hell happened to him.''

Donaldson shook his head. ''We aren't ready to make a move yet.''

''When you gonna make your move?''

''When we got something to move on. What do we got now? Your testimony? A convicted felon? A burglar? Fuck, anybody can buy wallpaper. Besides, even if we busted everybody in these pictures, it doesn't implicate the leaders. You've got to build a case like this slowly. You have to identify the kids, get to the parents who don't have their kids at risk. In San Jose they've blown a couple of big ones by being overanxious. Parents would rather see Vernon Cole walk than put their kid on the witness stand against him.''

''So what's your plan, Donaldson? Sit on your ass?''

''We're trying to get to their distribution point.''

''Yeah, and then?''

''Trace the money.''

''That might be a bit tough.''

Donaldson shrugged. ''Police work takes time. We'd try out our suspicions on some of the parents, except it would get back to Cole in a hell of a hurry.''

"But Harry, what about Harry?"

"Whatever they're going to do to him has already been done."

Charlotte said, "In the meantime, we've got a commission to get Cleomona out of there."

"She's in there, Donaldson. She's sixteen. Why don't you just go in there and pick her up?"

"Because we need a warrant, and as soon as we go in to get one, one of Dix's pals in the department would let him know, and then our whole game is blown."

Zank stared at him. "You don't give a fuck about Harry, Cleomona, or these kids. It's Dix you're after. Period."

Donaldson's cheeks reddened. "You know why you're a punk scuzball and why you're always going to be a punk scuzball, Zanca? Because you can't see the big picture. You do your fucking job and let me do mine. Go get the girl, that's what you've been paid to do. Forget the rest of it."

Charlotte said, "*Can* you get Cleomona out, Mr. Zanca?"

"I can get her out."

Zank started out the door, but then he turned and said, "Give me those pictures, Donaldson. There's somebody I got to show them to."

12

Zank stormed into his living room and slammed the door behind him.

"What's wrong?" Jill asked, jumping up from the couch, dropping the *World Book* she'd been reading on the floor. He stood in the middle of the room, glaring at her.

"What is it, Joey? What's happened?"

"Why don't you tell me?" He shoved the photos at her. Her eyes moved over them slowly. Her lips began to tremble. "Oh, God . . ."

Zank said, "That's what your pal Vernon Cole has been up to over there at Golden Sunrise and you knew it! You knew it and you did not one goddamn thing!"

She turned away from him, toward the window, clutching the curtain. She said nothing for a long time. He stood waiting, breathing heavily, his hands made into fists. Finally she turned back to him, large tears rolling down her cheeks. "I wanted to tell you. I'm just not a very brave person."

"If you knew this shit was going on, you had to call the cops! Anybody with a fucking ounce of brains would call the cops quick. These are kids! Little boys and girls!"

"I couldn't call the police." Her voice was barely audible.

"Why? Give me a reason. He drugged you or threatened you, something like that? You were scared, okay, but it had to be more than that."

She shook her head. "I wasn't drugged."

"Hypnotism? Brainwashing? I've read about things like that. It can make people do awful bad shit."

"No," she said. "I knew . . . I knew there were evil things going on. I poured myself a drink and told myself lies. I wanted Vernon to stop it. I tried to make him stop. But he wouldn't listen to me. He wanted me to . . . to do it too. To prove myself worthy of him, he said. But I wouldn't. I wanted him to want me so bad . . . but I still said no. Not with kids. That's when things went bad between him and me. That's when he threw me out."

"He threw *you* out? You mean you could have stayed after you knew this shit was going on?"

"Sounds stupid, probably, but I was trying to change things. But you run out and nothing gets better."

Zank paced around in a small circle, running his hands through his hair. He stopped pacing and turned to her. Her face had a cold expression and her body was rigid, like a beaten boxer expecting a blow. Finally, he said, "You got to be ringy in the head to stick around, not doing nothing about this. You maybe ought to talk to a doctor. Get your head right."

She wiped her eyes on her sleeve. "If you want me to leave, I'll leave."

"Did I say I wanted you to leave?"

"No."

"I want you to leave, I'll tell you." He started pacing around again. "Donaldson will want to talk to you. He's building a case against Cole and Dix."

"No," she said, shaking her head. "I don't want to talk to him."

"You're an accessory. Just knowing about it, they'll be able to hang something on you. I'll cut a deal with Donaldson, you'll walk. Probation, maybe, but no down time."

"Would I have to testify against Vernon?"

"You don't have to be scared. I'll protect you and so will the cops."

"I can't testify against Vernon."

"What the hell do you mean, you can't testify? The man's a fucking pornographer—a kiddie raper!" Zank turned suddenly and kicked the coffee table with his good left foot, bouncing it against the wall. "Sicko! Sicko! Sicko! The man's a fucking animal!"

"Whatever you want to call him, go ahead," she said in a sudden burst of emotion. "But he's still one of the greatest men that ever lived! He's a Rousseau, a Galileo, an Einstein! If they had recognized Vernon Cole instead of insulting him, he would have changed the world by now. He would have taught us all how to be free! How to love everyone! How to fill ourselves with greatness like his!"

"And how to take dirty pictures of kids!"

She turned away from him, going to the window and leaning her head against it. Her body sagged. "You don't understand, do you? I don't expect you ever will. How could you? You've never been touched by a god."

He stared at her for a long moment. "You're gonna see he ain't no god, if I find out he's hurt Harry Chow. I'm gonna break every one of the goddamn 212 bones in his body."

He went back to the roof of the paper box factory across the street from Golden Sunrise. He was taking five high-energy pills an hour. He watched who came and went from Golden Sunrise, noting what the security people did, how often the cops cruised by. He tried not to think of Jill. He tried to keep his mind on the case, but Jill kept popping into his head. Touched by a god. How goddamn idiotic. A child-fucking pornographer!

Then he thought of Nolan and remembered his story about the People's Temple and his nephew. Yeah, okay, so people got hooked on these goddamn hypnotists or whatever they were. You get hooked on anything, you can get unhooked. Maybe Nolan could talk to her. Nolan maybe could get her to see the light. Sure he could. Might take some time. But she'd come around. Get her to see she'd been brainwashed. Get her to a shrink, maybe. Give her a lot of love, show her the damage Cole had done.

First there was the business at hand. He had to get Cleomona out of there. He had to find out about Harry. First things first. Harry. Cleomona.

He watched the parents and domestic servants come and

go with children. Seeing the children angered him. He wondered which ones Cole was planning to use. He couldn't think about that. If he thought about that, he might go in there and tear the place apart.

A UPS truck made a delivery. The mail came. But no Vernon Cole. No Cleomona. No Harry Chow. At noon he went back to check on Harry's car. It was still there. There were two parking tickets now under the windshield wiper. Zank's mind was dull and fatigue was making him shiver. He lay down in the back of his car and went to sleep. At five-thirty in the afternoon his pager sounded. He drove over to Potrero Avenue, where he used a gas station phone to call in. Donaldson wanted him. He called the Police Department and they patched him through.

Donaldson said: "We found Harry Chow—we think."

"He dead?"

"Very."

"Geezus H. Christ."

"We need you for an ID."

Zank took a couple of deep breaths. "This the way you guys tell a guy his good buddy's dead? You just say *very*." Zank took another deep breath. "Where you at?"

"We're right behind his electronics shop. It's not pretty."

"I'll be right over."

"You aren't going to throw up, are you, Zanca?" Donaldson asked as soon as Zank drove up.

"No, Donaldson. I seen dead guys before."

"I just got to warn you, it's pretty grim."

Zank followed Donaldson up the alley between Harry Chow's electronics shop and the cut-rate liquor store next door. In back of the building half a dozen cops and lab men were milling about, looking for clues. Others were standing around, not doing anything. No one was saying anything. When death is around, most people shut up. Near the back door of the electronics shop stood a large plastic garbage can with a red piece of tape over it. The tape said, "Sealed by Coroner, City and County of San Francisco." The coroner's man standing beside the can nodded to Donaldson.

"This the guy?" the coroner's man asked.

Donaldson nodded, then said to Zank, "You sure you're not going to puke?"

"Let's just get it over with."

"Okay," Donaldson said. The coroner's man adjusted his glasses. He was in his twenties, big-boned, with a somber expression. The man peeled the tape carefully off the plastic garbage can and held it in his hand. Then he twisted the lid and opened the can. Zank looked inside. The stench of burned flesh wafted up at him. Zank looked at Donaldson, then at the coroner's man, then at the can. He stepped closer.

At first it didn't look like anything, just something burned and black on top of a body. But then he saw it was Harry's face. The features were charred, but they were recognizable. Zank turned away. His mouth went dry and for a moment the world seemed to spin under his feet. He managed to say, "What'd they do to him?"

"Cut him up, then poured lighter fluid on him and set him on fire."

"Geezus H. Christ," Zank said. He bolted suddenly and ran toward a chain-link fence, which was as far as he got when he heaved out everything that was in him. When he was done, he walked down the alley to the street, limping on his bad ankle, spitting as he went. Donaldson went with him. As they turned down the street, Donaldson touched his shoulder.

"I'm sorry, Joe," Donaldson said.

"It's okay, Donaldson."

"Can I get you anything?"

"I'll be okay, just give me a minute. I'm a tank, remember."

Zank had his eyes shut. He opened them now. The sunlight burned. He said, "They roasted him. Christ."

Donaldson didn't say anything.

"What do you think, Donaldson? Maybe they hit him first on the head and he died quick."

"Probably," Donaldson said. "Harry was married, wasn't he?" Donaldson asked.

"Her name's Wendy. She's pregnant."

"Shame," Donaldson said.

Zank spit again. "Cole is dead meat."

"You stay away from him, Zanca. No cowboy shit. We'll

get them, and when we do, we'll make it stick and they'll go to the joint for a long, long time. But you stay out of it. I mean it."

"Yeah."

They walked another half block.

"He looked like well-done hamburger," Zank said.

Donaldson said nothing.

"Who found him?"

"The garbage men."

"You got any gum on you, Donaldson?"

"I'm on a diet."

"Gum ain't fattening."

"I'd swallow it."

After a moment Zank said, "You gonna be able to keep this off the TV?"

"No."

"It'll be awful for Wendy."

"Can't be helped."

Zank stood at the curb and spit into the street a few times. Then he started walking again. He said, "Harry was an okay guy."

"I never knew him well. Busted him once for breaking and entering. He copped to some misdemeanor and walked."

"He always was a lucky son of a bitch."

"It maybe wasn't even Cole's people, Zanca. Harry had trouble with a Chinatown gang, the Wa Sing, too. Maybe they did it. They're brutal fuckers."

"It wasn't the Wa Sing. Me and Harry straightened that out last year. See ya around, Donaldson."

Zank turned and started back up the block.

"Where you going?"

"None of your goddamn business."

He knocked softly on the door. He hoped to hell she wasn't in. But he could hear footsteps. His heart froze. Then: "Yes?"

"Joe Zanca."

The door opened. Wendy Chow looked at him and her large brown eyes opened wider. "What is it? Is he hurt?"

"Sit down, okay?"

"Is he hurt bad, what is it?" She grabbed his arm. "He's dead, isn't he!"

Suddenly Zank didn't seem to have breath enough to speak. He gulped for air. "Wendy, listen, please."

"Shut your mouth, don't say he's dead!"

He wrapped his big arms around her trembling body.

"He's run off with another woman!" she cried. "He's in jail! He went to China. He's not dead, I won't hear it!"

He held her tight as her body shook with sobs. He hadn't moved out of the doorway.

Finally she stopped crying and looked at him with cold eyes. "Was he doing it for money or a favor?"

"Both."

"How much money?"

"Two thousand dollars."

"For lousy money?" She pulled away from him.

"He took risks," Zank said. "The business is risky. But it wasn't the money this time. I tried to keep him out of it. Honest to Christ, I told him no."

"How'd he die?"

"Stabbed right through the heart. He didn't suffer even for a minute, the coroner said."

She stood frozen for a long moment, her eyes fixed straight ahead, apparently at nothing in particular. She said, "I'm going to have an abortion."

"You don't have to decide that now."

Her eyes were growing vague. "Every time I heard him mention your name, Zank, I got a little sick to my stomach. He had no business dealing with you. With him it was all a fantasy. He wasn't in your league. Why couldn't you see that?"

"I should have seen it."

"I'll hate your guts as long as I live, Joe Zanca."

"You got the right."

Gunther said, "When we had the old San Francisco Seals we had real baseball. The Pacific Coast League. Those guys were players, know what I mean?" It was late and red lines streaked the lower quarter of Gunther's eyes.

Zank said, "Fuckin' A right. I 'member. I was a little kid, but I 'member."

Gunther said, "We used to go out to Seals Stadium and see 'em play L.A. Beers were twenty cents, hot dogs a quarter—no, other way around."

Zank said, "Tha's right, other way 'round."

Gunther stopped wiping the bar and said, "You drivin', Zank?"

"Nope."

"Good."

A guy on the next stool said, "The Giants suck."

Zank turned to him. The guy's edges were blurred.

"Everybody knows the Giants suck," Zank said, then added, "You ever see a guy cooked into hamburger?"

"Sure, I seen hamburger."

"Hey, Gunther, you ever see a guy cooked into hamburger?"

"What guy?"

"Any guy?"

"No. You want another rum and coke?"

"Yeah. More rum this time. Make it a double-quadruple-dupple."

"Sure, Zank."

Gunther poured his drink and passed it to him over the bar.

"It's that asshole manager McKlintock who's fucking up the Giants," Gunther said.

The guy on the next stool said, "McKlintock's okay. He's just got the personality of a cardboard box with nothing written on it."

Zank flexed his fingers. "Broke another knuckle."

Gunther said, "Let me see." He looked at it with a squinted eye. "Ohhhh, yeah, shit, she's busted good."

"When I was boxin', I used to bust it regular."

"Don't it hurt?"

"Damn right it hurts." He flexed his fingers again, then made a fist. "You know these are lethal weapons? I mean, I can go to the can just for saying I'm going to punch your lights out. That would be the same as threatening you with a gun. I'm gonna punch a lot of guys' lights out for good." He drank his rum and coke and made a face at Gunther. "No matter what you do to it, it still tastes like puke."

"To a lot of guys it tastes good."

"They got their taste in their assholes. I got an ankle that feels like an elephant sat on it."

"How'd you do that?" Gunther asked. He was shaking a drink for somebody and looked to Zank in his blurred vision like a cartoon of a guy using a hammerjack.

"How'd I do what?" Zank asked.

"Hurt your ankle?"

"Fell off my bike. This a quadruple-quadruple?"

"They call it a Zombie."

Zank drank it down. The room rocked back and forth. He held onto the bar to steady himself. He took a deep breath and said, "Zombie, that's good, zombie-wombi-double-quadruple."

The guy on the next stool slipped away into a blur.

Somebody behind Zank said, "Hello, Joey."

He turned around. He blinked. It might have been Jill, or it might have been a hallucination. He wasn't sure.

"You want to talk about it?" the specter said.

"Talk 'bout what?"

"You really are juiced."

Gunther said, "Take him home, Jill."

Jill pulled on Zank's arm. Zank felt himself sliding off the stool, felt himself drifting toward the front door. Outside there was a drizzling rain.

"I just been thinking." Zank said, concentrating on the lines of the sidewalk to keep going straight. "Harry got barbecued."

"I know. It was on the TV."

"My mistake, taking him in there."

"You can't take the blame. There was no way for you to know."

"Harry read comic books, you know that?"

"No, did he?"

Zank had his tongue out, collecting raindrops. He said, "Where we going?"

"I'm taking you home." She held the door of her car open for him. He got in. She drove.

Along the way he hummed to himself. She found a place to park in front of the building. They got out and started walking to his apartment.

"What time is it?" he asked.

"Time for you to be in bed."

"That late, eh?" He started humming "I Left My Heart in San Francisco." "Time me, let's see if I can go five minutes without thinking about Harry. Harry knew karate. Said he did. Maybe he did know a little something. That's a fact. It's 'portant to remember the facts at a time like this." Zank stopped walking suddenly and looked at Jill. "When I used to fight—now see if you can follow this—when I used to fight, I mulched a lot of guys. Made them into hamburger. The other guy never really had a face and name. He was there to punch and I punched him. I punched him, he punched me. I keep asking myself the key question."

"Which is?"

"Am I the kind of guy who can kill somebody? I mean just go out and drop the hammer on them? That's tough-guy talk. Drop the hammer. You say drop the hammer, you don't have to say kill. But that's what it is. Can I just kill, *bango*, just like that? Think about that one. It's the key question."

"Are you that kind of guy?"

"Don't know."

They went up in the elevator. He kept humming. Once they entered the apartment, he stopped humming and said, "They made Harry into hamburger, and Harry was my pal. He was my pal. I got him killed."

"Let's go away, Joey. Let's go to New Guinea. Antarctica. Anyplace."

He stepped back from her, shaking his head. "No, no, no, no, no, no, no. I got business."

"It's wrong to get even for things. You can never get even. If he thinks you're trying to get him, he'll get you first."

"I'm gonna get more than just even."

"Listen," she said. "I'll go to the cops about Vernon. I'll testify. I'll say anything you want me to say—only, please, Joey, for me, don't kill him. Please."

He stared at her for a long moment, while his sluggish

brain analyzed what she'd just said. "Don't believe you'd testify against the asshole."

"I will. I want to."

"You can unswear to anything you swear to. He's a god, said so yourself."

"Whatever he may or may not have done, you don't have the right to kill him. Can you hear me?"

"I hear you."

"Nobody elected you God."

"Nobody elected him God."

He kicked off his shoes and dropped onto the couch.

"Vernon didn't kill Harry. It's not his way."

"Don't be so simple."

"You're not the man I thought you were."

"I don't make it right with Harry, I ain't no kind of man at all."

In the morning she was gone. So were her clothes. No note. No good-bye. No nothing.

"Ruby, honey, hey, how are ya?"

"Who's callin'?"

"It's me, baby, Joe Zanca."

"Joe Zanca? Ah don't know no Joe Zanca. Never heard the name in my life. Only Zanca Ah know is the Zanca who fixes my car whenever it needs it, and he's a gentleman."

"I got to see you, Ruby."

"Ah don't see strangers. Sorry, whoever you are."

"How about I buy you lunch?"

"What kind'a lunch? A hot dog lunch or a French restaurant lunch?"

"Prime rib down at Victoria Station."

"Ah might be persuaded. What you want in exchange, Mr. Stranger?"

"A small favor."

"Ah might not want to do no small favor."

"It's such a tiny favor, I'm sure you'll want to do it even for a total and complete stranger."

"We'll jus' have to see, won't we?"

* * *

The waiter took their order and poured some red wine into Ruby's glass. Zank said he didn't want any wine. He wanted to keep his mind clear now until this thing he had to do was done. Ruby smiled at him from across the table. She was a large black woman, nearly Zank's height, with cocoa-brown skin, sparkling black eyes, and bright red painted lips; her arms jangled with gold bracelets and her dress was a blaze of color. She looked, Zank thought, like she was always ready to go and party. He was damn glad to see her. They were sitting in the last booth in a railroad boxcar that had been converted into a restaurant. Zank was damn glad to see her.

"Zanca, yo' not lookin' so good." Her eyes narrowed with concern.

"Heavy night last night, Ruby."

"Yo' gettin' on in years, Ah guess."

"Must be."

"Ah seen in the *Chron* this mornin' 'bout Harry Chow. Seems to me now, yo' and Harry Chow was very good friends."

"Yeah."

She nodded. "Ah got it now," she said softly. "Yo' want to talk to mah brother, Bad John."

"That's right, Ruby. I need Bad John in a bad way."

"Yo' still with The Agency?"

"You know I can't answer that."

"The Agency not gonna like it, yo' go and start blowin' people away."

"Harry got made into a crispy critter and I know who done it. That's all there is to it."

She shrugged. "The dead don't care."

"Well, I care."

She touched his hand. "Okay, Ruby understands."

"Where's Bad John?"

"He in the can up in Washington State."

"Christ!"

She leaned across the table and whispered, "What kind of hardware yo' lookin' to buy?"

"Something heavy."

"What 'bout that guy in Oakland. C.C.?"

"Don't trust him."

She glanced around. "Ah knows a guy."

"Can you trust him?"

"As much as you can trust anybody who ain't yo' mother."

She took a slip of paper out of her pocket and handed it to him. "Here's his number. He got good stuff, but it won't come cheap."

"Thanks, Ruby." He slid out of the booth.

"The prime rib ain't here yet."

"Sorry, Ruby, I got to get on with it."

"Look, Zank, even though yo' a turkey, yo' ever need a little love and affection, you got my number."

"Thanks, Ruby."

"O. Henry your name?" Zank asked the man behind the wheel of the battered old pickup.

"You Conrad?"

"Yeah."

"Get in."

"I'd rather not leave my bike here."

"Park it in the woods, nobody'll fuck with it."

Zank pushed the Kawasaki off the pavement and covered it with brush. They were on a country road off Highway 17 in the Santa Cruz Mountains, sixty miles south of San Francisco. Not much traffic. Zank crossed over to where the driver was waiting for him next to the pickup. The man wore faded overalls and cowboy boots. A burn scar on the side of his neck stood out like a string of jelly beans. He frisked Zank thoroughly and professionally before letting him in the truck. Okay, Zank thought, the guy's careful. That's a good sign. He's a pro. They drove southeast on dirt roads, stopping every once in a while to look for helicopters and tracking vehicles.

The driver said, "In this line of work you either watch your ass or kiss your ass good-bye."

"Same in my line of work," Zank said.

They turned down a dirt road that passed through dense pine groves until they came to a small clearing. The driver stopped the truck.

"Get out. Somebody'll be along directly."

Zank got out and the man in the truck drove away. A moment later, Zank heard: "Hey, you."

He turned around and saw a man in jeans and a T-shirt, with a square face and cruel eyes. His belly was folded over his jeans and a faded tattooed snake crawled up his right arm. "Ruby send you?"

"Yeah," Zank said.

"Who's her brother?"

"Big Bad John."

He motioned for Zank to follow him. It was a short walk down a trail to another clearing. A creek ran through it, and on the far side were some sandstone cliffs. Fresh man-sized targets were spaced along the cliff.

"This way," the man said.

Zank followed him to the far edge of the clearing, where a pile of cut pine boughs covered some rectangular boxes.

"What you lookin' for?" the man asked.

"Heavy duty stuff."

"What kind of job you got to do?"

"The messy kind."

"You want an M-16, an AK47 . . . how about a combat shotgun?"

"Shotgun."

"Gas or pump?"

"Gas."

He nodded. He obviously appreciated a customer who knew what he wanted. "Nine, ten, twelve gauge?"

"Nine."

"You mad at somebody?"

"When I hit 'em, I want to make sure they don't get up off the ground."

"Okay. You want hot loads with Teflon ball bearings? Tear a man apart up to thirty feet or so. Sure you wouldn't want something that gives you a little more range?"

"I want to be looking at his face when I give him his send-off."

"Then the nine gauge is your baby. We got one Shaefer nine-gauge gas loader, and one Woller—they're made in Australia." He hesitated. "The Woller is a little slower, but I like it better. Dependable."

"How much slower?"

"One, maybe two-tenths of a second."

"Okay, let's go with dependable."

The gun dealer spit and opened a box, removed a black-barreled shotgun and handed it to Zank. It looked strangely ominous. This gun had one purpose only. Not just killing, but dismembering. Zank hefted it, sighted down it, opened the breach.

"Looks like it's never been fired."

"All my stock's brand new."

"Traceable?"

"Not to me, but don't get caught with it."

Zank admired it for a moment, running his hand up and down the stock. He liked the feel. "How much?"

"With fifty shells, one thousand. It's a good price."

"Can I try it?"

"Sure." He handed Zank a couple of shells. Zank shoved them in. "All you got to do is push the safety forward and point," the gun dealer said. "Whoever's in front of you will no longer have to file his income tax."

Zank stood on the near side of the creek and pointed at the first target, about twenty feet away. He stared at the target until he could imagine Cole's face and form and condescending smile. He imagined Cole taking a little girl, stripping her, and mounting her. He saw him burning Harry alive. He saw him putting wires on Jill's head. He pulled the trigger. The thunderous boom sent birds flying in all directions and the target disintegrated into a thousand fluttering pieces of paper. A chunk of sandstone the size of a beach ball was missing from the cliff.

In Zank's mind he could see Cole's body blown apart and bloody on the ground. For a moment he felt excited as he imagined Cole's lifeless body before him. An arm gone. Head like a squashed melon. He held the image in his mind for a long moment. The feeling of excitement drained. Vomit rose in the back of his throat.

Finally, the gun dealer said, "Sweet, ain't she?"

Zank looked down at the gun in his hand. Goddamn, it was trembling. He could feel a cold sweat on the back of his shoulders. He handed the gun back to the gun dealer.

The gun dealer said, "What's the matter man, too much gun for you?"

"Yeah, I guess maybe I ain't Luca Brasi, like I thought I was."

13

Zank stood at the corner of Fifth and Bryant, across the street from the Bryant Street police station, and watched Donaldson's car pull out of the driveway to the underground garage, make a turn on Bryant, cross three lanes of traffic, and pull up to the curb. Donaldson reached over and opened the door. Zank got in. Donaldson waited for a car to clear the intersection, then made a right turn on the red and headed for the Interstate 280 freeway.

Donaldson said, "Word is, Vernon Cole is still breathing, how come?"

"Look Donaldson, just because you see in the movies all the time Sicilians don't give a shit and can kill a man as easy as a butcher kills a chicken, it ain't so. But don't you worry about Vernon Cole. The fucker's going to get his, you can bet your fucking pension on it."

Donaldson grunted. "So you turned pussy, that what you're saying?"

"Yeah."

After a moment Donaldson said, "Maybe there's hope for you as a human being after all."

Zank turned to him. "If I had bought him his lunch, would you be buying my ticket to the gas chamber?"

"Sure. But I'd thank you for taking care of Cole. And I'd have seen to it that you got a nice obituary. Hungry?"

Donaldson reached over and opened the glove box. Inside were a half-dozen packages of Twinkies.

"Have one," Donaldson said, dropping a package on Zank's lap. He took two for himself. They were on the elevated freeway now, cruising over Hunters Point, the industrial section of the city.

Zank opened the Twinkies, took one out and bit into it. "Thought you were on a diet," he said.

"A foolish consistency is the hobgoblin of little minds."

"Ralph Waldo Emerson said that. My cellie at Q was always quoting people. You learn a lot in the joint."

"Is there anything you don't know, Zanca?"

"I don't know how to nail Cole. Jill's gone too."

"The one you said was your sister?"

"Yeah. We had something going. This fucker Cole has got her so she don't know if she's getting up or going to bed. She fucking begged me not to kill him."

"She'll be back. A prince like you, how could she stay away?"

"Funny, Donaldson. You ought to go on Johnny Carson."

"What's the matter with you? You scared? I never seen you look scared before."

"I've been scared plenty of times."

"If you're scared, get yourself a good pair of Nikes and run your ass off," He chuckled under his breath.

Zank took another bite of his Twinkie. "I think you like to see me sweat, Donaldson."

"It's just you were always so damn cocky. Pissing on cops."

After a moment Zank said, "Since the minute I seen Harry in that garbage can, I ain't quite as cocky. But it ain't just me I'm worried about. Cole gets his hands on Jill, no telling what he might do to her. He thinks she's been helping me."

Donaldson stuffed half a Twinkie into his cheek. While he chewed, a yellow Corvette streaked past. He sat upright. "I ought to go after that turdball." Then he eased back. "What the hell, the Highway Patrol'll get him."

Zank said, "How do I nail Cole so he stays nailed?"

Donaldson eased back into his seat. "How to nail Cole. Hmmmmmmmm. You got to get him with his stash of pictures, his records, and maybe get some of his people to rat on him. And we don't want just him, we want the organization. And we want to get the guy who's fronting for him."

"You figure that guy is Dix."

Donaldson grinned at him. "You got enough clairvoyance to be a detective."

"You've got to tell me what to do, Donaldson."

"I don't know what to do exactly. Spook him. Shake him up, I don't know. Get him to go for his stash."

"You think he would if he figured the cops were closing in on him?"

"He'd probably want to destroy the evidence or get the stuff safe—them pictures are worth a lot of bread."

Zank crumpled his Twinkies wrapper, rolled down the window, and pushed the wrapper out.

"Hey!" Donaldson said. "That's a three-hundred-buck fine!"

"You rather I litter your car?"

Donaldson blinked a couple of times. "You got a point there. The department don't like us leaving shit in the cars." He looked around for a highway patrol car, then handed his wrappers to Zank. Zank stuffed them out the window.

"If we made him think we were closing in on him," Zank said, "maybe he'd just make a phone call or send one of his flunkies to destroy the shit."

"It's possible, but a paranoid schizoid like him isn't likely to trust anybody."

"How many men can you get to help with surveillance?"

"What the hell you think I am? I told you, Dix is an untouchable. Me and an assistant DA name of Frick, that's it. That's the team. Nobody else is in on this, period. My neck is out there three fucking miles."

"I'll get Vernon Cole together with his stash, Donaldson, but you got to be ready day and night to come in and make the bust."

Donaldson reached under his seat, pulled out a small two-way radio, and handed it to Zank. "Twenty-four hours a day, all you got to do is press that button."

The knit hat pulled down over his head, the fake scar on his face, the thick wad of tissue in his cheeks, and the dark glasses were a guarantee the clerk would never recognize him. He probably wouldn't have remembered him anyway, since all he seemed to be looking at was his figures, his forms, and his hangnail. Mostly his hangnail.

"Man, these little suckers hurt," he said.

"Sure do," Zank said.

The clerk was fortyish and balding. He parted his hair low on the left side and combed it over the top of his head to hide the baldness. His eyes drifted over Zank's bruised and scarred face, but he didn't say anything.

"You wanted what now?" the clerk asked.

"The Ford van. The dark blue one."

"Twenty-four a day, one thirty a week."

"A couple days ought to do it."

"Visa, MasterCard, or two hundred deposit—and we need a driver's license."

Zank gave him the two hundred and his driver's license.

"Richard Conrad?"

"That's me."

"Okay, then . . . here's your receipt and the keys. The little key is for the locking gas cap. You want insurance to cover the thousand dollar deductible in case you have a wreck? It's six bucks a day extra."

"I'll take my chances."

The clerk bit on his hangnail. "Your funeral."

He stopped off at the Electronic Marvel Shoppe and picked up a couple of homing devices and a receiver. Wendy Chow wasn't there, but Cynthia Sung, the clerk, let him go into Harry's office and take what he needed. She checked first with Wendy to make sure it was okay.

Zank put an air mattress and a sleeping bag in the back of the van, along with a camp cook stove, an ice chest full of Cokes, three gallons of fresh water, extra clothes, sandwiches, six cans of beans, six cans of Dinty Moore's beef stew, two loaves of sourdough French bread, two jars of peanut butter, and a bag of apples. Maybe, he figured, he was going to have to wait them out. He was prepared to last a week. He parked in the five hundred block of New York, far enough away that no one would take notice of the van, yet close enough that he could see what was going on through his binoculars. He had the homing device receiver tuned to the frequency of the tiny transmitter Harry had put in the station wagon. He kept the two-way radio that Donaldson had given him inside his jacket. And he kept the .44 magnum in his belt.

It was late on a Friday afternoon when he began his surveillance. Parents came to pick up their kids. The nursery school staff went home. Security guards came and went. He didn't see any of Cole's people. It got dark at eight-thirty. At nine the redheaded man came out, got into the station wagon, and drove off. Okay, asshole, let's see what you're up to.

Zank followed him. The man drove to a supermarket on Army Street, went in and bought six bags of groceries, loaded them into the station wagon and drove back to Golden Sunrise. He carried the bags in by himself in three trips, locked the car, and went inside. No one came or went after that. At ten the lights on the bottom floor went out. At midnight a light on the second floor went out.

Zank wrapped himself in his sleeping bag and daydreamed about Jill. He was fatigued, and his mind drifted like a dustball in the breeze. He'd get her straightened out. A good shrink would fix her up. Maybe take a while, but then it would be great. He pictured the two of them on a bay cruise, pretending to be tourists from Omaha. Then they were camping in the High Sierras, going to the boxing matches at the Oakland Coliseum and sitting in the front row, and sunbathing at Stinson Beach. She'd be zoomo in a bikini, he thought. He saw them eating spaghetti with clam sauce at Vanessi's, the best Italian restaurant in North Beach, and he'd have the little quartet play something romantic.

Thinking of Jill made him anxious to get the business with Cole over with. He was worried about her. He had no idea where she might be. Sober, she'd stay away from Cole and his men, but drunk she might do anything. The quicker he got things settled with Cole, the sooner he could turn his full attention to Jill.

He took some speed just after three in the morning. The dawn came under a heavy cloud cover, painting the bottoms of the clouds orange. The shadows in the alleyway alongside

Golden Sunrise turned from black to deep purple before they vanished. There was a heavy dew on the van's windshield.

It was Saturday morning. No one came or went except the mailman, who delivered only a few letters. Zank stayed in the van all day except for two trips to a gas station to relieve himself. At ten that night he ran out of patience. Gotta know who's in that goddamn building. Only way to find out is to get them to come out.

And he knew just how to get them to do that.

He started up the van, turned down Twenty-fourth Street, went south to Army, then east to the Bayshore Freeway, heading for the Bay Bridge. Twenty-five minutes later he was pulling into the driveway of a small bungalow on East Thirteenth Street in Oakland. There were lights on inside. Two motorcycles were parked by the front steps. An old Jeep parked in the driveway on blocks looked as if it had been parked there for a thousand years. The front yard was mostly dirt. A sloppily painted sign on the porch said: THE DOG DOES NOT BITE. BEWARE OF THE PEOPLE. Underneath was a skull and crossbones.

Zank stayed in the van and blew the horn. After a few moments the porch light came on, and then a guy came out on the porch with a beer can in his hand, blinking in Zank's headlights. He wore a T-shirt with a skull on the front and was unshaven and needed a haircut. He looked hungry and unloved.

He said: "What the fuck you want?"

Zank stuck his head out the window. "Looking for C.C. He around?"

The guy didn't answer. He went back inside and a moment later a big man with a beard came out. He was wearing jeans and a T-shirt with grease all over it. It was C.C.—Cecil Collins, Zank's first cellmate in San Quentin. C.C. had been convicted of raping a nine-year-old girl, and never showed remorse, even when the other cons beat the hell out of him.

Zank said, "How come you ain't dead yet?"

"Who's that? Joe Zanca? Well, well, fuck me in the ass, if it ain't mister clean jeans hisself."

Zank got out of the van, leaving the motor running and the headlights on. He came to the bottom of the stairs leading up to the porch. Two guys, the one with the beer and another one with a girl on his arm, stood behind C.C. in the doorway. Up close the girl had wild hair and wild eyes.

"Hear you're in business," Zank said.

C.C. spit. "Gotta eat."

Zank said, "Need a smoke grenade and I need it now."

C.C. laughed. "What makes you think I'd give you shit?"

" 'Cause you're in business and I'm a paying customer."

"That's different. I usually get a hundred bucks. For you, it'll be *two* hundred."

C.C.'s two friends and the girl laughed at that.

Zank reached into his pocket, took out two bills, and handed them up to C.C., who sniffed them, rubbed them, and stuck them in his pocket. He moved inside; the door closed. Zank waited. Five minutes later C.C. came back out and tossed a small, cylindrical grenade to Zank.

C.C. said, "You know how it works? You pull the pin and throw it. Think you can remember that okay?" Everyone laughed.

Zank tossed it up in the air and caught it. "This don't make a lot of nice heavy smoke, I'm coming back and stuff it in your nose. Think you can remember that?"

Nobody laughed at that; they could see he meant it.

By eleven-forty Zank was on the roof of the building across the railroad tracks from Golden Sunrise. The throw would be about thirty feet. A cold wind was blowing, but the night was clear. He carried two rocks with him.

There were only a few lights on at Golden Sunrise. The entire first floor and third floor and all but two rooms on the second floor were dark. The window in Cole's office was still boarded up. He would have only one shot, so he'd better make it good. He threw a rock first and smashed in a window. Bull's-eye. Then he quickly pulled the pin on the grenade and threw it. He heard it hit the floor inside.

Okay, everybody. Fire drill time.

More lights came on inside the building. Smoke began to billow out. Smoke alarms went off. He watched the exits. Two young women came out in night clothes, then half a dozen kids. Then the red-haired man, followed by four security guards. That was it. No Cleomona, no Vernon Cole.

It was one-fifteen in the morning when Zank got back to his apartment. There was a gusting, cold wind blowing from the north as he got out of the van half a block down the hill. He was feeling the effects of having gone nearly three days with barely three hours' sleep. His legs were stiff and aching, his mouth full of bile. The ringing in his ears, he guessed, was from the speed. It was quiet as he made his way up the hill and already his mind had gone ahead of him to the soft, warm bed. A car went by with three young women in it singing boisterously. They waved at him. One gave him the finger. He smiled and turned his collar up against the wind. How wonderful to be young and stupid.

He glanced up at his apartment and saw the light on in his living room. He always left it on. But there was something else. A faint, reddish glow reflected off the window for a moment. Somebody smoking a cigarette? Jill?

He fought back the impulse to run up the stairs and find out. No, no. Better to check things out first. He stood in the shadows across the street for a few minutes looking up at the windows of his apartment. Nobody looked out. Nobody moved around. There were lights on in a second-floor apartment he knew belonged to an old lady who never shut them off. She was deathly afraid of the night and slept only in the daytime. He looked up and down the street. Nothing out of the ordinary. Nobody around. He looked up again, this time towards Nolan's apartment. The living room was dark.

Zank limped up the street past the apartment house and looked down the alley on the south side of the building. Nobody there. He looked up to Nolan's bedroom window. The light was on. Reading, maybe, Zank thought. So nothing was wrong. He must have imagined the glow. Speed hallucinations. But then again, Vernon Cole hadn't come out of Golden Sunrise, which meant he had to be someplace else.

Zank made his way down the alley cautiously and turned the corner in back of the building. He pulled the magnum out of his belt and cocked it. It was dark, but he could see a car parked in the building manager's space. The building manager only came in the daytime. It was a BMW four-door. He checked the doors and found them unlocked. Nobody, he thought, leaves a BMW around unlocked. Nobody with a brain in his melon. He got in the car. No papers in the glove box or in the pockets on the doors.

He looked up at the fire escape. It had a retractable ladder pulled up to the second story and he couldn't figure any way of getting to it. So he circled around in back of the building again and let himself in the back door with his key. Moving as quickly and as silently as he could up the darkened back stairs on his tender ankle, he paused briefly on each landing to listen. He heard nothing. His hand gripped the butt of the gun firmly and he could feel it getting greasy with sweat. His breathing was quick now, choppy, and the drumming of his heart filled his head.

He stopped at the door to the hallway on the third floor and tried to look through the crack, but couldn't see anything. He moved down the hallway, hugging the wall to minimize the creaking of the floor. He expected that if they planned to gun him down in the hallway it would be now, in a sudden burst from his apartment or maybe Nolan's. He was ready to drop to the floor and fire. He figured to risk head shots to whoever came at him and take them out quick.

The drumming of his heart quieted now, and his mind was clear. He paused at Nolan's door. All he could hear was the faint sound of music playing downstairs in one of the apartments. He passed the gun to his left hand and wiped the sweat off his right palm. It struck him that maybe the fatigue had gotten him and he was like a kid afraid of the dark. So he hallucinated a little reddish glow. It didn't mean anything. The BMW out back didn't mean anything. But he wasn't taking any chances. Not with a guy who'd fucking cook your brains.

Still, he didn't go near his door. It was five feet from Nolan's, on the other side of the hall. He moved past it down the hall to the front stairs and checked the landing. He saw nobody and heard nothing.

He went down the front stairs, out the front door, and limped back to the van. He kept looking up to see whether anyone was looking out the window. He didn't see anyone.

At the van he picked up one of the homing devices he'd gotten from the Electronic Marvel Shoppe and the tire iron from the van's tire-changing kit. Then he opened the engine lid and took out the dipstick, wiping the oil on his pant legs. He limped back up the street and down the side alley to the rear of his building.

He put the homing device on the BMW, up behind the back bumper. Then he went back upstairs to the second floor and knocked softly on the door to 2B. He stuck the magnum in his belt under his shirt and waited. After a moment an eye appeared in the little peephole, then an old woman opened the door. "Zanca, Zanca, Zanca," she muttered. 'What the hell you want?" She smelled of cheap port wine.

"Lost my keys. Okay if I go out on your fire escape?"

She frowned and said it was okay for him to pass, but she didn't like it. He gave her a ten dollar bill. She kissed it, and tried to kiss him.

"Hey, lady, it's only ten bucks, cool it."

He made his way up the fire escape by inches, feeling his way in the darkness with his hand in front of him, looking for wires. At the flat part of the fire escape he found one. An electronic sensor guarding the part of the fire escape that ran along the side of his apartment. He stepped over it, being very careful not to disturb it. He continued checking for more wires, but didn't find any. He came next to his living-room window and took a look inside. The shade was drawn, but there was a slit between the shade and the window frame and he managed to see part of the room. Goddamn. He had company.

Vernon Cole was sitting on the couch with a gun in his lap. Next to him sat Cleomona, and next to Cleomona sat Jill. Her eyes were half closed and she was gently weaving back and forth. Drunk, Zank thought. Or drugged. The fuckers.

Zank moved around and looked in the other direction. Two of Cole's men were standing by the door. One he had met before—Black Eyes. He had an automatic in a shoulder holster; the other had a short-barreled pump shotgun. Black Eyes was smoking a cigarette and his eyes were pinched together. The other one had corn-yellow hair and freckles and looked about fourteen, but he had to be older. He was sweating with fear, his breathing shallow and irregular.

Suddenly Zank heard a noise below him and looked down. A drunk was singing "My Body Lies Over the Ocean" to himself while he peed in the alley. Christ.

Zank looked back into the living room. Cole was heading for the window. Zank backed down the fire escape and hugged the wall. He heard the window open and saw the movement in the shadow from the window on the building next door. Someone in the living room said: "A street person relieving himself."

The window closed.

Zank moved back up the fire escape and checked inside the living room again. Cole was up now, pacing around with his automatic cradled in his arms. His small, black eyes were the size of raisins. Zank figured he was on something too. Something to keep him sharp, yet quell the fear. If I dump Cole, Zank thought, what are his chumps gonna do? Lose their goddamn heads and shoot wild? Rush the fire escape and fire on him where there was no cover? Pump a couple into Jill? He couldn't risk it.

He looked at Jill. She had a bruise over her right eye. So, somehow they'd found her. Beat her. Made her take them to his apartment. Her eyes looked dull, but she seemed to know what was going on. Hang tight, Jill, sweetheart, I'm gonna get you out of there.

The kid with the freckles and the corn-yellow hair said something, then went down the hall. Zank retreated to the kitchen window. The kid came into the kitchen, turned on the light, got a beer out of the refrigerator, rummaged around for an opener, turned off the light, and went back to the living room.

Zank slipped the dipstick he'd taken from the van between the top window and the bottom and pushed it along the crack until it hit the lock. Gradually, he put pressure on it and pushed the lock open. His mouth was dry now and he was sweating as much as the kid. He had to be absolutely silent. He took hold of the bottom of the window and eased it up slowly, slowly. When the window was open a foot or so, he squeezed inside.

He could hear the music in the living room. Someone was moving around. Someone spoke, but he couldn't make out what was said. Then someone else said: "He should have been here at least an hour ago."

"He'll be here, David, have patience."

David, Zank figured, was the kid with the corn-yellow hair.

Someone said, "Have a beer."

Another voice: "Think I will." Must be Black Eyes, Zank thought.

Footsteps came toward Zank down the hall. He wrapped his magnum in a kitchen towel and positioned himself behind the door. He waited and didn't move. The footsteps came closer. Black Eyes came through the door and looked at the refrigerator; Zank hit him hard with the towel-wrapped gun. There was an umph sound, like a football being kicked.

Black Eyes' head snapped back and he coughed before he sagged to his right. Zank eased him to the floor, then hit him again to make sure he stayed down.

"Connie?" Cole called from the living room.

Zank put his hand over his mouth and answered for the man on the floor. "Yeah."

"Get me one too."

Zank put the gun back in his belt, then went to a kitchen drawer and pulled out a piece of string. He slipped quietly back out onto the fire escape and tied the string to the trip wire, then went back into the kitchen and stood by the door with the light off.

"Hey, Connie, hurry up with the beer."

Zank pulled on the string. An electronic beeper sounded from the living room.

Cole's hushed voice said, "On the fire escape!"

Zank heard running in the hallway coming toward him. He stood behind the door and waited. The kid with the corn-yellow hair came bursting into the kitchen just as gunfire erupted on the fire escape. The kid tripped over Black Eyes on the floor, kept his balance, righted himself, and swung his gun in Zank's direction. He was half a second late. Zank clubbed him with his gun. The kid went down.

Nothing happened for a moment. Not a sound. Nothing. Then Zank heard a rushing movement. The front door slammed.

With his magnum in his hand, cocked and ready, Zank went slowly down the hall and peered into the living room. The lights were off. He couldn't hear any breathing. No one was moving. He stood still and waited. Then he heard a car scream down the alley and turn up the street. He didn't move. They could still be waiting for him. He knew the homing device was good for half a mile, and to go half a mile wouldn't take long. By the time he got to his van they would already be out of range.

Suddenly the front door opened. "Joseph?" It was Nolan.

"Right here, Nolan." He switched on a light.

"They've gone. What happened?"

'Some creeps were laying for me," Zank said, heading back into the kitchen. He picked up Black Eyes first and put him in a chair, then the kid with the corn-yellow hair. He quickly tied them up with extension cords, then threw water on their faces. Black Eyes didn't respond, except for a groan, but the kid came around.

"Jesus, what hit me?" he said.

"It's what's gonna hit you," Zank said. "Tell me where Cole went."

The kid looked at Zank with terrified child eyes, blood streaking down his face, and said, "We don't know, honest to Christ." Tears gushed up.

Zank hit him. The kid's chair, with him in it, spilled over onto the floor. Zank reached down and snatched the kid off the floor, chair and all, and set him back up again. The kid whined.

Nolan stood in the doorway. "He said he did not know."

"Get outta here, Nolan. Somebody must've heard the shots and called the cops, so we ain't got much time."

"If you are going to be a beast, Joseph, I'm going to watch."

"Okay, watch." Zank grabbed the kid by the throat. "I asked you where Cole went."

The kid shook his head. "Cole never tells nobody where he's going next, honest, Mr. Zanca." Blood and spit bubbled out of his mouth and splattered on his shirt. Zank hit him again, two hard rights straight into his face. His broken knuckle hurt, but he ignored the pain. The kid's head jerked back and forth with the blows. He whined again. The whining was lower in his throat now and came out his nose, where two streams of blood flowed. The bridge of his nose was mashed flat against his face. He shut his eyes tight. The lids were puffy and red. Zank had him by the collar and shook him. "Tell me, asshole, I'll beat you till your goddamn brains run out your nose."

Nolan said, "Please don't do this, Joseph. Please." Nolan took hold of his right arm and held it tight.

"They got Jill!"

Nolan let him go. His eyes went wide.

"Jill? How? Who?"

"This asshole's boss." He hit the kid again. The kid fainted.

Before Zank could revive him, he heard police sirens. He stuck his .44 under his shirt and headed out the door.

"Wait, Joseph, let the police handle it!"

"Not a fucking chance, Nolan."

14

He drove the van recklessly through the streets, with the receiver tuned to the frequency of the homing device he'd put on the BMW, but he didn't pick up anything. He drove over to Golden Sunrise and circled around the block. No BMW. No signal. Nothing. Sweat ran down his face. He headed in the direction of the wharfs, then back toward downtown. Nothing. Not a goddamn tweet. He started imagining Jill getting her brain burned, and it made his pulse race.

He was heading for Third Street when he realized he was going in circles. He pulled over and came to a stop. He had to get his thoughts in order or he wasn't going to get anywhere. He got out and walked back and forth next to the van, running his hands over his head. For the first time in his life he thought of calling the police, but that would alert Dix, probably, so that was out.

Okay, the homing device on the BMW was good for maybe half a mile. San Francisco was seven miles by seven miles. If Cole was still in town, Zank figured he could find him—all he had to do was cover the city in a logical pattern. He couldn't keep swinging wild. He had to go about it right. Methodical.

He got back in the van and continued on to Third Street, where he turned south then headed east past the Cow Palace and over to the outer Mission. He was calmer now. He figured he would make the City into a phonograph record, starting on the outside and making smaller and smaller circles until he got to the center. Gotta do it right.

It was four in the morning by the time he got to the beach and followed the Great Highway to Golden Gate Park. Here the fog was thick and swirling in from the dark, vast Pacific. He swung into the park and the receiver blipped. It would sometimes pick up a cosmic ray or something and just go off. That was probably what it was, but he pulled over to the side of the road and listened for another anyway. There wasn't another.

He paused for a moment and calculated how long it would take him to cover the City the way he was doing it. Eight, ten hours, maybe. He was trying to figure out a better pattern when it hit him that he had better check out Supervisor Dix. California Park Drive was just a little off his circular route.

He swung around and turned right on the Great Highway, heading north. A cop car whizzed past him with the red bubble-gum machine on top flashing, but no siren. Then another. Saturday night in a big city.

He went down Geary, made a left on Thirty-eighth Avenue, and headed for the Sea Cliff section and California Park Drive. The light on top of the receiver started flickering, the buzzer started buzzing, and Zank knew he was in business. He rolled down his window and let a little cool air in. Okay, Mr. Cole, I got my hook into you good.

He drove by Supervisor Dix's big house and the beeps got louder and the flashing light on top of the receiver flickered brighter. He glanced at the house. There were lights on inside, both in the garage and upstairs. He didn't slow down. Past the house the beeps grew quieter. No doubt about it, the BMW was in Dix's garage.

Mole Allen once said the thing that counts most in the ring—and in life—is luck. And Mole should have known, Zank thought, he was an unlucky son of a bitch. At the moment Zank was feeling lucky. And alert. He turned around in a driveway and parked along a row of hedges. It was quiet. The fog was thick, forming droplets on the windshield. He waited. A private security service car drove by. Zank switched the beeping receiver off and slouched down. The driver looked the van over but kept going.

Zank turned on the receiver again. The beep was louder now. It meant the BMW was on the move and coming at him. There were the headlights now just in front of him. He slouched down again and let the car go by. It looked like Cole, Cleomona, and Dix inside. Now where the hell was Jill? He doubted Dix would leave her at his house. Unless they had dropped her off somewhere, there was only one place she could be: in the trunk.

Zank started up the van, pulled out into the street, and followed them at a distance. A dial on top of the receiver indicated which direction the signal was coming from. Twice the BMW made figure eights around a couple of blocks to check any tail, but since Zank had the receiver and knew just where they were he didn't have to worry about it. He just pulled over and waited for them. They were heading in the direction of downtown.

After the BMW turned up Van Ness it stopped doubling back. Zank had them in view now. Okay, now we got you. The traffic had picked up; he wouldn't be quite so noticeable. The BMW turned right at Bay Street and headed down toward Fisherman's Wharf. But it didn't get that far; it turned off at Columbus and pulled into the parking lot of the Surfview Motel. Zank cruised past, made a right and then another right, pulling into the driveway of the parking lot behind the motel.

The motel was out of business. The windows were boarded up. A huge sign along the side of the building said: AVAILABLE. Through the fog Zank could see three figures come down the side of the building and go in through a door. Two men and a woman. The woman could have been Cleomona. Zank sat and waited, listening to the foghorns on the bay. Minutes passed; nothing happened. Zank got edgy, but he didn't get out of the van. He was playing it safe. Wait it out.

It was just after 4:45 when headlights appeared at the front of the building and a car drove into the parking lot, stopped, and a man got out. It was the redhead from Golden Sunrise, and there was another man with him. Zank couldn't see what he looked like until they walked under the light at the back of the building. A fleshy creep in a suit and tie, maybe fifty, fifty-five. He was looking around as if he half expected a cop to jump out from every pothole in the parking lot. Zank didn't recognize him, but he figured he was maybe the retailer. You sell pictures, you need outlets. Scum bastard. The redhead knocked at the door; after a moment they were let in.

A couple minutes later the redhead came out with Dix, both carrying boxes. Inventory, records, shit like that, Zank thought. They put the boxes in the trunk of the BMW and went back inside. So Jill wasn't in the trunk. Zank had three quarters convinced himself she was in there. So they must have dropped her off someplace before they went to Dix's place. That, or they just killed her. Oh, God, no, no, no.

The panic was back for a moment. He sat frozen at the wheel. Easy now, he told himself. No time to lose control. Think it through, think it through. One step at a time. Wait it out, wait it out.

Ten minutes passed. No one went in or out. Zank didn't move. His shirt had soaked through with sweat. He kept pounding his fist into his hand. His knuckles hurt, but the pain relieved the anxiety. He got an apple out of the bag, took a bite, and tossed the rest out the window. He turned the radio on low and listened to a talk program. They were arguing the merits of a homosexual rights bill. Both the caller and the talk-show host thought homosexuals were a mistreated minority. Not in San Francisco, Zank thought. He turned the radio off. He chewed some Juicy Fruit. Ten more minutes passed. The redhead came out alone, put some more boxes into the BMW, then got into the car he came in and left. Zank sat up. Maybe they were done with business.

He turned the radio back on. There was a woman caller now. She was saying in the calmest of voices that the talk-show host was an idiot.

Suddenly Cole and Cleomona came out and headed half in a run for the front of the building and the BMW. Zank started up the van, turned around, and pulled into the street without turning on his lights. He made a quick swing around the block and clicked on his receiver. The BMW was a couple of blocks ahead. They went up Columbus, turned on Broadway, and through the tunnel. Zank stayed well back. On the other side of the tunnel the fog was heavy in patches.

It was getting light. The overcast was heavy, so there was little chance of seeing the sun, but the dawn was coming. The BMW turned on Laguna, turned again on Sacramento, and headed west. He cut over a block to Jackson and drove parallel to them. They stopped between Webster and Mason. Zank made a right and then another right on Sacramento, cruising slowly. The signal was loud and clear.

It was a middle-class neighborhood, mostly stately old Victorians mixed together with forties and fifties cracker-box buildings. In the middle of the block was a large, white, brick apartment house with a driveway around back. That's where the beep was loudest. The BMW was either in the basement parking garage or in the driveway behind the building.

Zank pulled in across the street and parked by a fire hydrant. It was raining. He turned off the engine and waited. Images of Jill getting her brains cooked pushed their way into his head. A car went by. Then a taxi. A woman in a nurse's uniform came out of a nearby apartment house, got into an old Toyota, and drove off. A moment later another woman came out under a large black umbrella and walked to the corner. A couple minutes later a car picked her up. Zank turned on the radio and listened to the news. A young father in San Jose had raped his fourteen-year-old daughter and in his guilt had taken an axe and cut off his sex organ. The newsman apologized for ruining everyone's breakfast, but it was news and he was, he said, obliged to report it. Zank turned the radio off.

Zank checked the load and action of his .44 magnum and put it back into his belt. He watched the rain streak down the windshield. He stuffed his mouth with two more sticks of gum. He turned the radio back on. The news people were talking about Princess Diana hatching another royalette.

The front door of the apartment house opened and someone came out. Whoever it was stayed in the shadows for a moment, then started walking toward him. It was Cleomona. Zank grabbed his gun and looked around, thinking she might be a setup to draw him out. But he didn't see anyone else. He got out and limped across the street to meet her.

"Vernon said I was to give you this."

Cleomona dropped the homing device into Zank's hand. She kept looking back at the apartment.

"Where's Jill?"

"He's got her in a closet. I told you not to mess with Vernon, but you wouldn't listen. He's got her locked in a closet back there and he's setting the place on fire!"

"What apartment? Show me!"

He grabbed her and pulled her along to the building and through the front doors. Smoke detectors had set off the fire alarm. Tenants flooded into the halls. Cleomona shouted above the din of the alarms: "Down the hall to the end, on the right!"

Zank let go of her and raced down the hall. He tried the door and found it unlocked. He burst in. The place was full of smoke and flame. "Jill! Jill!"

From beyond the flames he heard Jill's voice: "Get out of here, Joey, get out!"

He started into the mass of flames, but the heat drove him back. He went out into the hall and found a fire extinguisher, ran back into the apartment, and started spraying. Most of the fire was from a pile of trash piled in the middle of the living room. The flames died down, then quickly flared up again. He held his breath as long as he could, but then he had to inhale. "Jill! Where are you?"

There were doors everywhere. Zank heard pounding on one of them. But which one? For a moment he was overcome by smoke and the flames seemed to spin around him. "Jill! Jill!"

"Here, over here!"

The bedroom.

He leapt over a pile of burning seat cushions and through a door. In the bedroom the mattress blazed. Flames were shooting up the drapes and snaked across the ceiling. The dense smoke blinded him. He felt along the walls, coughing, his eyes feeling as if on fire. "Jill! Jill!"

"In here!"

The door was a few feet away, nailed closed. He kicked it open. Jill collapsed, choking, into his arms. He stumbled across the room and smashed out a window. He dropped her carefully into the driveway, then went out after her, lifted her up, and hurried toward the street.

They were around the corner at the rear of the building when the gas lines exploded, sending flaming debris raining down the length of the driveway.

Zank pushed the button on the hand-held radio Donaldson had given him. It buzzed. Static, then a voice: "Yeah?"

"Donaldson?"

"Zanca?"

"Cole's porno stash is at the Surfview Motel on Columbus near Bay. Better hurry, I think Dix is down there emptying out the joint. Least he was an hour or so ago. Cole tried to burn me up and he's made off in a tan BMW, license 1NAT245X."

"Wait a minute, how do you know Dix is at this motel?"

"I followed him there an hour ago."

"Why the fuck didn't you call me then?"

"They had Jill."

He could hear Donaldson groan. "This better be righteous stuff, Zanca, I don't like getting up out of a nice warm bed just because some turd has my number."

"I ain't in the mood for getting insulted, Donaldson. You can either go back to bed or you can go and put some kiddie fuckers in the can, it's up to you."

Zank clicked off the radio and got out of the van.

The firemen were still inside the building. The tenants stood around under umbrellas waiting for word that it was okay to go back inside. Zank went over to the Fire Department rescue van. The medics were standing around waiting for the fire marshal to tell them there were no more injured persons to collect. Zank got into the back of the rescue van.

Jill lay on the stretcher. She smiled at Zank. "Thank you, Joey." Her clothes were torn and smudged, she was cut and bruised, but her eyes were bright.

"How are you?" Zank asked, kneeling beside her.

"I'm all in one piece. Want to hear something really weird? I made a deal with God. He gets me out of the fire, I'll be a good nurse and really behave. No more hooch. So now I've got to keep my promise."

"That'll be no problem at all."

"That's not all that was going through my head, Joey. It was what I'd done, and knowing if I ever saw you again I was going to have to tell you."

"Tell me what?" He held her hand.

"I went to Vernon and told him I was staying with you. I wanted to make peace. I didn't want you killed, I didn't want him killed. I didn't want anyone killed. He said he was ready to make peace and that Cleomona would have to go back to her mother. She seemed to go along with the idea. I took her to your place to wait for you, and Vernon, Connie, and David followed. Pretty stupid, wasn't I? I suspected something, but I wanted so much to believe him that I did."

"It doesn't matter, it's all over now." He was stroking her hair.

"You forgive me?"

"You were trying to do the right thing, what's to forgive?"

"Can we go up in the Sierras someplace, make that training camp where I can be the nurse?"

"Yes."

"When I was locked in that closet with the fire eating at the door, after I made my deal with God, that's all I could think about. Being up there with the trees, with Vernon Cole and everything that's happened behind us."

"Sounds good to me," Zank said. "And no booze anywhere near the place."

"Not a drop," she said, shaking her head.

"Let's not even have a TV. We won't get a newspaper. We'll just let the damn world go where it wants to go. We'll read the *World Book*, that's it."

"Okay," she said.

"Nolan can come too. He can make his sculptures."

"He just might like to do that. There's one thing, Joey," she said softly. "Please hear me out."

"Whatever you want, you just ask."

Her eyes narrowed. "You got to forget about Vernon Cole."

"Forget what about Cole? What the hell are you talking about?"

"Listen to me. He's on his way to Brazil with Cleomona

and he's never coming back. When he gets down there, he might be able to fulfill his ambition. He's got to have that chance.''

Zank pulled back. ''Ambition? Chance? What the hell are you talking about? He's a kiddie raper! He killed Harry and he tried to kill you and me! I'm going to put him in the can. Geezus, Jill, I made a deal. I got to take Cleomona home to her mama if I can.''

''If you try to stop him, there's no telling what he might do. He'll take hostages. He's got a gun. He'll shoot too. You've got to make sure the police don't bother him. Just let him go, everything will be all right. In a few hours he'll be on a plane and he'll be gone forever.''

Zank shook his head slowly, then he kissed her. ''I'm gonna have him down on the ground looking up before he even knows what hit him.''

''No, Joey, please, just leave him be.'' Her voice cracked.

''He's running scared now, Jill. We'll take him easy. Donaldson will have an APB out on him, he can't get far. I'll see you later at the hospital.''

She grabbed his arm. ''If you put him away, Joey, I couldn't stand it. . . .'' Tears flooded into her eyes.

''Take it easy, Jill. Relax. You're out of it. It's gonna be a piece of cake.''

''You don't get me. Listen. You can't go after Cole.'' She raised up on an elbow. ''I'm not going to try to explain it. I feel something for him that I could never feel for an ordinary man. If you kill him or send him to jail, I could never live with you. Every time I looked at you, I'd think of what you did to him and I'd hate you.''

''What the hell kind of shit is this? We're talking about a goddamn sicko who just tried to burn you up.''

A paramedic stuck his head in the door and said, ''We have to be going now, sir.''

''In a minute!'' Zank snapped.

Jill said, 'Ride to the hospital with me, Joey. I'll get checked out, we can be on our way to the Sierras this afternoon. I want it so badly. Please.''

He wiped a tear from her cheek. ''I'm sorry,'' he said. ''Harry's dead. Cleomona's got to go home.''

"I'm begging you to leave him alone. What do you want me to do? We can have a life! All you got to do is walk away!"

"I can't, Jill."

She let go of his arm. For a moment she said nothing. Then the streams of tears started flowing. She turned her face away from him.

Watching the emergency van drive off down the street, siren wailing, Zank felt suddenly alone and empty. *Every time I'd look at you . . . I'd hate you.*

He shook his head.

He went over to his van, started it up, and headed down the street. At the corner of Divisadero he paused for a moment and waited for the cross traffic to clear. He could turn right and follow the emergency van to the hospital and make it all right with her, or he could turn left and head for the airport. He watched the emergency van disappear into the distance.

Then he headed for the airport.

"No, I don't think so. . . ." the ticket agent said, staring at the picture of Cleomona.

"She's my half sister, her name's Cleomona Fisk. I've got to find her. She's running away with a no-good snake and won't answer a page."

"You say she'd have come through this morning?"

"Maybe within the last half hour."

She stared at the picture, her eyes narrowed with concern. "I'm just awfully sorry."

"Thanks anyway," Zank said.

"Are you okay?" she asked him. "You look sort of messed up."

"A fire at my apartment this morning."

"Gee, you certainly are having a run of bad luck."

Zank moved away from the Continental ticket counter and tried TWA. He checked with the skycaps in front of the terminal. He'd asked the parking patrol people and the taxi drivers, but no one had seen her.

The only direct flight to Brazil was a four-thirty flight to Rio. There were dozens of other ways to get there in a hurry, he soon found out. They could take United, American, or Delta to Miami, then TWA to Rio, or take any of six different domestic carriers to JFK and get a connecting flight. Then there was People's Express, Air Cal, or P.S.A, and a half-dozen others to L.A., where they could connect with Japan Airline's afternoon flight to Caracas. Checking the passenger lists of all the possible combinations would take a week. Besides, they were probably traveling under phony goddamn names.

He was working in the direction of the North Terminal, questioning everyone along the way who looked as if they worked there. He went up the escalator and was heading for the Japan Airlines desk when, goddamn, there right in front of him was Vernon Cole, wearing a long gray coat, dark glasses, and a wide-brimmed felt hat that sat jauntily on his head. He'd shaved his beard and cut and darkened his hair. He had Cleomona in tow; she was wearing a scarf over her head and looked, he thought, scared as hell.

They didn't spot Zank, who made a quick right turn and fell in behind them. He followed them down the long corridor, heading for the TWA gates at the end of the terminal. Zank kept looking around at the rest of the crowd, wondering whether Cole might have someone backing him up, but it didn't look like it. Cole stopped at a trash can and dropped something in it. His gun, no doubt. Zank smiled. Suddenly he felt very good. Gonna K.O. the son of a bitch yet.

Cole and Cleomona went through the metal detectors and continued on.

Zank dropped his magnum into the same trash can Cole had used. Then he went through the metal detector and continued down the corridor. Cole was hurrying now, Cleomona running to keep up. They turned down a long empty corridor leading to the TWA gates at the end of a long concourse. Zank rushed to catch them. Cole looked over his shoulder and saw Zank. He pulled on Cleomona and they moved along faster to a lounge area, where they stopped to wait for Zank to catch up. The lounge was full of people, mostly Japanese tourists. Many of them with kids. As Zank came running up, Cole started to say something, but Zank didn't wait for the words to clear his lips and hit him with a right cross. Cole stumbled backward and dropped onto the floor.

Cleomona threw her arms around Zank. "No! Get back! We'll be killed!"

"Enough, Cleomona!" Cole yelled, sitting up, rubbing his jaw. Blood trickled out the corner of his mouth. He looked around at the startled tourists. "No problem," he said, "everyone just stay calm."

Zank said to Cleomona, "He didn't come through that metal detector with a gun. His baby-raping days are over."

"Child love," Cole said, "is an ancient and honored tradition in many cultures of the world, cultures much older and wiser than yours."

"Is Jill okay?" Cleomona asked.

Zank nodded without taking his eyes off Cole. "Come on, Cole," he said. "You got an appointment with twelve good citizens who'll let you know what they think of your ancient and honorable tradition."

"If I get up, will you knock me down?"

"Not unless you run for it."

"Why should I do that?" He got to his feet. "Look at him, Cleomona," he said. "So puffed up with pride and arrogance." He sneered at Zank. "You stupid ape, you actually think you've won, don't you?"

"I'd rather have you dead, but you're going to the joint, and I guess that's good enough. I been there. Know what they do to guys who mess around with kids? One guy, name of Packman—something like that—they cut his nuts off and stuffed them in his mouth. You're going to be a big celebrity in the joint, Cole. I got friends still in there. I'm gonna see to it they know all about you."

"Mr. Zanca, if I had more time I'd have you pay for your meddling with a long and excruciatingly painful death. But I've a plane to catch, so I'll make this brief." He looked around to make sure he wasn't being overheard. The tourists had backed away; no one wanted to be involved. "See this?" Cole said, opening his coat to show Zank a small cord hanging down from the pocket with a small ring on the end of it. "The lining of this coat is stuffed with A-90 plastique. Two-point-three pounds of it. If I pull this, the three of us—and anyone else within three hundred yards—will go to heaven. You *do* believe in heaven, don't you, Mr. Zanca?''

For the first time Zank could see in the glow of his eyes the fullness of his insanity.

"It's true," Cleomona said anxiously. "It's really true. For once in your life don't be stupid."

Cole said, "Mr. Zanca, you insignificant nothing. Hear this, you amoeba. If that plane doesn't take off for any reason whatever, everybody in it is dead, understand? And if it turns around anyplace, that's it—tragedy will strike. Got it?''

"I got it."

Zank felt like a wall had caved in on him.

"Don't feel so bad, Mr. Zanca. In a battle of wits it's the intelligent that win. You've just been competing in the wrong arena." He turned and started heading toward the boarding area, pulling Cleomona along with him.

"Hold it a second, Cole," Zank said.

Cole and Cleomona stopped and turned back toward Zank.

Zank said, "Leave Cleomona."

Cole shook his head, baffled. "Why would I do that? She's a wonderful comfort."

"I ain't letting you go with Cleomona."

"Just how do you intend to stop me?"

"I can stop you."

"And get everybody blown up?"

Zank took a couple of steps closer to him. "Listen, Cole, you take her out of the country, she's dead anyway. You'll just use her just like you been using her until one day you'll dump her. Leave her with me."

Cole's eyes darted around. "If I pull this cord, you're dead, Zanca."

"The same goes for you."

"Don't do this," Cleomona said to Zank.

Now Cole's eyes were shifting back and forth between Cleomona and Zank. He had his hand inside his coat.

Zank said, "No bluff, Cole. You walk two steps closer to that plane, I'm going to be all over you like a tiger on a fat pig."

Cole stood frozen. The confidence drained from his face. His mouth twitched. Then he shoved Cleomona toward Zank.

"Take her—good-bye, Cleomona, say hello to Mama!" He turned and hurried down the corridor.

Zank watched him go.

"Good-bye, Vernon," Cleomona said after he was long out of earshot. "Sure has been fun."

Cole disappeared around a corner. Zank turned and started down the corridor with Cleomona. Then he stopped. Goddamn, this ain't right. Wherever the son of a bitch goes there's gonna be more kids and more Harrys cut up, roasted, and put in garbage cans.

"What're you thinking?" Cleomona asked.

"I'm thinking luck maybe is running with me and I ought to go running with it."

A security man was running toward them, huffing and holding his belly as he ran. Zank took out his Sgt. Veracruz badge. "Here, hold this girl, she's wanted for dope smuggling. Take her back down by the snack bar and hold on tight!"

"Yessir, yessir!" He took hold of Cleomona's wrists.

Zank started after Cole. He ran up the corridor and turned toward the exit gates.

Cole, standing in line at the check-in desk, glanced back over his shoulder and saw him coming. His eyes flooded with terror. He turned and ran, heading for an emergency exit. Zank caught up with him, grabbed him by the shoulder, and spun him around. Cole reached inside his coat, but Zank hit him, sending him crashing into a wall.

"You son of a bitch," Zank screamed at him, "you really think you can bluff me like that!"

"No bluff, I've got explosives!"

Zank looked around. There were half a dozen people nearby. Better to risk a half dozen than three hundred passengers on an airliner. "Everyone out, this guy's got a bomb!"

The passengers scattered in all directions.

Zank said to Cole: "Okay, pull the string, asshole. Come on, pull it! Pull it!"

"We'll all be blown up!"

Zank hit him hard in the gut, then again. "Do it, chicken fucking shit! Come on, do it!"

"We'll all die!" Cole screamed, scrambling to his feet,

scampering toward the exit. Zank caught him, spun him around, and hit him on the side of his face. Blood ran down Cole's chin and he spit pieces of tooth. Zank hit him with a hard, straight right. Cole dropped to his knees, putting his hands up in surrender. Zank didn't accept the offer; he hit him on the jaw and laid him out on the carpet.

Zank stood over him, waiting for him to move. He didn't. A few moments later the security man and Cleomona approached cautiously. "It's all over," Zank said to the security man, then added, "That coat's wired with explosives." The security man approached Cole hesitantly. "Hurry up," Zank said, "get the damn coat off him before he comes around." Cole was moaning and rocking back and forth now, his face swollen and blood running from his mouth.

"He don't look like much now, does he?" Zank said to Cleomona. She didn't answer him. She was staring at Cole with her mouth half open.

The security man removed Cole's coat and put handcuffs on him.

"Stay with him," Zank said to the security man. "Come on, Cleomona."

She said, "You knew he loved himself too much to blow himself up, didn't you?"

"I was hoping," Zank said.

15

Zank parked the van in front of Gertrude Fisk's Victorian farmhouse. The old Buick was still sitting and rusting in the driveway. It was ten in the morning; the sky was overcast. A gusting wind stroked the branches of the barren trees in the orchards surrounding the house.

Zank shut off the engine and turned around to Cleomona. She'd been stretched out in the back, sleeping most of the time. All she said on the way was that Cole had gone off his noodle.

"You're home, Cleomona."

She raised her head from the sleeping bag and said, "Fuck." She rubbed her eyes.

Zank said, "That's awful language on a girl."

"I'm an awful girl." She said it matter-of-fact. No apology. But maybe with just a little regret, Zank thought. Cole threatening to kill all those people, including her, had maybe wised her up a little.

"You been through a lot," Zank said. "People are gonna help you now, you'll see. I brought two other youngsters home, and they both are doing real good now."

She climbed into the passenger seat and looked around. "Yeah, but this is such an unhappy place, who could do well here?"

"Maybe you can make it happy if you try."

"Maybe," she said, but there wasn't much hope in her voice. "I guess now that she's dying, I ought to do the daughterly thing."

"If it don't work out, you can find me in the City. I know a place you can stay, real nice. It's for women who get beat by their men. I know the woman who runs it, she'll let you stay."

"I got places to go. I can take care of myself."

Zank looked at her. Maybe she was planning to leave as soon as he was down the road, he thought. He wouldn't put it past her. But that wasn't his business. He opened the door, but before he got out, he said, "You mind if I ask you something about Jill?"

"Shoot."

"Cole give her a drug or something?"

"Why do you ask that?"

"Even though he put her in that closet, she still wanted me to let him go."

Cleomona laughed. "He owns her. Possession."

"Owns her? What the hell you mean, he owns her?"

"Ever read about the Japs ramming their planes into ships on purpose? Kamikazes, they called them. Like that."

"Divine wind."

"Pardon?"

"Kamikaze means divine wind."

"Yeah, well, anyway it means follower. Total follower. That's Jill. She's like my old lady. My old lady is full of the Bible, Jill's full of Vernon Cole. Once you give your soul, it's given, baby, that's it." She scissored the air with her hands.

"How come you wised up?"

She shrugged. "I was never all the way there, I guess. It was fun being with Vernon. Kicks." She smiled at Zank. "Kids love sex, and so do I. I like getting my picture taken—not shocked are you? Selling the pictures was my idea. Vernon needed money. What the hell. I was all for Vernon. Great guy, lots of balls. But when I seen him put Jill in that closet, I said to myself, you're next, kiddo. I didn't want none of that scene."

"It's wrong, what you did with them kids. You got to know that."

"Right, wrong, they're just words. Good, bad. What the fuck's the difference? I'm bad, just like my mama always said, so big deal."

"You're just mixed up, that's all. You'll get straightened out."

"Yeah, think so? Don't worry yourself. I know whatever I want in life, I can find a way to get it."

"I hope," Zank said, "that what you want is good for you."

She gave him a smile. "What fun is that?"

They got out of the van. The driveway was muddy and they had to thread their way around the puddles to the flagstone walk leading up to the porch. Zank looked up at the windows and didn't see anyone. The place seemed deserted. An empty wind blew from the south.

"When I was little I wanted a pony," Cleomona said. "My daddy got it for me, but one day while I was at school, Mama sold it. She was a bitch even then. My daddy and me, we were tight. Mama couldn't stand that."

Zank's legs were stiff with fatigue. He rubbed the stiffness out of them. They climbed the front stairs and knocked on the door. Footsteps. Then the front door opened. Gertrude Fisk stood stone still in the doorway, the big gold cross hanging from her neck.

"Hello, Ma," Cleomona said.

Gertrude Fisk stared at her daughter with eyes like black poker chips on her pale white skin. "Never thought . . . never hoped . . ." Tears flooded into her eyes.

Neither moved to touch the other. Cleomona stepped inside, but kept her distance from her mother.

"I didn't expect you today," Gertrude Fisk said. "But come in, come in." She turned to Zank. "Thank you, sir, oh, thank you! I'll write a letter to your company, tell them how wonderful you are. Thank you again." She started to close the door.

"I'd like to see Cleomona settled in," Zank said, holding the door. "You don't mind, do you?"

She hesitated, glancing at Cleomona. Then she said, "Why, sure. Come in, Mr. Conrad." She clapped her hands together. "We'll have a real homecoming, won't we now."

Cleomona held her mother's arm going up the stairs. "I wanted to come home right away when I heard you were sick, Ma, but this mean man, Vernon Cole, just wouldn't let me."

"That's all behind us now, dear," her mother said.

Mrs. Fisk served tea and bologna sandwiches in her kitchen. The kitchen was overheated and cluttered, the dirty dishes piled high in the sink. There was a faded, red-checkered cloth on the table, and the calendar on the wall was three years old and featured pictures of cats. While Zank and Cleomona ate the sandwiches, Mrs. Fisk kept going in and out of a bedroom with broom and dust cloths, clean sheets, pillowcases, a comforter. "Got to be right," she said, "got to feel welcome."

"Don't tire yourself, Ma."

"I won't, I'm just so tickled to have you home." She went back into the bedroom.

Cleomona seemed pleased, Zank thought. When she'd finished eating she said, "Maybe she has changed. Maybe we can make peace before she goes."

"I think you will," Zank said, getting to his feet.

Cleomona smiled. "Funny how she doesn't scare me anymore. Vernon taught me how not to be afraid of anything, so something good came out of it."

Mrs. Fisk came back from the bedroom carrying a large cardboard box. "Wait 'till you see what I got for your homecoming," she said. She opened the box. It was a white satin dress.

Cleomona came to her feet, her mouth wide. "Oh, Ma!" she gasped. "It's beautiful!" Suddenly she caught herself by the chair and lost her balance. Zank grabbed hold of her.

"What's the matter?" he asked.

"Must be the excitement," Cleomona's mother said, coming to her side.

Cleomona sat back down. "I got real dizzy there."

"She never was a very strong child," her mother said.

"Maybe she ought to lie down," Zank said. "She slept most the time on the way out here."

"You want to lie down, child?" Gertrude Fisk asked. "Or wouldn't you rather try on the dress? I'm dying to see how you look in it."

"I'm all right," Cleomona said to Zank, getting back up on her feet. "Stay a few minutes and see me in the dress, okay?"

"Sure."

She excused herself and went into the bedroom to change.

Gertrude Fisk said, "Sure is nice to have her home."

Zank thought her smile seemed penciled on her flat, cold features. Her eyes were empty.

"What you gonna do if she wants to leave?" Zank asked.

"She's not leaving."

"But what if she decides she wants to?"

Her eyes grew serious. "That is none of your affair, now is it?" she said sharply. "You best mind your own business."

Zank was feeling too tired to argue. "Yeah, I guess I should mind my own business." He finished off his tea, stood up and looked at his watch. "I'd better be heading back . . . maybe I'll see her in the dress some other time."

"Come by whenever you wish," she said, suddenly more cheerful.

"Thanks for the lunch."

The penciled smile melted into a real one. "Well, you're welcome." Her eyes were filled with warmth. "Did you have much trouble finding Cleomona?"

"It was a piece of cake. I'd like to say good-bye to Cleomona."

"All right."

Gertrude Fisk went to the bedroom door and knocked softly. She listened. No answer. She opened the door. Zank looked over her shoulder. Cleomona had the dress on, but she was slumped in a chair in front of the vanity.

"Poor dear is so tired," Mrs. Fisk said. "Help me to lay her on the bed, would you, Mr. Conrad?"

"So tired," Cleomona mumbled. "What's wrong with me?"

Zank laid her on the bed. He checked her eyes. Her pupils were large and didn't shrink in the light. Cleomona's mother covered her with a large white comforter with red roses on it. "There, there, Cleomona, have a nice rest."

Zank and Mrs. Fisk went back out into the kitchen. "What did you drug her with?" Zank asked. He smelled Cleomona's teacup. "What was it?"

Mrs. Fisk's expression had turned cold again. "Isn't none of your business."

"I ain't leaving here till you tell me."

She pursed her lips. "Seconal."

"Why?"

"You have no right to be asking me questions. I've paid for your services. You were hired to bring Cleomona back, and you've done just that. I thank you. You've been well paid. Now leave." She pointed to the door.

Zank didn't move.

"If you don't leave, Mr. Conrad, I'm going to call your superiors."

Zank put down the cup. "I want to know what you plan to do," he said.

"And what if I don't want to tell you?"

"Then I'll take Cleomona with me."

She folded her arms across her chest. "All right, if you *must* know," she said through tight lips, "I have people coming over here tonight that are supposed to be able to straighten up her mind. I've seen certain photos of Cleomona with no clothes on. Dirty pictures of her doing evil things—with children. That private-eye Stroud brought the pictures to me. Do I have to say it all?"

"You aren't going to harm her?"

She shook her head. "She's my daughter, why would I harm her? I only want what's best for her and her immortal soul."

Zank looked into the bedroom at Cleomona. She was beautiful in the white satin dress. Angelic. Zank looked at Gertrude Fisk. "You said you have people coming over tonight? Who are they?"

"The man coming tonight is Dr. Stephen Harris and some of his staff. Dr. Harris is a local man, but very good. Your own people recommended him. Call him if you wish, the phone is downstairs in the hall."

"Where's your phone up here?"

"It's my phone, and I don't let nobody use it. Downstairs, that's the public phone." Her lips were drawn tight against her pearl-white teeth now. "You do understand why I had to drug her, don't you? You said so yourself, she'd be hard to handle. At any moment she could change her mind and just run off God knows where. I'll bet she was fixing to go the minute you left. You can't believe anything the girl says. I'm sure you know that. Don't trouble yourself, Mr. Conrad, Cleomona is in very good hands."

"I think I will call that doctor. Harris, you said his name was?"

"It isn't necessary to bother Dr. Harris."

"I'm gonna bother him anyway."

She clenched her teeth. "If you must, you must."

She stood at the top of the stairs glaring at him while he went down to use the phone. He got the number out of the book and dialed. The receptionist answered. He mentioned Mrs. Fisk and the receptionist put him right through to the doctor. He turned away from Mrs. Fisk's stare. The doctor came on the line.

"My name is Richard Conrad, Doctor. I'm calling just to double check and make sure everything is all right for tonight up here at the Fisk place."

"Who did you say you are?"

"Richard Conrad. I'm a friend of Cleomona's. I brought her home just now."

"What's this about tonight?"

"Her mother tells me you're coming over tonight to begin deprogramming her daughter."

A heavy sigh came over the line. The doctor said, "I've been monitoring Mrs. Fisk almost daily. What's this about deprogramming? Did you say her daughter is home? I think that may not be a good situation—Mrs. Fisk has been having a very bad time lately with a lot of paranoia about her daughter. I don't think this would be a good time for a visit."

"What do you mean, paranoia?"

"Mrs. Fisk thinks her daughter is inhabited by the spirit of the Devil."

"You aren't coming over tonight?"

"I wasn't planning to."

Zank looked back to the top of the stairs. Mrs. Fisk was gone.

Zank dropped the phone and raced back up the stairs and down the hall to Cleomona's bedroom. The door was locked. There was organ music coming from inside the room, ponderous funereal music. He threw his shoulder against the door. It didn't budge. He hit it again and again.

"Leave us alone!" he heard from the other side.

"Don't do anything, Mrs. Fisk, the doctor wants to talk with you!"

"Go away!"

Zank backed up a few feet and threw himself at the heavy door. The doorframe splintered but the door didn't open. He threw himself at it again. His shoulder ached. He hit it again. It split more. He threw himself at it again and again and it finally split open. He pushed his way in.

Gertrude Fisk, draped in a heavy black and red-hooded robe, was standing over the bed with a long, thin-bladed knife in her right hand, poised above Cleomona. In her other hand was a large silver crucifix. She looked at Zank with wide open eyes. She was standing on the opposite side of the bed, perhaps fifteen feet away.

"She's possessed," she hissed. "We got to get the devils out of her."

Zank couldn't see any blood. Cleomona was breathing regularly and softly on the bed.

"I know she's possessed," Zank said. He didn't move. He was watching the knife. He'd had a crazy sparring partner once and he knew you never argued with what they said. Not ever. He stood perfectly still so as not to make her jumpy.

Gertrude Fisk said, "She slept with her own father. She corrupted him."

"Nothing about her surprises me."

"Made him a sinner. To see the Devil living in your own daughter and not being able to do nothing? But the Lord took my husband, and now he's calling for Cleomona." She raised the knife.

"You better watch out," Zank said. "You punch her with that knife, it's gonna let the Devil out into this room." He took a chance and inched closer.

"What do you mean?"

"That cross might scare him, but without an open window he could just go into you—or me."

Her eyes danced with momentary confusion.

Zank said, "Do you know how to handle this? You got to do it just right or the Devil can just crawl up your arm and into your mouth."

"I don't care, so long as he's out of Cleomona."

"Why don't you let me do it? I've done dozens of them. I know just how to do it. You twist the knife when you ram it in the heart, it catches old Satan napping. Here, let me open the window too, so he'll have someplace to flee when he sees that cross."

Her eyes measured the distance between Zank and the window and between the window and herself.

"Open the window," she said.

He kept his eyes on the window and not on her. He walked purposefully over to the window and opened it. A fresh burst of air flushed through the room.

"There," he said, sitting on the window ledge. He was at the foot of the bed. "I don't think this music is right either." She was next to the stereo.

"The music is right." She wiped her face on her sleeve. "You're getting me all confused. I got to get this done with." The knife went up over her head.

"Wait, wait!" Zank said, drawing his scapula out of his shirt. "See this, it'll protect you. The Devil can't stand the sight of the Sacred Heart of Jesus—let me put it on you." He held it out to her, waiting.

"Stay back, don't come no closer!" she ordered.

"Don't you see the picture? It's Jesus." He was just a couple of feet from her, almost close enough. "Here, take it, you don't want the Devil getting in you."

Cleomona moaned suddenly.

"That's the Devil!" Gertrude Fisk shouted, "Out Satan!" She brought the knife up over her head and brought it down in an arc, driving it toward Cleomona's chest.

'Nooooo!" Zank yelled, leaping, trying to catch the blade with the flat of his hand, but it sliced through his palm and into Cleomona's chest; she sat up with a gasp. Zank reached across and slammed his left hand into the mother, knocking her back into the wall.

"It's done!" she cried.

Zank jerked his impaled hand from Cleomona; blood spurted from the hole in her chest onto the white dress, turning it a deep purple.

Cleomona clutched at his shirt, whispering, "Fucking bitch ruined the dress."

Zank used a sheet for a compression bandage, trying to stop the torrent of blood pulsing from her chest, but it was useless.

"You gotta know I had no idea," Zank stammered.

She nodded, then closed her eyes and was gone.

For a long moment he stood over her without moving. Mrs. Fisk said, "Our job is done, Mr. Conrad." She walked out of the room.

In death Cleomona's face seemed to swell, and had already turned waxy.

Zank covered her over with a blanket, turned off the organ music, and walked out into the living room. Gertrude Fisk was rocking in her chair, holding her mother's picture on her lap, humming to herself. Zank stood over her, staring at her, but said nothing. Blood dripped from his hand onto the floor. She didn't look at him, she just kept rocking and humming.

He thought about Charlotte and The Agency and how they must have checked out Gertrude Fisk and probably knew what they were taking on when they took her money; that she might do something to harm her daughter. Maybe that's why Stroud wouldn't take the case, he thought. Maybe that's why the price was high. A wave of nausea and revulsion flooded over him. He'd brought her home for this. What a goddamn idiot.

He went downstairs and out the front door into the clean air. He sat in his van for a while, wrapping his hand with strips of gauze. It burned, but it didn't hurt much. He wanted it to hurt bad and never stop hurting.

The overcast was breaking up. Off to the east he could see the snowcapped peaks of the High Sierras in the distance, and he thought of the training camp he was going to have there someday for young boxers. Kids like Davy Swan, who had the talent and were going to be up there some day. Kids that had it all ahead of them. He started the engine, backed out of the driveway, and headed down the road toward Gehenna.